Jake.

He pushed his way out of the crowd and stood smiling up at her.

Zoe didn't faint with relief, didn't gasp, didn't reveal in any way that she recognized him. Instead she looked down at him very deliberately, as if she were checking out the new man, the handsome stranger in town.

He was dressed the same as the rest of the men, in blue jeans and a worn denim work shirt. But the faded jeans hugged his thighs, and the shirt fit perfectly over his very broad shoulders. He was heart-stoppingly, impossibly beautiful, his eyes a shade of molten blue.

Jake had been looking her over as thoroughly as she had been looking at him, and now he smiled. And that was all he had to do. His smile promised everything. His smile promised heaven.

And he was good. For a minute he almost had her believing it, too.

Dear Reader,

What is there to say about a month with a new Nora Roberts title except "Hurry up and get to the store!" *Enchanted* is a mysterious, romantic and utterly irresistible follow-up to THE DONOVAN LEGACY trilogy, which appeared several years ago and is currently being reissued. It's the kind of story only Nora can tell—and boy, will you be glad she did!

The rest of our month is pretty special, too, so pick up a few more books to keep you warm. Try *The Admiral's Bride,* by Suzanne Brockmann, the latest TALL, DARK & DANGEROUS title. These navy SEAL heroes are fast staking claim to readers' hearts all over the world. Read about the last of THE SISTERS WASKOWITZ in Kathleen Creighton's *Eve's Wedding Knight.* You'll love it—and you'll join me in hoping we revisit these fascinating women—and their irresistible heroes—someday. *Rio Grande Wedding* is the latest from multiaward-winning Ruth Wind, a part of her MEN OF THE LAND miniseries, featuring the kind of Southwestern men no self-respecting heroine can resist. Take a look at Vickie Taylor's *Virgin Without a Memory,* a book *you'll* remember for a long time. And finally, welcome Harlequin Historical author Mary McBride to the contemporary romance lineup. *Just One Look* will demand more than just one look from you, and it will have you counting the days until she sets another story in the present day.

And, of course, mark your calendar and come back next month, when Silhouette Intimate Moments will once again bring you six of the most excitingly romantic novels you'll ever find.

Enjoy!

Leslie J. Wainger
Executive Senior Editor

Please address questions and book requests to:
Silhouette Reader Service
U.S.: 3010 Walden Ave., P.O. Box 1325, Buffalo, NY 14269
Canadian: P.O. Box 609, Fort Erie, Ont. L2A 5X3

THE ADMIRAL'S BRIDE

SUZANNE BROCKMANN

INTIMATE MOMENTS®

Published by Silhouette Books

America's Publisher of Contemporary Romance

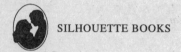 SILHOUETTE BOOKS

ISBN 0-373-07962-1

THE ADMIRAL'S BRIDE

Copyright © 1999 by Suzanne Brockmann

This edition published by arrangement with Harlequin Books S.A.

® and TM are trademarks of Harlequin Books S.A., used under license.
Trademarks indicated with ® are registered in the United States Patent
and Trademark Office, the Canadian Trade Marks Office and in other
countries.

Visit us at www.romance.net

Printed in U.S.A.

Books by Suzanne Brockmann

Silhouette Intimate Moments

Hero Under Cover #575
Not Without Risk #647
A Man To Die For #681
Prince Joe #720
Forever Blue #742
Frisco's Kid #759
Love with the Proper Stranger #831
Everyday, Average Jones #872
Harvard's Education #884
It Came Upon a Midnight Clear #896
The Admiral's Bride #962

*Tall, Dark & Dangerous

SUZANNE BROCKMANN

lives just west of Boston in a house always filled with her friends—actors and musicians and storytellers and artists and teachers. When not writing award-winning romances about U.S. Navy SEALs, she sings in an a cappella group called Serious Fun, manages the professional acting careers of her two children, volunteers at the Appalachian Benefit Coffeehouse and always answers letters from readers. Send her an SASE along with your letter to P.O. Box 5092, Wayland, MA 01778.

For Nancy Peeler.
We miss you guys!

Prologue

Vietnam, 1969

Sergeant Matthew Lange had been left to die.

His leg was badly broken and he had shrapnel embedded in his entire right side. It hadn't hit anything vital. He knew, because he'd been hit hours ago and he wasn't dead yet. And that was almost a shame.

His morphine wasn't working. He not only hurt like hell but he was still alert enough to know what was coming.

The soldier next to him knew, too. He lay there, crying softly. Jim was his name. Jimmy D'Angelo. He was just a kid, really—barely eighteen—and he wasn't going to get any older.

None of them were.

There were a dozen of them there, United States Marines, hiding and bleeding in the jungle of a country too small to have been mentioned in fifth-grade geography class. They were too badly injured to walk out, but most of 'em were still conscious, still alive enough to know that sometime within the next few hours, they were going to die.

Charlie was coming.

Probably right before dawn.

The Vietcong had launched a major offensive yesterday morning, and Matt's platoon had been one of several trapped by the attack. They were now God knows how many clicks behind enemy lines, with no chance of rescue.

Hours ago, Captain Tyler had radioed for help, but help wasn't coming. There were no chopper pilots insane enough to fly into this hot spot. They were on their own.

But then the bomb dropped—close to literally. Well, at least it would be dropping literally, come morning. The captain had been ordered out of the area. He was told that in an attempt to halt the Vietcong, the Americans would be napalming this very mountain in less than twelve hours.

There had been twenty injured men. They'd outnumbered the uninjured by more than two to one.

Captain Tyler had played God, choosing the eight least wounded to drag out of there. He'd looked at Matt, looked at his leg, and he'd shaken his head. No. He'd had tears in his eyes, not that that helped much now.

Father O'Brien had been the only one to stay behind.

Matt could hear his quiet voice, murmuring words of comfort to the dying men.

If Charlie found them, he'd use bayonets to kill them. He wouldn't want to waste bullets on men who couldn't fight back. And Matt couldn't fight back. His right arm was useless, his left too weak to shoulder his weapon. Most of the other guys were worse than he was. And he couldn't picture Father O'Brien picking up someone's machine gun and giving Charlie a mouthful of lead.

No, bayonets or burning. That's what their future had come down to.

Matt felt like weeping along with Jimmy.

"Sarge?"

''Yeah, Jim. I'm still here.'' Like Matt might've walked away.

''You have a family, don't you?''

Matt closed his eyes, picturing Lisa's sweet face. ''Yeah,'' he said. ''I do. Back in New Haven. Connecticut.'' He might as well have said Mars, it seemed as far away. ''I got two boys. Matt, Jr., and Mikey.'' Lisa had wanted a little girl. A daughter. He'd always thought there'd be plenty of time for that later.

He'd been wrong.

''You're lucky.'' Jimmy's voice shook. ''I don't have anyone besides my ma who's gonna remember me. My poor ma.'' He started to cry again. ''Oh, God, I want my ma....''

Father O'Brien came over, but his calm voice didn't cover Jimmy's sobbing. The poor bastard wanted his ma.

Matt wanted Lisa. It was the stupidest thing. When he'd been there, back in that stifling little crummy two-bedroom apartment in one of the worst neighborhoods in New Haven, he'd thought he'd go absolutely mad. He hated working as a mechanic, hated the way his money was already spent on groceries and rent before he even brought home his paycheck. So he'd re-upped. He'd told Lisa he'd reenlisted for the money, but the real truth was he'd wanted to get the hell out of there before he suffocated. And he'd left, even though she'd cried.

He'd married too young—not that he'd had a real choice about it. And he'd liked it, at first. Lisa, in his bed every night. No need to worry about getting her pregnant, since he'd already done that. He'd loved the way she'd grown heavy with child, with *his* child. It made him feel like a man, even though at twenty-two, fresh out of the service, he'd been little more than a child himself. But when the second baby had come right after the first, the weight of his responsibilities had scared him to death.

So he'd left. He'd come here, to Nam.

It was much different from his first tour, when he'd been stationed in Germany.

And right now all he wanted was to be back in Lisa's arms. He was the stupidest fool in the world—he didn't realize how much he had, how much he truly loved that girl, his wife, until he was hours away from dying.

Bayonets or burning. "Dear God."

Father O'Brien's soft voice had quieted Jimmy, and he now turned to Matt. "Sergeant—Matthew. Would you like to pray?"

"No, Father," he said.

Not even prayer could help them now.

"Their captain just left them there?" Lieutenant Jake Robinson kept his voice even, kept his voice low, even though he absolutely could not believe what his chief had just told him. Wounded marines, left behind by their CO in the jungle to die. "And now the good guys are going to finish them off with friendly fire?"

Ham nodded, his headphones still plugged into the radio, his dark eyes grim. "It's not as heartless as you're thinkin', Admiral. There's only a dozen or so of them. If Charlie isn't stopped before he gets to the river, we'll have casualties in the thousands. You know that." He spoke in a barely audible voice, too.

The enemy was all around them tonight. And well they should know. Jake's team of Men with Green Faces, U.S. Navy SEALs, had spent the past twenty-four hours marking the Vietcongs' location in this target area. They'd radioed the info in and now had exactly four hours to get out before the bombing raid began.

"Only a dozen men," Jake said. "Or so. Any chance of giving me an exact number, Chief?"

"Twelve wounded, one priest."

Fred and Chuck materialized from the jungle. "Only nine wounded now," Fred corrected him in his soft Southern drawl. "We found 'em, Admiral. Near a clearing, like they hoped a chopper would be able to come in and grab 'em. Didn't approach—didn't want to get their hopes up if we didn't think we could help. What we could see, three of 'em are already KIA.''

KIA. Killed in action. It was one of Jake's least favorite acronyms. Along with POW and MIA. But he didn't let his aversion show on his face. He never let anything like that show. His men didn't need to know when he was shaken. And this one had shaken him, hard. The commanders-in-chief knew those men were there. U.S. Marines. Good men. Brave men. And those commanders had given the order to proceed with the bombing regardless.

He met Ham's eyes and read the skepticism there.

''We've pulled off some tough missions before,'' Jake said. His words were as much to convince himself.

Ham shook his head. ''Nine wounded men and seven SEALs,'' he said. ''Against thirty-five hundred Vietcong? Come on, Lieutenant.'' The chief didn't need to say what he was thinking. This wasn't just a tough mission, it was insanity.

And the chief had called Jake by his true rank, a sign of his disapproval. It was funny how accustomed he'd become to the nickname this team of SEALs had given him—Admiral. It was the ultimate expression of respect from this motley crew, particularly since he'd gone through BUD/S cursed with the label Pretty Boy, PB for short. Yeah, he liked Admiral much better.

Fred and Chuck were watching him. So were Scooter and the Preacher and Ricky. Waiting for his command. At age twenty-two, Jake was one of the two old men of the team—a full lieutenant having served three back-to-back tours of duty in this hell on earth. Ham, his chief, had been there with him for the last two. Steady as a rock and, at twenty-seven years of age, as gnarled and ancient as the hills. But he'd never questioned Jake's authority.

Until now.

Jake smiled. ''Nine wounded men, seven SEALs and one

priest," he pointed out lightly. "Don't forget the priest, Ham. Always good to have one of them on our side."

Fred snickered, but Ham's expression didn't change.

"I wouldn't leave *you* to die," Jake quietly told the man who was the closest thing to a friend he had in this armpit of a jungle. "I will not leave those men out there."

Jake didn't wait for Ham's response, because frankly, Ham's response didn't matter. He didn't need his chief's approval. This wasn't a democracy. Jake and Jake alone was in command.

He met Fred's eyes, then Scooter's and Preacher's and Rickie's and Chuck's, infusing them all with his confidence, letting them see his complete faith in their ability as a SEAL team to pull off this impossible task.

Leaving those poor bastards to die was not an option. Jake couldn't do it. Jake *wouldn't* do it.

He turned to Ham. "Get on the radio, Chief, and find Crazy Ruben. If anyone'll fly a chopper in this deep, it'll be him. Pull in all those favors he owes me, promise him air support, and then get on the wire and get it for him."

"Yes, *sir*."

Jake turned to Fred. "Go back there and get their hopes up. Get them ready to move, then get your ass back here on the double." He smiled again, his best picnic-in-the-park smile. The one that made men under command believe they'd live to see another sunrise. "The rest of you gentlemen get ready to cut some very long fuses. Because I've got one hell of a plan."

"They musta parachuted in!" Jimmy had real excitement in his voice. "Listen to that, Sarge! How many of 'em do you think are out there?"

Matt painfully pulled himself up, trying to see something, *anything* in the darkness of the jungle. But all he could see were the flashes in the sky from an enormous battle just off to the west. Deep in VC territory. "God, there must be hundreds."

Even as he said the words he couldn't believe it. Hundreds of American soldiers, appearing out of nowhere?

"They had to've dropped 'em in," Jimmy said again.

It seemed impossible, but it must have been true—because there came the air support, then, big planes screaming overhead, dropping all kinds of nasty surprises on Charlie.

Two hours ago a big, dark-skinned man had appeared, rising out of the jungle like an apparition, his face savagely painted with green and brown, a cammy-print bandanna tied neatly around the top of his head. He'd ID'd himself as Seaman Fred Baxter of the U.S. Navy SEALs.

Matt had highest rank among the men left behind, and had asked what the hell a sailor was doing this far inland?

Apparently there was a whole group of sailors out there in the jungle. A team, Baxter had said. Jake's team, he'd called them, as if that meant something—whoever the hell Jake was. And they were going to get Matt and Jimmy and the rest of 'em out of there. Stand ready for extraction, Baxter had said, and he'd disappeared.

Matt had been left wondering if the entire conversation hadn't been some weird morphine hallucination. Seals. Who would name a special forces group after a circus animal? And how the hell was an entire *team* of them going to get out of the jungle with nine wounded men?

"I've heard of the SEALs," Jimmy said, as if he'd somehow been able to follow Matt's drug-hazed thoughts. "They're some kind of demolitions experts. Even underwater, if you can believe *that.* And they're kinda like ninjas—they can move right past Charlie—within *feet* of Charlie—without being seen. They go miles behind the line in teams of six or seven men and blow stuff up. And I don't know what kind of voodoo they use, but they always come back alive. *Always.*"

Six or seven men. Matt looked up at the flashes of explosions lighting the sky. Demolitions experts... No. Couldn't be.

Could it?

"Chopper!" Father O'Brien shouted. "Praise our Lord God Almighty!"

The roar was unmistakable. The hurricane-force wind from the blades felt like a miracle. Holy Jesus, they actually had a chance.

Tears were running down the padre's round face as he helped the medics lift the wounded men up and into the chopper. Matt couldn't hear him over the roar, over the sound of weapons discharging as the men with green faces suddenly appeared, keeping Charlie back, away from the clearing. Matt didn't need to hear O'Brien to know that his mouth was moving in a continuous prayer of thanks.

But Matt wasn't Catholic, and they hadn't made it out yet.

Someone lifted him up and the sudden knifelike pain in his leg made him scream.

"Sorry, Sergeant." The voice held the quiet confidence of a seasoned officer. "No time to ask where it hurts."

And then the pain was worth it, because he was inside, his cheek pressed against the olive-drab U.S.-made riveted metal of the chopper floor. And then they were lifting up and away, on an express flight out of hell.

But fear cut through his waves of relief. Dear God, don't let them have left anyone behind!

He forced himself over, onto his back, and the pain nearly made him retch. "Head count!" he somehow managed to shout.

"We got all of you, Sarge." It was the steady voice of the man who'd carried him aboard. He was crouched by the open doorway, a grenade launcher in his arms, aiming and firing even as he spoke. He was younger than Matt had imagined from his voice. He wore no insignia, no rank, no markings on his camouflage gear at all. Like the other SEALs, his face was streaked with green and brown, but as he turned to glance over his shoulder at the wounded men, Matt could see his eyes. They were an almost startling shade of blue. And as he met Matt's gaze, he smiled.

It wasn't a tense, tight grimace laced with fear. And it wasn't a wolfish expression of adrenaline-induced high. It was a calm, relaxed, "let's get together and play softball sometime" kind of smile.

"We got everyone," he shouted again, no room for doubt in his voice. "Hold on, Sergeant, it's going to be a bumpy ride, but we *will* get you out, and we *will* get you home."

When he said it like that, as if it were an absolute truth, even Matt could believe him.

The hospital was the pits, filled with pain and stink and death, but Matt knew he was only going to be there a little while longer.

He'd been given his orders, his medical discharge. He was going home to Lisa.

He was going to walk with a limp, probably for the rest of his life, but the doctors had managed to save his leg. Not bad for a guy who'd been left for dead.

"You're looking much better today." The nurse that stopped by his bed and checked his leg was a pretty brunette with two deep dimples in her cheeks when she smiled. "I'm Constance. You can call me Connie for short."

He hadn't seen her before, but he'd only been here about forty-eight hours. He'd spent most of that time in surgery and recovery.

"Oh, you're one of Jake's Boys," Connie said as she checked his chart, her Georgia peaches-and-cream accent suddenly hushed with respect.

"No," he said, "I'm not a SEAL. I'm a sergeant with—"

"I know you're not a SEAL, silly." She dimpled up again. "Jake's SEALs don't turn up in our hospital beds. We sometimes have to give them extra penicillin, but perhaps I shouldn't mention that in mixed company." She winked.

Matt was confused. "But you said—"

"Jake's *Boys*," she repeated. "That's what we call you—the wounded men that Lieutenant Jake Robinson brings in. Someone started keeping count here at the hospital about eight months ago."

At his blank look, she tried to explain. "Jake has developed the habit of resurrecting U.S. soldiers from the dead, Sergeant. Last month, his team liberated an entire prisoner-of-war camp. Don't ask me how, but Jake and his team came out of that jungle with seventy-five POWs, each one looking worse than the last. I swear, I cried for a week when I saw those poor souls." She shook her head. "I think there were ten of you this time, weren't there? Jake's up to…let's see…I think it's four hundred and twenty-seven now." She dimpled again. "Although if you ask me, he should get extra points for the priest."

"Four hundred and…"

"Twenty-seven." Connie nodded, taking his blood pressure, her touch businesslike, impersonal. "All of whom owe their lives to him. Of course, we only started counting eight months ago. He's been in-country much longer."

"A lieutenant, huh?" Matt mused. "My *captain* couldn't get even get one single chopper to fly in to pull us out."

Connie bristled. "Your captain is a word I will not use because *I* am a lady. Shame on him for leaving you boys that way. He better not come to *this* hospital for his annual checkup. There are a dozen doctors and nurses who are *dying* to get a chance to tell him to turn his head and cough."

Matt laughed, but then winced. "Captain Tyler tried," he said. "I was there. I know he tried. That's what I don't understand. How could this lieutenant make things happen when a captain couldn't?"

"Well, you know Jake's nickname." Connie looked up from her gentle but methodical checking of his shrapnel wounds. "Or maybe you don't. His teammates call him Admiral. And it wouldn't surprise me one bit if he made it to that rank someday. He's got something about him. Oh, yes, there's something very special in those blue eyes.''

Blue eyes. "I think I met him," Matt said.

"Sergeant, you wouldn't just *think* it if you'd met him. You'd know it. He has a face like a movie star and a smile that makes you want to follow him just about anywhere." She sighed, then smiled again. "Oh, my. I am getting myself worked up over that young man, aren't I?"

Matt had to know. "So how *did* a lieutenant manage to get all those soldiers dropped into the area? There must've been hundreds of them, and—''

Connie laughed but then stopped, her eyes widening as she looked at him. "My goodness," she said. "You don't know, do you? When I heard about it, I didn't quite believe it, but if they managed to fool *you,* too…''

Matt just waited for her to explain.

"It was a ruse," she said. "Jake and his SEALs rigged a chain of explosives to fool the VC into thinking we'd launched a counteroffensive. It was just a distraction so he could get Captain Ruben's chopper in to pull you out. There weren't hundreds of soldiers in that jungle, Sergeant. What you saw and heard was solely the handiwork of seven U.S. Navy SEALs, led by one Lieutenant Jake Robinson.''

Matt was floored. Seven SEALs had made him believe there was a huge army out there in the darkness.

Connie's dimples deepened. "Gracious, that man might be more than an admiral someday. He just might go all the way and become our president." She raised her eyebrows suggestively. "I'd give him *my* vote, that's for sure.''

She made a note on Matt's chart, about to move on to the next bed.

"Connie?"

She turned back patiently. "Sergeant, I can't give you anything for the pain for another few hours."

"No, that's not… I was just wondering. Does he ever come around here? Lieutenant Robinson, I mean. I'd like to thank him."

"First off," she said. "As one of Jake's Boys, you and he are on a first-name basis. And secondly, no. You won't see him around here. He's already back out there, Sergeant. He's sleeping in the jungle tonight—that is, if he's sleeping at all."

Chapter 1

The Pentagon.

Dr. Zoe Lange gazed out the window of the limo as the driver pulled up to the *Pentagon*.

Damn.

She was way underdressed.

Her boss, Patrick Sullivan, had told her only that she was a candidate for an important and potentially long-term assignment. Zoe had figured that appropriate dress for such a meeting meant comfortable—blue jeans, running shoes, a T-shirt with a little blue flower print, and hardly any makeup. She was who she was, after all. If she were going to join a long-term mission, everyone might as well know exactly what to expect right from the start.

She didn't dress up unless she had to.

Unless she were going someplace like, oh, say, the Pentagon.

If she'd known she was coming to the Pentagon, she

would have put on her skintight black cat suit, her three-inch heels, dark red lipstick and worn her long blond hair in some kind of fancy French braid, rather than this high-school cheerleader ponytail she was wearing. Because men in the military tended to think female agents who looked like Emma Peel or one of James Bond's babes could hold their own when the going got tough. But little blue flowers, nuh-uh. Little blue flowers meant they'd have to hand her hankies to mop her frightened tears. Never mind the fact that little blue flowers didn't compromise her ability to run hard and fast, the way three-inch heels did.

Well, okay. She was here now. The little blue flowers were going to have to do.

She put on her sunglasses and picked up her oversize handbag that doubled as a briefcase and let herself be escorted by the guards into the building, through all the security checkpoints and into a waiting elevator.

Down. They headed down, further even than the B that marked the basement floor. Even though no more letters or numbers flashed on the display over the door, they kept sinking. What could possibly be this far down besides hell?

Zoe smiled tightly at the idea of being summoned for a meeting with the devil himself. In her line of business, it was entirely possible. She just hadn't expected to meet him here in D.C.

Finally the elevator stopped and the doors opened with a subdued chime.

The hallway was a clean off-white and very bright, not the dimly lit, smoky magentas and red-oranges of hell. The guards waiting for her outside didn't carry pitchforks. Instead they wore naval uniforms. Navy, huh? Hmm, wasn't *that* interesting?

U.S. Navy Lieutenant Clones One and Two led her down that nondescript corridor, through countless doors that opened and closed automatically. Maxwell Smart would've been right at home.

''Where are we heading, boys?'' Zoe asked. ''To the Cone of Silence?''

One of the lieutenants looked back at her blankly, either too young or too serious to have seen all those late night *Get Smart* reruns she'd watched as a kid.

But as they stopped at an unmarked doorway, Zoe realized her joking question had been right on the mark. The door was ridiculously thick, reinforced with steel, layered with everything else—lead included, no doubt—that would render the room within completely spy-proof. No infrared satellites could look through *these* walls and see who was inside. No high-powered microphones could listen in. Nothing that was said inside could be recorded or overheard.

It was, indeed, the equivalent of Maxwell Smart's Cone of Silence.

The outer door—and it was only the first of three she passed through—closed with a thunk, followed by the second. The third door was like a hatch on a ship—she had to step over a rim to get inside. It, too, was sealed tightly behind her.

Apparently, she was the last to arrive.

The inner chamber was not a big room. It was barely sixteen by thirteen, and it was filled with men. Big men, wearing gleaming white naval dress uniforms. The glare was intense. Zoe resisted the urge to pull her sunglasses down from where she'd pushed them atop her head as they all turned to look at her, as they all rose to their feet in a unison display of chivalry.

She looked at them, scanning their faces, looking for someone, *anyone* familiar. The best she could do was count heads—fourteen—and sort through the various ranks on their uniforms.

''Please,'' she said, with her best professional smile. ''Gentlemen. No need to stand on my account.''

There were two enlisted men, four lieutenants, one senior chief, two commanders, a captain, a rear admiral lower grade and three—count 'em, *three*—full-grade admirals, complete with scrambled eggs on the hats that were on the table in front of them.

Seven of the men were active-duty SEALs. Two of the admirals wore budweisers, as well—the SEAL pin with an anchor and an eagle in flight gripping Poseidon's pitchfork in one talon and a stylized gun in the other—which meant they'd been SEALs at one time during their long military careers.

One of the SEALs—a blond lieutenant with an even, white-toothed smile and a much too handsome face, who looked as if he might've come straight from the set of *Baywatch*—pulled out a chair for her. Nodding her thanks, she sat next to him.

"Name's Luke O'Donlon," he whispered, holding out his hand.

She shook it quickly, absently, smiling briefly at both O'Donlon and the SEAL on her other side, an enormous African-American man with a shaved head, a diamond stud in his left ear, and a wide gold wedding band on his ring finger. As she set her bag down in front of her, her attention was held by the men on the other side of the big table.

Three admirals. Holy Mike. Whatever this assignment was, it required this spy-proof room and three full-grade admirals to launch it.

The admiral without the budweiser had snow-white hair and a face set in a permanent expression of disgust—as if he carried bad fish in his inside jacket pocket. Stonegate, that was his name. Zoe recognized him from his newspaper picture. He was always showing up in the Washington *Post*. He was part politician, something she didn't quite approve of in a man of his rank and standing.

Beside her, O'Donlon cleared his throat and gave her his most winsome smile. He was just too cute, and he knew it, too. "I'm sorry, miss, I didn't catch your name."

"I'm afraid that info's need-to-know," she whispered back, "and probably beyond your security clearance level. Sorry, sailor."

The senior chief next to her overheard and deftly covered his laughter with a cough.

The admiral who had reclaimed his seat next to Stonegate had a thick head of salt and pepper hair. Admiral Mac Forrest. Definitely a cool guy. She'd met him at least twice in the Middle East, the last time just a few months ago. He nodded and smiled as she met his eyes.

The admiral on Mac's left—the man directly across the table from her—was still standing, his face hidden as he quickly rifled through a file. "Now that we're all here," he said, "why don't we get started."

He looked up then, and Zoe found herself looking into eyes that were amazingly, impossibly blue, into a face she would've recognized anywhere.

Jake Robinson.

The one and only Admiral Jake Robinson.

Zoe knew he was in his early fifties—he had to be unless he'd performed his heroics in Vietnam as a twelve-year-old. Still, his hair was thick and dark, and the lines around his eyes and mouth only served to give his handsome face strength and maturity.

And handsome was a complete understatement. Jake Robinson was *way* beyond handsome. He needed a completely new word invented to describe the sheer beauty of his face. His mouth was elegant, gracefully shaped and ready to quirk up into a smile. His nose was masculine perfection, his cheekbones exquisite, his forehead strong. His chin was just the right amount of stubborn, his jawline still sharp.

Lieutenant Cutie-Pie sitting next to her—now *he* was merely handsome. Jake Robinson, on the other hand, was the Real Deal.

He was looking around the table, quickly making introductions that Zoe knew were mostly for her benefit. Everyone else here knew each other. She tried to listen. The two enlisted SEALs were Skelly and Taylor. One was built like a pro football linebacker, the other looked like Popeye the sailor man. Which was which, she didn't have a clue. The African-American senior chief was named Becker. She'd met O'Donlon. Hawken, Shaw, Jones. Try as she might to memorize names, to attach them permanently to faces, she couldn't do it.

She was too busy flashing hot and cold.

Jake Robinson.

Great glorious God, she was being given a chance to work a long-term assignment under the command of a living legend. His exploits nearly thirty years ago in Vietnam *were* legendary—along with his more recent creation of the Gray Group. Robinson's Gray Group was so highly classified, so top secret, she could only guess the type of assignments he handed out. But she *could* guess. Dangerous. Covert. Intensely important to national security.

And she was going to be part of one.

Zoe's heart was pounding as if she had just run five miles. She took a deep breath, calming herself as the admiral introduced her to the rest of the room. By the time fourteen pairs of very male eyes focused on her, she was completely back in control. Calm. Cool. Collected. Positively serene.

Except thirteen of those fourteen pairs of very male eyes didn't seem to notice how absolutely serene she was. Instead, they all focused on her ponytail and her little blue flowers. She could read their speculation quite clearly. She was the secretary, right? Sent in to take notes while the big strong men talked.

Guess again, boys.

"Dr. Zoe Lange is one of *the* top experts in the country—possibly in the world—in biological and chemical weapons," Jake Robinson told them in his husky baritone voice.

Around the room, eyebrows went up. Zoe could almost smell the skepticism. Across the table, the admiral's eyes were sparkling with amusement. Clearly, the skepticism's stench was strong enough for him to smell it, as well.

"Dr. Lange works for Pat Sullivan," he added matter-of-factly, and the mood in the room instantly changed. The Agency. He didn't even need to say the name of the organization. They all knew what it was—and what she did for a living. Admiral Robinson had known exactly what to say to make them all sit up and take notice of her, little blue flowers or not. She sent him a smile of thanks.

"I truly appreciate your being able to join us here today, Doctor." The admiral smiled at her, and it was all Zoe could do not to melt at his feet.

It was true. Everything she'd ever read or heard about Jake Robinson's smile was absolutely true. It was warm and genuine. It was completely inclusive. It lit him from within, made his eyes even more blue. It made her want to follow him anywhere. *Anywhere.*

"It's my pleasure, Admiral," she murmured. "I'm honored that you invited me. I hope I can be of assistance."

"Actually—" his face sobered "—it's unfortunate that we need your assistance." He looked around the table, all amusement gone from his eyes. "Two weeks ago, there was a break-in at the Arches military testing lab just outside of Boulder, Colorado."

Zoe stopped watching the man's eyes and started paying attention to his words. A break-in. At Arches. Holy Mike.

She wasn't the only one shifting uneasily in her seat. Beside her, Senior Chief Becker was downright uncomfortable, as were most of the other SEALs. Like Zoe, they all knew what was tested at Arches. They all knew what was *stored* there, as well. Anthrax. Botulinum toxin. Sarin. The lethal nerve gas VX. And the newest man-made tool of death and chemical destruction, Triple X.

The last time Zoe had been in Arches, she'd written a hundred-and-fifty-page report on the weaknesses in their security system. She wondered now if anyone at all had bothered to read it.

"The break-in was done without force, without forced entry, even," the admiral continued. "Six canisters of a deadly nerve agent were removed and replaced—it was only by dumb luck we discovered the switch.''

Zoe couldn't stand it a minute longer. ''Admiral, what exactly was taken?''

Stonegate and several of the other high-ranking officers were looking at her as if she deserved to get her mouth washed for speaking out of order. But she didn't give a damn. She needed to know. And Jake Robinson didn't seem to mind.

He met her gaze steadily, and she saw the answer in his eyes even before he opened his mouth to speak. It was the worst possible scenario she could imagine.

Trip X. *Six* canisters? Oh, God.

She realized she'd said the words aloud as he nodded. ''Oh, God is right,'' he agreed with rather grim humor. ''Dr. Lange, perhaps I could impose upon you to explain exactly what Triple X is, as well as our options for dealing with this little problem.''

Little problem? Holy Mike, this was no *little* problem. ''Our options for dealing with it are extremely simple, sir,'' she said. ''We have only one option—there are no choices here. We need to find and regain possession of the missing canisters. Believe me, gentlemen, Triple X is not something we want floating around out there. And particularly not *six* canisters' worth.'' She looked at the admiral. ''How in God's name did this happen?''

''How's not important right now,'' he told her almost gently. ''Right now we need to focus on *what*. Please continue, Doctor.''

Zoe nodded. The thought of six canisters of Triple X set loose on the unsuspecting world made her blood feel like ice water as it flowed through her veins. It was terrifying. And she wasn't used to feeling terrified, even though her job was a frightening one most of the time. She spent hours upon hours learning the awful details of all the different weapons of mass destruction that were out there, ready to wreak havoc on the planet. But she'd learned to sleep dreamlessly at night, untouched by nightmares. She'd learned to sit impassively while reading reports of countries that tested chemical weapons on prisoners and the infirm. Women and children.

But six missing canisters of Trip X…

That scared her to death.

Still, she took a deep breath and stood up, because she'd also learned how to give tight, to-the-point, emotionless information even when she was badly shaken.

"Triple X is currently the nastiest chemical weapon in the world," she reported. "It's twenty times more potent than the nerve agent VX, and like VX, it kills by paralysis. Get a noseful of Triple X, gentlemen, and you choke to death, because your lungs, like the other muscles in your body, slowly seize up. Trip X or Tri X or T-X. It's all the same thing—airborne death."

Zoe moved around the table to the white board that was on the wall behind Admiral Robinson. She picked up a marker and scribbled the two chemical components on the board, labeling them A and B.

"Trip X is a triple compound, which makes it far more stable to store and transport. It also makes it far more adaptable as a weapon." She pointed to the board. "These two compounds are stored dry, in powder forms that are, on their own, relatively harmless. But just like Betty Crocker's dromedary gingerbread mix, just add water. And then it's time to put your gas mask on. Instant poison. It's that easy, boys. You get me two balloons, about a teaspoonful each of Trip X compounds A and B, both harmless in dried form, remember, and a little H_2O laced with some acid or lye, and I can make a weapon that will take out this entire building—the entire Pentagon—as well as a good number of people on the street. Water sealed in one balloon, which is tucked inside of the other, which is also filled with air and that little bit of compounds A and B. A little acid or lye in the water eats through the rubber. Balloon springs a leak, water hits old A and B. It causes a chemical reaction that creates both a liquid and a gaseous form of Triple X, sending it out into the air, and eventually through the building's ventilation system, killing everyone who comes into contact with it.''

The room was dead silent as she put the marker down.

Jake Robinson had taken his seat as she'd started her little lecture, turning to face her as she'd stood in front of the white board. She was directly in front of him now. He was close enough to reach out and touch. And smell. He wore a subtle amount of Polo Sport—just enough to smell completely delicious.

She drew in a deep breath to steady herself—and to remind herself that although her world was fraught with evil, there *was* good in it, too. It held men like Jake Robinson.

''That's what two teaspoons of Trip X can do, gentlemen,'' she said. ''As for six *canisters…*'' She shook her head.

''I know it's hard to imagine a disaster of this magnitude,'' the admiral said quietly, ''but in your opinion, how many thermos-size canisters would it take to wipe out this city?''

''Washington, D.C.?'' Zoe chewed her lower lip. ''Rough guess? Four? Depending on which way the wind was blowing.''

He nodded. Clearly he'd already known that. And *six* were missing.

She looked around the room. ''Any other questions?''

Senior Chief Becker lifted his hand. ''You said our only option was to find the Triple X and regain possession of it. Is there any way to destroy it?''

''The two powders can be burned,'' she told him with a tight smile. ''Just don't put the fire out with water.''

Lieutenant O'Donlon raised his hand. ''I have a question for Admiral Robinson. After two weeks, sir, you must have some idea who was behind the theft.''

The admiral stood up. He towered over her by a solid six inches. She started toward her seat, but he caught her elbow, his fingers warm against her bare skin. "Stay," he commanded softly.

She nodded. "Of course, sir."

"We *have* identified the terrorist group that stole the Trip X," Jake told them, "and we also believe we've found the location of the missing canisters."

Everyone started talking at once.

"That's *great*," Zoe said.

"Yeah, well, it's not as great as it sounds," the admiral told her in a low voice. "Nothing's ever that easy."

"When do we ship out?" she asked just as quietly. "I'm guessing our destination is somewhere in the Middle East."

"Guess again, Doctor. And maybe you should wait for all the facts and details before you agree to sign on. I've got a feeling you're not going to like this assignment very much."

Zoe met his steady gaze with an equal air of calm. "I don't need to know the details. I'm all yours—if you'll have me."

It wasn't until the words left her mouth that she realized how dreadfully suggestive they were.

But then she thought, why not? She was attracted to this man on virtually every level. Why not let him know it?

But something shifted in his eyes, something unidentifiable flitted across his face, and she realized in another flash that he wore a wedding band on his left hand.

"I'm sorry, sir," she said swiftly. "I didn't mean for that to sound—"

His smile was crooked. "It's okay, I know what you meant. It's a juicy assignment. But you won't be going to the Middle East." He turned and knocked on the table to regain the room's attention. "The terrorists who took the Triple X live right here in the United States. We've traced the canisters to their stronghold in Montana. They're U.S. citizens, although they're trying hard to secede from the union. They're led by a man named Christopher Vincent, and they call themselves the CRO, or the Chosen Race Organization.''

The CRO.

The admiral glanced at her, and Zoe nodded. She knew all about the CRO. And this was what he'd meant about waiting to find out the details. The CRO was mysogynistic as well as being neo-Nazi, antigovernment and downright vicious. If Jake Robinson's plan was to send her into the CRO fortress as part of an undercover team assigned to retrieve the Trip X, it wasn't going to be fun. Women were treated little better than slaves in the CRO. They served, silently, tirelessly, unquestioningly: They were treated as possessions by their husbands and fathers. And they frequently were physically abused.

Jake was passing around satellite photos of the CRO headquarters—a former factory nestled in the hills about two miles outside of the tiny town of Belle, Montana. Zoe was familiar with the pictures, and with the extensive high-tech security the independently wealthy CRO leader, Christopher Vincent, had set up around the place.

If the lab in Arches had had even *half* the security of the CRO headquarters, this wouldn't have happened.

''We don't want to get in by force,'' the admiral was saying. ''That's not even an option worth considering at this point.''

Admiral Stonegate spoke up. ''Why not simply evacuate the surrounding towns and bomb the hell out of the bastards?''

Admiral Forrest rolled his eyes. ''Yeah, Jake,'' he said. ''That worked so well at Waco.''

''Surround 'em, then,'' Stonegate suggested, unthwarted and possibly even unaware of Mac Forrest's sarcasm. ''Give our soldiers gas masks and let the CRO use the Triple X to wipe themselves out.''

Admiral Robinson turned to Zoe as if he'd sensed her desire to respond.

''There are a number of reasons we wouldn't want to

risk that,'' Zoe explained. ''For one, if they waited for the right weather conditions—strong winds or even rain—the amount of Trip X they've got could take out more than just the immediately surrounding area. And then there's the matter of runoff. We don't know what would happen if that much Trip X got into the groundwater. We don't have enough data to know the dilution point—or, to be perfectly honest, if there even *is* a dilution point.'' The room was silent, and Zoe knew they were all imagining a lethal poison spreading through the groundwater of the country, making its way down to the Colorado River.... She took a deep breath. ''I'll say it again, gentlemen, our sole option in this situation is to retrieve—or destroy—the six canisters of Triple X in its powder form.''

''My plan is to continue surveillance,'' Admiral Robinson said. ''I've already got teams in place, watching the CRO fort, trailing everyone who goes outside of their gates. We'll continue to do that, but we'll also be sending someone inside to track down the exact whereabouts of the Triple X. That's not going to be easy. Only CRO members are allowed in.''

Senior Chief Becker lifted his hand. ''Permission to speak, sir?''

''Please. If we're going to work together as a team, let's not stand on formality.''

Becker nodded, but when he spoke, it was clear he chose his words carefully. ''I think it's obvious that I'm not likely to be accepted as a member of the CRO any time in the near future. Seaman Taylor, here, either. And as for Crash—Lieutenant Hawken—his face may be the right shade of pale, but it's only been a year since he was on the national news. He's got to be too well-known. And while my intent is not to suggest that lieutenants O'Donlon, Jones and Shaw aren't capable of a mission of this magnitude, sir, it seems to me we might want to have a team leader with more experience. I'm sure either Captain Catalanotto or Lieutenant Commander McCoy of Alpha Squad would appreciate the chance to be included in this op.''

The admiral listened carefully, waiting courteously until the senior chief had finished, despite the fact that Zoe could tell from his body language that everyone he wanted to be part of this operation was already right here in this room.

''I appreciate your thoughts, Senior Chief. And I'm aware of both Joe Cat and Blue McCoy's well-deserved reputations.'' He paused, glancing around the room before he casually dropped his bomb. ''But I'll be leading this team, hands-on, from out in the field. And I'll be the one gaining entry into the CRO fort.''

Chapter 2

Jake lifted his hands, halting the words of outrage, doubt and concern. He was too old to go into the field. He was too out of touch. It had been years since he'd last been in the real world. It was too dangerous. What if he were killed? What if, what if, what if?

"Here's the deal," he said. "I know Christopher Vincent. I met him about five years ago—he had a book published by the same company who released my wife's art books. We met at a party in New York, and I talked to him for a very long time. He's extremely dangerous, a complete megalomaniac. And it just so happens that he liked me. I know with a little help and the right cover story, I can get us inside."

"Admiral, this is highly irregular and—"

Jake cut Stonegate off. "And six missing canisters of T-X isn't?" He looked around the room. "I didn't call you here to ask your permission. *I* run the Gray Group. *I* call the shots. And this *is* a Gray Group mission. The President gave me this assignment with a direct order not to fail.

Those of you who haven't worked for the Gray Group before need to know that I don't take that order lightly. What I need right now from the SEALs and from Dr. Lange is to know whether or not you want to be part of my team.''

He hadn't even put the final ''m'' on team before Zoe Lange spoke up, her clear alto voice ringing out into the room. ''I'm in and I'm behind you one hundred percent, Admiral.''

She was just too cute, standing there in her blue jeans and blue-flowered T-shirt. She looked like a college student, but Jake knew better. She was Pat Sullivan's top operative. She'd come highly recommended. She was bright, she was beautiful and she was so freshly young it almost hurt to look at her.

Her hair was blond, long and straight. She wore it in classic California-girl style, with no bangs to soften her face. But she had a face that didn't need softening—it was already soft enough. She had baby-smooth skin, a face that was nearly a perfect oval, and equally perfect, delicately shaped features. From her fair skin and her light coloring, he'd expected her eyes to be blue. But they weren't. She had brown eyes. Not a light, hazel shade of brown, but deep, dark chocolate brown.

Was it possible for someone with eyes that dark to be a natural blonde? He knew exactly how to find out.

I'm all yours—if you'll have me.

Don't go there, pal! She hadn't meant it that way.

Jake focused his attention on his SEAL team. Harvard Becker. He'd never worked with the African-American senior chief, but when it came to electronic surveillance, he was the best. And right now Jake needed the best.

Seamen First Class Wesley Skelly, short and skinny, and Bobby Taylor, built double-wide, could've been any of the enlisted guys he knew back in Nam. Loyal to the bitter end, they drank too much, played too hard and were always right where you needed them, when you needed them. Right now, their loyalty was to Harvard, though, and they waited for their senior chief to nod his acceptance before they, too, agreed to sign on.

Lieutenant Billy Hawken, nicknamed Crash, was Jake's wife, Daisy's, cousin. Jake had helped raise him from the time the boy was ten. He thought of him as a son, but there was real reservation in the kid's eyes as he gazed at Jake across the table. *Are you sure you know what you're doing?* He could read the words in Billy's eyes as clearly as if he'd spoken them aloud.

Jake nodded. Yeah. He knew exactly what he was doing. He'd thought about it long and hard. This was more than just an excuse to get back into the real world. Although— he couldn't kid himself—he did want to do it just a little too much. Still, the timing was right and he trusted himself, trusted his instincts.

Billy turned to look at Lieutenant Mitchell Shaw, sitting on his right. Mitch and Billy had both worked for Jake's Gray Group more times than any of them could count. Mitch had been there at the conception of the group. He'd been part of the first mission. At five feet ten, he was shorter than most of the other SEALs, lean and compact, with long, dark hair and hazel eyes that gave nothing away.

Including his doubt.

His silence broadcast that, though, loud and clear.

Jake knew how Mitch thought, and he could practically see the progression that led to the lieutenant's short nod. He was in—but only because Mitch believed he and the rest of the SEALs would be able to keep Jake out of harm's way.

Jake was going to have to set him straight, but not here, not now.

"I'm in," Lieutenant Luke O'Donlon announced, his words echoed by Lieutenant Harlan Jones. Lucky and Cowboy. Both blond and blue-eyed, Jake had chosen them based on their fair-skinned complexions as well as their reputations. Both were hotshots, that title well-earned, and both would be accepted into the CRO as easily as possible, if they had to go that way.

And that was that. He had his team. The SEALs had all agreed, if not quite as enthusiastically as Zoe Lange.

"Gather your gear, gentlemen—and Doctor," Jake said, glancing at the young woman. "And prepare to meet at Andrews in two hours. Bring a sweater or two. We're going to Montana."

Senior Chief Harvard Becker was the first to reach the door. He hit the buzzer that signaled the guards in the outer chambers and the hatch swung open. The SEALs cleared out, none of them uttering another word.

They probably knew Admiral Stonegate would handle all the uttering necessary.

"I will be registering my official protest," he told Jake stiffly. "An admiral's place is not in the field. You are far too valuable to the U.S. Navy to put yourself into a position of such high risk that—"

"Didn't you hear anything Dr. Lange said?" Jake asked the older man. "With the magnitude of this kind of potential disaster, we're all expendable, Ron."

"It's been years since you've been in the field."

"I've been keeping up," Jake told him evenly.

"Mentally, perhaps, but physically, there's just no way—"

Since he'd gotten out of the hospital, Jake had put himself into the best physical shape he'd been in since Vietnam. "I can keep up physically, too. Ron, you know, fifty-three's just not that old—"

"Dammit, this is all John Glenn's fault."

Jake had to laugh. "Excuse me for laughing in your face, pal, but that's ridiculous."

Stonegate was offended. "I *will* be registering a protest."

"You do that, Admiral," Jake said, tired of the noise. "But not until this mission is over. Everything you've heard today in this room is top secret. You leak *any* of it—

even in the form of a protest, and I will throw your narrow-minded, pointy ass in jail.''

Well, that did it.

Stonegate stormed out.

Mac Forrest followed. ''And I'll help,'' he murmured to Jake with a wink. ''Anything I can do, Jake, you just let me know.''

The room was finally empty.

Jake drew in a deep breath and let it all out in a rush as he collected and organized his notes and papers.

That had gone far better than he'd hoped. He'd been sure his age was going to be an insurmountable issue, that none of his first choice of SEALs would accept the assignment. He'd gone so far as to have his hair colored for the occasion, covering the silver at his temples with his regular shade of dark brown. He'd figured looking as young as possible couldn't hurt.

And it *had* made him look younger, there was no doubt about it.

He'd liked the way his colored hair looked more than he cared to admit. But he had admitted it. He'd forced himself to confront the issue. He hated the thought of growing old. He'd fought it ever since he'd turned thirty with every breath he took, cutting red meat and high-cholesterol-inducing foods out of his diet. Eating health foods and sea-weeds and exercising religiously every day. Aerobics. Weights. Running.

He hadn't lied to Ron Stonegate. He *was* in top-notch, near-perfect shape, even for a man fifteen years his junior.

There was only one type of exercise he no longer participated in regularly and that was—

Jake closed his briefcase with a snap and turned around and found himself staring directly into Zoe Lange's eyes.

Sex.

Yes, it had definitely been nearly three years since he'd last had sex.

Jake swallowed and forced a smile. ''God, I'm sorry,''

he said. "How long have you been standing there? I didn't realize you were still in the room."

She shifted her briefcase to her other hand, and Jake realized that she was nervous. He made Pat Sullivan's top operative nervous.

The feeling was extremely mutual—but for what had to be an entirely different reason. He found her attractive, college-girl getup and all. *Much* too attractive.

"I just wanted to thank you again for including me in this assignment," she said, all but stammering. She was trying so hard to be cool, but he knew otherwise.

"Let's see if you're still thanking me after you get an up-close look at the CRO compound." Jake headed for the door to get away from her subtle, freshly sweet scent. She wasn't wearing perfume. He had to guess it was her hair. Hair that would slip between his fingers like silk. If he were close enough to touch it. Which he wasn't.

"I've spent years in the Middle East. At least I won't have to walk around wearing a veil in Montana." She followed, almost tripping over her own feet to keep up. "I'm just…I'm thrilled to be working with you, sir."

He stopped in the corridor just outside the third door. There was no doubt about it. "You've read Scooter's damn book."

For seventeen years, that book had been coming back to haunt him. Scoot had written his memoirs about his time in Nam. Who knew the monosyllabic, conversationally challenged SEAL was a budding Hemingway? But he'd written *Laughing in the Face of Fire* both eloquently and gracefully. It was one of the few books on Nam that Jake had actually almost liked—except for the fact that Scooter had made Jake out to be some kind of demigod.

Zoe Lange had probably read the damn thing when she was twelve or thirteen—or at some other god-awful impressionable age—and no doubt had been carrying around some crazy idea of Lieutenant Jake Robinson, superhero, ever since.

"Well, yeah, I've read it," she told him. "Of course I've read it." She was looking at him the way a ten-year-old boy would look at Mark McGwire or Danny Sosa.

He hated it. Hero worship without a modicum of lust. What the hell had happened to him?

He'd turned fifty, that's what. And children like Zoe Lange—who hadn't even been born during his first few tours in Vietnam—thought of him as someone's grandpa.

"Scooter exaggerated," he said shortly, starting down the hall toward the elevators. He was mad at himself for giving a damn. So what if this girl didn't see him as a man? It was better that way, considering they were going to be working together, considering he was *not* interested in getting involved with her. *"Extensively."*

"Even if only ten percent of the stories he told were true, you would still be a hero."

"There's no such thing as a Vietnam war hero."

"You don't really believe that."

"Yeah? You can't be a hero alone in a room. You need the crowd. The ticker-tape parade. The gorgeous blonde rushing the convertible to kiss you silly. I know—I've seen pictures of U.S. soldiers coming home after the Second World War. *They* sure as hell didn't get egged by college students."

"The Vietnam era was a confusing time in history."

Jake winced. *"History.* Jeez, it wasn't *that* long ago. Make me feel old, why don't you?"

"I don't think you're old, Admiral."

"Okay, then start by calling me Jake. You're on my team, we're going to get to know each other pretty well by the time this is over." Jake stopped at the elevators and punched his security code into the keypad. "And I am old. I've been around a half a century, and I've seen more than my share of terrible, violent, monstrous acts. The things people do to each other appalls me. But I'm going to use that in my favor. Everything I've seen and learned is going to help me keep Chris Vincent and the CRO from doing some awful, permanent damage to this country that I love.''

She laughed. Her teeth were white and straight. ''And you claim you're not a hero.'' The elevator doors slid open and she followed him inside. ''I think you're wrong. I think you *can* be a hero alone in a room. I think you would've shied away from the ticker-tape parade anyway.''

''Are you kidding? I would've eaten it up with a spoon.'' He punched in the code that would take them to the ground floor. ''Look, Doc, I appreciate your support, I do. Just...don't believe everything you read in Scooter's book.''

''Four hundred and twenty-seven.''

''Four hundred and twenty-seven what?''

''Men.''

His first thought was surely a sign that he'd had sex on his mind far too frequently of late. But there was no innuendo in Zoe Lange's face, no hint of a suggestion in her eyes that she wanted Jake to be number four hundred and twenty-eight in a very, very long line. In fact, such a long line, it was preposterous. He tried not to laugh and failed. ''I cannot begin to guess what you're talking about. I mean, I'm trying, but...'' He laughed again at his own cluelessness. ''You've lost me, Doctor.''

''My father was number four hundred and twenty-seven,'' she said quietly. ''He's one of Jake's Boys.''

Jake didn't know what to say.

It happened sometimes. Someone would come up to him with emotion brimming in their eyes and shake his hand, whispering that their husband or son or father was one of Jake's Boys. As if he still had some kind of hold over them. Or as if, upon saving their lives, he'd somehow become responsible for them until the end of time.

He'd learned to be courteous and brief. He'd shake their hand, touch their shoulder, smile into their eyes and pretend he remembered Private This or Corporal That. The truth was, he didn't remember any of them. The faces stuck in his mind were only of the men he hadn't been able to save. The men who died, who were already dead. Empty eyes. All those awful, empty eyes...

"Sergeant Matthew Lange," she told him. "He was with the forty-fifth—"

"I don't remember him." He couldn't lie to this woman. Not if she was going to be on his team.

She didn't even blink. "I didn't expect you to, sir. He was only one out of hundreds." She smiled and reached out to take his hand, to squeeze his fingers. "You know, I owe *my* life to you, as well. I wasn't born until a year after he came home."

Which meant her father was probably younger than Jake was.

Perfect.

His one completely loyal ally, the one person on his team who honestly didn't have any reservations about his age or ability, had just managed to make him feel undeniably old.

And not just old, but *nasty* and old. Like some kind of complete degenerate.

As he gazed into her perfect brown eyes, as she held onto his hand and he felt the warmth and strength of her fingers, the smoothness of her skin against his palm, he forced himself to admit that for the first time in the two and a half years since Daisy had died, he'd finally met a woman he could imagine himself making love to.

And he didn't want that. He didn't want to imagine himself capable of wanting anyone but the only woman he'd ever loved, the woman he *still* loved. But he couldn't deny that he missed sex, that he wanted sex. And he didn't know how to reconcile his physical needs with the indisputable fact that Daisy was forever gone.

Forever, permanently gone. And she wasn't coming back.

For just a second, he let himself really look at Zoe Lange. She was brilliant, she was brave, she was tough, yet her beauty held a sweetness to which he was powerfully drawn.

Her eyes were alight with intelligent wit, her mouth quick to smile. Her laughter was contagious, and her body...

Jake let himself look, for just a second, at Dr. Zoe Lange's near-perfect body. Her legs were long, her jeans slightly loose on her hips and thighs. She was not particularly tall, not particularly short, but average wasn't a word that could ever be used to describe her. Her arms were well-toned, lithe. She was trim in all the right places, and, God, all right, *yes,* he *was* a breast man, and she had a body that pushed all his buttons in a very big way. Her T-shirt clung to her full figure enticingly, making her demure little flowered print look decadent and sexy.

In a flash, in his mind's eye, Jake saw her, tumbled back on his bed with him, her T-shirt and jeans gone, his mouth locked on hers, her perfect breasts filling his palms, his body buried deeply inside her as they moved together and...

Oh God, oh God, oh *God.* Sheer wanting slammed into him so hard he nearly gasped aloud. But that wanting was followed just as quickly by guilt and shame.

He still loved Daisy. How could he still love Daisy and want someone else so badly?

Sweet Lord, he missed her so much.

The hole in his gut that he'd been trying to heal for nearly three years tore wide open.

And he released Zoe's hand and took a step backward, bumping awkwardly against the elevator wall. He realized almost instantly that he was well on his way to becoming completely aroused. Ah, jeez, terrific. Just what he needed—a souvenir from his little guilt trip.

He didn't know whether to laugh or cry.

So he did neither, casually holding his briefcase in front of him.

Zoe kept her eyes carefully on the numbers above the elevator door, and he knew she'd seen something in his eyes that embarrassed her. No wonder—he'd been eyeing her like the hungry old fox checking out the gingerbread girl. Good job, Robinson. Way to feel even older and nastier. And somehow it was even worse since his attraction was clearly one-sided.

But when she turned toward him, she was the one who apologized. "I'm sorry," she said. "I didn't mean to embarrass you. You must get approached by people all the time and—"

"I like it when they've done something really right with their lives—the way your father obviously did. He must be very proud of you. God knows I'd be proud as hell if you were *my* kid." He tried his best to sound fatherly. But all he sounded was pathetic.

She smiled tentatively. "Well, thanks."

The elevator opened, and this time Jake stood back, courteously letting her out first. She looked both ways, up and down the deserted corridor as the elevator doors closed behind them.

"Exit to the street's down that way." Jake pointed. "Take the—"

"First right," she said. "I know, thanks. Listen, Admiral—"

"Jake," he said. "Please."

"Actually, Admiral works a little better for me."

"All right," he said quickly. "That's fine. It's not like I'm ordering you to call me Jake or anything. It's not like—"

"I know." She tried to meet his gaze, but couldn't hold it this time. She was nervous again. "I was just... I can't help but wonder about your willingness to put yourself at risk. I mean, you've earned the right to sit back and command safely from behind a desk, sir. And I can't imagine your, um, wife is very happy about your decision to go back into the field. Particularly after that assassination attempt a few years ago. You were in the hospital for months."

Jake had been around long enough to recognize a fishing expedition when he heard one. But what information exactly was Zoe Lange fishing for? Was she looking to find his motivation for taking the mission or his reason for looking at her as if he wanted to eat her alive?

He had no need to hide anything from her—well, except for the extremely unprofessional fact that nearly every time he looked at her, he pictured her naked. And even if thoughts of Daisy didn't stop that, all he really had to do was think about those missing canisters of T-X. *That* cooled him down pretty damn instantly.

"I know that's an extremely personal question," she continued quickly, "and you can tell me it's none of my business if you want and—"

"Daisy, my wife, died of cancer," he told her quietly. "It'll be three years ago this Christmas."

"Oh," she said. "I'm so sorry. I didn't know."

"And I think you're probably right. If she were still alive, I'd be thinking long and hard about the risks of this mission. But even if she were still alive, I wouldn't be able to avoid the fact that I've got a connection to Christopher Vincent. I know I can get into the CRO's inner sanctions. It's just, this way, it makes the choice a complete no-brainer."

She was looking at him with compassion in her eyes, and he glanced away, unable to bear the thought of looking closer and seeing her pity.

"You better go pack," he said brusquely. "We go wheels up in ninety-eight minutes. If you make us wait for you, trust me, the team will never let you live it down."

"Don't worry, Jake," she said. "I'll be the first one on the plane."

He watched her walk away, and before she took that right corner, she looked back and gave him a smile and a little wave.

And it wasn't until he was in his office, changing out of his ice-cream suit and into black BDUs, that he realized she'd called him Jake.

Chapter 3

Zoe itched to call Peter.

Five months ago, she would have. She would have called on a secured line and she would have said, "What does it mean—a man's been a widower for nearly three years, and he still wears his wedding ring?"

Peter would've said, "That's obvious. He uses the ring to keep women from coming too close."

And *she* would have said, "I think he still loves her."

And Peter would've snorted and said, "Love's a myth. He just hasn't met anyone who could replace his dead wife. But you better believe when he does, that ring will come off faster than you can spit. The hell with him. What do you say you and I meet in Boston next weekend and set the Ritz Carlton aflame?"

But that's what Peter would've said five months ago. Before he'd discovered that love was indeed *not* a myth.

Her name was Marita and she was a TV news anchor based in Miami. She was of Cuban descent and lovely, but Zoe wasn't even remotely jealous. Well, maybe she was a *little* jealous—but only of the fact that Peter, restless, hungry, insatiable, cynical superagent Peter McBride had finally found complete inner peace.

Zoe was jealous of that. She'd liked Peter—she'd even loved him more than a little, but she knew just from one conversation with him after he'd met Marita that he finally had a shot at true happiness.

And Peter deserved that.

Zoe had liked talking to him, liked the way he could always make her laugh. And she had liked making love with him the few times a year that their work for the Agency brought them into each other's presence.

But she'd known from the start there could be no permanence in their relationship. She was too like him. Too restless, too hungry, too damned insatiable, too jaded by a world bent on destroying itself.

She hadn't spoken to Peter in five months, assuming his new bride wouldn't appreciate his getting phone calls from a former lover. But she missed his friendship. She missed talking to him.

She missed the sex, too. It had been safe. She'd never once been in danger of completely losing her heart.

"So," she said to Peter, even though he wasn't there, "what does it mean that I'm packing my sexiest underwear and this little black nightgown?"

"To wear in Montana in September?" he would have mused, lifting one elegant eyebrow. "You're in trouble, Lange."

"You wouldn't believe the way he looked at me in that elevator." Zoe closed her eyes, momentarily melting just from the heat of the memory. "Dear God, I *am* in trouble."

"Doing your boss is bad office politics," Peter would have reminded her. "But on the other hand, he's not really your boss, is he? Pat Sullivan is. So, go for him. You've been fantasizing about the guy for years—how could you not go for him? And if he's looking at you like that... I'm surprised you didn't make a move right then and there. It wouldn't've taken much to disable the security cams in the elevator and…"

"He'd been giving me go-away signals from the moment we met." She pulled her warmest sweaters from her closet shelf. Her warmest sweaters—and her skimpiest tank tops. Shorts. Her bathing suit even. It was a bikini—Rio cut. Not quite a thong, but not quite demure, either. Maybe she'd get lucky and they'd have Indian summer. "Besides, at the time I thought he was still married."

"Ooh, there are those upright, golden, Girl Scout morals, shining through again." When Peter said it like that, it was as if it were something she should be ashamed of.

"He seemed so embarrassed by the fact that he finds me attractive. As if it made him feel, you know, *guilty.*" She'd come full circle. "He definitely still loves her. In his mind, he *is* still married."

"So what are you going to do?" Peter would've asked.

Zoe zipped and shouldered her bag. "He's a really good guy, Pete. I'm going to try to be his friend."

He'd always hated it when she called him Pete. "And for that you definitely need all that underwear from Victoria's Secret?"

"Six missing *canisters* of Trip X," she said, and Peter's evil spirit was instantly exorcised, instantly gone.

She had a job to do. A very, very important, life-or-death job.

Zoe grabbed her briefcase, grabbed her laptop and locked her apartment door without looking back.

Day two. Oh-three-hundred.

Jake had been out most of the night, silently creeping along the perimeter of the CRO compound with Cowboy Jones. Lieutenant Jones's father was a rear admiral. Jake had figured that out of everyone on the team, Jones would be most at ease with buddying up with a man of his rank.

He'd been wrong.

Ever since they'd inserted in Montana, his entire team

had been treating him with kid gloves. Let me carry that for you, Admiral. I'll take care of that, Admiral. Why don't you just stand aside and let me handle that, Admiral. Sit down, Admiral. You're getting in the way.

Well, okay. No one had said that last bit, but Jake knew they'd been thinking it.

Even Billy Hawken, the closest thing to a son Jake had ever been blessed with, had pulled Jake aside to tell him in a low voice that the technological advances in the surveillance gear in just the past few years had changed both the hardware and the software completely. If Jake needed any help understanding the readouts or if he needed any assistance with the equipment, Billy was standing by.

And no doubt if Jake needed helped cutting his food, Billy would do that for him, too.

What, was he suddenly ninety years old? And hell, even if he *was* ninety years old, that didn't automatically mean his brain had turned to oatmeal.

As they'd done the sneak and peek, Jones kept asking him if he'd seen enough, if he'd wanted to turn around and head back to camp.

The night had been crisply cold, but Jake had wanted to examine every square inch of the CRO compound he could see from the outer fence. He'd squinted through his night-vision glasses until his head had ached, and then he'd squinted some more. He'd done a complete circuit, and he'd lingered longer than he otherwise might have at the main gate, simply to show Jones he was capable of doing a complete, thorough job.

Except Lucky and Wes had been sent after them, to see what was holding them up. Jake and Cowboy had run into the pair on the trail. It was obvious that his team had sent them out as a search-and-rescue party to drag the old admiral in from wherever he'd gotten himself entangled in barbed wire.

It was discouraging, to say the least.

Jake needed these men to trust him. He needed their support, one hundred percent.

Because he *was* going in there. He'd figured out a plan— and Zoe Lange's somewhat different surveillance tonight had given him cause to believe it would work.

She sat across from him now, in the main trailer.

Bobby and Wes had gotten hold of four beat-up old recreational vehicles that afternoon, and the SEALs had already outfitted them with enough surveillance equipment to make a destroyer sit low in the water. They were parked in a KOA campground fifteen miles south of Belle—just a group of happy campers, in town to do some hunting.

Zoe stood up and opened the refrigerator, helping herself to a can of soda. Something without caffeine. She didn't look tired despite the late hour, but then again, he hadn't expected her to.

Jake had been taking care to keep his distance from her from the moment he'd stepped on the plane at Andrews. He hadn't gotten too close, had barely let himself look at her. But he allowed himself to watch her now as she spoke.

"The name of the bar is Mel's, and it's owned by Hal— Harold—Francke, spelled with a c-k-e. I didn't meet him. Apparently he doesn't come in often on Wednesday nights. The waitress I did meet was named Cindy Allora. She said Hal's always looking for new hired help." She smiled. "I guess he's a dirty old man with a wandering pair of hands, and the turnover rate of waitresses at Mel's is high."

A dirty old man. Jake tried not to wince visibly as she sat at the table.

Zoe looked different tonight. The flower-print T-shirt was gone. She was dressed all in black. Slim black flares, black boots, black hooded sweatshirt that slipped off one shoulder to reveal her smooth tanned skin and a body-hugging black tank top, its thin straps unable to hide the straps of her black bra.

She was wearing quite a bit of makeup, too. Dark liner around her eyes, thick mascara, deep red on her lips. She wore her hair down, loose and windswept around her shoulders.

She looked dangerous. Wild. Completely capable. And sexy as hell. Hal Francke would hire her on the spot. And then he'd be all over her.

"Maybe this isn't such a good idea," Jake said. "Maybe you could get a job working checkout at the supermarket."

She lifted an eyebrow lazily. "And I could communicate with you by semaphore flags when you came into town?" She leaned forward slightly. "You know as well as I do the CRO men come to town and go to the bar. Only the women go into the supermarket."

Jake refused to let himself look down her shirt. He kept his gaze staunchly focused on her dark brown eyes. "It just…it seems unfair. A scientist of your knowledge and ability. I'm not only asking you to wait tables, but virtually guaranteeing you're going to get groped as well."

She laughed. "You haven't worked with women much, have you, sir?"

"Not as team leader, no."

"Let's just say if it happens, it won't be the first time I've been groped while on assignment. And if letting Hal Francke cop a feel in the back alley helps keep me where I'll be of most assistance to you…" She spread her hands in a shrug.

Jake laughed in dismay. "God. You're serious."

"It's no big deal." She took a sip of her soda. "You know, Jake, I just don't take sex as seriously as I think you do."

Sex. God. How did their conversation get onto *that* topic? She was more than just dressed differently tonight, she was looking at him differently, too. Just a few days ago he'd felt bad because there hadn't been a bit of attraction in her eyes. Now she was holding his gaze rather pointedly. Now she was smiling just a little bit too warmly.

It made him nervous as hell.

And they were talking about sex. But he couldn't steer

the conversation in a safer direction. Not yet. First he had to ask. "Are you telling me you'd *sleep* with this guy?"

"I think of my body as just another of my assets," she told him, a small smile playing about the corners of her lips. "I don't mind showing it off if it gets me closer to my goal. It's amusing, actually, to see the way men can be manipulated—" she leaned closer again and lowered her voice "—just by the whispered suggestion of sex." She laughed, and her eyes seemed to sparkle. "Look at you. Even *you* aren't immune."

"Me? I'm... I'm..." His face was heating in a blush, as if he were fourteen again. How did she know? He'd been purposely playing it super cool. Mr. Extra Laid Back. It had required superhuman effort, but he *hadn't* looked down her shirt. His gaze slid there now, and he quickly shut his eyes. "I'm only human." Damn, and he'd been trying so hard not to be.

"Try human *male*," she said, laughter in her voice. "I swear, men fall into one of two categories. You have the men who are totally controlled by sex, and you have the men—like you—who spend all their time trying to protect women from the men who are totally controlled by sex. Either way, it's a complete manipulation."

She stood up, peeling off her sweatshirt. "I walk into Mel's bar dressed in my little tank top. You're sitting at the bar, and maybe you're not controlled by sex per se. Maybe you *don't* catch sight of me in the mirror and try to imagine me naked."

Jake did his best not to react. How could she know? There was no way she could have read his mind.

She sat next to him, sliding onto the bench beside him. "Maybe I sit down next to you and you glance over, and you think, gee, what's that nice woman doing in here alone? Maybe you don't notice what I'm wearing, maybe it has no effect on you, and you think, gee, she has pretty eyes." Her smile clearly said, *yeah, right.* "And you look up, and you notice about five big drunk guys getting ready to approach me, and you think, she's not going to like it when those clowns put their hands all over her. And you stand up, you move closer. You're ready to save the day."

She smiled. "Like it or not, notice 'em or not, babe, you've just been manipulated by my breasts."

Jake had to laugh. He put his head in his hands.

"God, the awful thing is that you're absolutely right. I just never thought of it that way." He looked at her from between his fingers. "Look, we need to focus on how you're going to get that waitressing job at Mel's, and what's going to happen after you're established there."

She stood up, slipping her sweatshirt over her shoulders. "Cindy invited me to a party at her friend Monica's house on Saturday afternoon. Hal Francke is going to be there. I thought it would be smart to manipulate him into approaching and asking me to work for him. That way if anyone in the CRO gets suspicious and starts checking into me, they'll find out I'm just another girl Hal found at some party. It's a little less suspect than if I go into Mel's and fill out a job application."

"It's also a little less certain," Jake pointed out. "I mean, you don't know for sure he's going to offer you the job."

Zoe gave him a look. "It's a hot tub party, Jake. He'll offer me the job."

Hot tub. Jake cleared his throat. Hot tub.

"Don't worry, I'll keep my bathing suit on," she assured him with a smile.

Somehow that didn't make him feel any better.

"So after I get this job waitressing at Mel's, what then?" she asked. "I mean, obviously, I'll be in place to act as a go-between for any communication between you and the rest of the team."

He nodded. "It might be a while before I can come into town. I know the CRO rules are pretty complicated—I might have to pass some sort of loyalty test before I have free run of the place. But once I do come into the bar, I'll, um…'' He managed a weak smile. ''Well, I'll hit on you. I'm sorry—but I think that's the cleanest way to explain why we're going to spend so much time whispering into each other's ears. If you could set it up—tell people you're a little older than you really are, they might believe there could be something between us.''

Zoe's heartbeat tripled in time. Jake Robinson was going to hit on her. They were going to spend time cozied up together. True, it was only to pass information, but she could go far on a fantasy like that. She kept her voice low and controlled. ''I think we can make them believe we're attracted to each other. Our difference in ages is not that big a deal.''

''I'm old enough to be your father.''

''So what? You can pretend you're going through some kind of midlife crisis, and I'll let everyone know I prefer more mature men. Experienced men.'' Gorgeous, incredibly buff, blue-eyed, heroic men…

''I just don't want it to come off as such an obvious setup. You know, the first time I come into the bar… A beautiful young woman like you…''

''Jake, the first time you go into that bar, the women are going to be lining up to meet you. I'll have to fight to get to the front of that line.'' She laughed in disbelief at the look on his face. ''You'd think after fifty-three years of looking into the bathroom mirror every morning, you might've noticed you're the most handsome man on the planet.''

His laughter was tinged with embarrassment. God, he really didn't know what he looked like, did he?

''Well, thanks for your vote of confidence, but—''

Zoe wanted to reach for his hand to squeeze it, to reassure him that this would work, but she didn't dare touch him.

''I'll set everything up,'' she said. ''I'll set up the fact that I'm looking to have a fling, too.''

''Not just a fling,'' he corrected her almost apologetically. "I'm going to need a way to get you into the CRO compound. I'll need your expertise in there to help me find the missing canisters of T-X. And the only way for a woman to get inside is…"

"Through marriage."

Her laughter sounded almost giddy to her ears. This assignment was a dream assignment to start with, Hal Francke's anticipated groping aside. She was working with Jake Robinson, the man who had always been her own personal poster model for the word *hero*. Whenever she'd imagined her perfect man, he'd always had Jake's steely nerve, his long list of achievements, and yes, his deep blue eyes.

And now this dream assignment was going to have her pretend she was marrying her hero. He was going to have to kiss her, hold her in his arms. To *marry* her. Could it possibly get *any* better?

Yes, he could kiss her, and mean it. And maybe, just maybe she could make that happen.

"It won't be real," he told her hastily, misreading her laughter. "The way I understand it, Christopher Vincent performs any wedding ceremonies among his followers. There's no paperwork or licenses filled out. They don't believe in state intervention when it comes to marriage."

He looked at his hands, at the wedding ring he wore.

"It won't be real," he said again, as if he were trying to convince himself of that fact.

Zoe sat across from him, her elation instantly subdued. "Are you sure you want to do this?" she asked him quietly. "You'll have to take off your wedding ring."

Jake looked at his left hand again. "I know." He fingered it with his thumb. "That's okay. It doesn't really mean anything anyway. We were only married a few days before she died."

Wait a minute… "Crash told me you and Daisy were together for just short of forever."

"Daisy didn't believe in marriage," he told her simply.

"She only married me at the end, because it was the only thing she had left to give me." He took off the ring, letting it spin on the table in front of him.

"You must really miss her."

"Yeah. She was pretty incredible." He caught the ring deftly, midspin, and slipped it into his pants pocket. "I should probably get used to not wearing this."

He looked so sad, Zoe ached for him. "You know, Jake—we could think of another way to do this."

He met her eyes. "I suppose I could call Pat Sullivan and see if Gregor Winston's available to take over for you."

Zoe reacted. "Gregor's not *half* as qualified as—"

Jake was smiling at her. "As you are," he finished for her. "Yeah, that's why I requested you."

"But he's a man," she pointed out unnecessarily. "He could get into the CRO without having to marry you."

"Thank goodness." Jake's smile faded as he gazed at her. "Look, I'm all right with this, Zoe. But if it makes *you* feel uncomfortable…"

She looked at his hands, now ringless. He had big hands, with neat nails and broad, strong fingers. She even found his hands outrageously attractive.

Uncomfortable was not the word to describe the way she felt about this assignment.

She tried to make a joke. "Are you kidding? I have no problem letting Hal Francke grope me. Why should it bother me if I have to let you do the same?"

It wasn't true. The part about Hal. Despite what she'd told Jake, she hated it when men touched her, when she had to use her body in any way while on the job. But there were times when dressing seductively got her further. And as for letting men touch her…

She'd learned to pretend it was nothing, to be flip about it. She was a tough, professional Agency operative. She shouldn't give a damn about something as meaningless as that. And although she also pretended her casualness extended all the way to the act of sex, she'd always drawn the line well before that. Always.

"Are you telling me you'd *sleep* with this guy?" Jake had asked about Hal Francke.

She'd purposely sidestepped his question, avoiding a direct answer. It wouldn't do her a bit of good to make her team leader believe she needed to be protected. As nice as it might be in some fantasy to have Jake ready to rush to her side, to protect her from the Hal Franckes of the world, this was reality.

And if he thought she was weak—in any way—she'd spend this entire mission inside the safety of the surveillance van.

"I'm going to have to make it look real," he told her. "You know, when I come into the bar."

"I will, too," she told him. "So don't freak out when I grab your butt, all right?"

He laughed, but it was decidedly halfhearted, and she knew what he was thinking. The last woman to grab his butt had been his wife.

Zoe pushed herself up and out of the booth, tossing her empty soda can into the recycling bin. "Do you want…" She stopped. It seemed so forward of her to ask—and that wasn't even considering her suggestion implied a lack of ability on the admiral's part.

But he could read her mind. "You're afraid I'm going to get stiff," he said, then winced realizing his poor word choice. "Tense up," he quickly corrected himself. "You're afraid I'm going to tense up."

Zoe couldn't keep from laughing, and Jake joined in, shaking his head. "Jeez," he said. "This *is* awkward, isn't it?"

She held out her hand to him. "Come here."

He hesitated, just looking at her, a curious mix of emotions in his eyes. He shook his head. "Zoe, I don't think…"

"Just come here."

With a sigh, he slid from the booth, the powerful muscles in his arms standing out in sharp relief as he pushed himself up. Dressed the way he was in a body-hugging black T-shirt and black BDU pants, she could see he was in better shape than most men half his age. He looked like some kind of dream come true. Why couldn't he see that?

"I don't need to, you know, practice this," he said, even as he took her hand. "It's not like it's something I've forgotten how to do."

"But this way, the mystery's gone," she told him. "This way you don't have to spend any time in the bar thinking about the fact that Daisy was the last woman you held in your arms. This way you'll be able to concentrate on making it look real, on getting the job done."

She slipped her arms around him, but he just stood there, arms at his side, swearing very, very softly.

"Come on, Jake," she said. "This is just make-believe." She said it as much to remind herself of that fact.

He smelled too good. He felt too good. His body fit too perfectly with hers.

And slowly, very slowly, he put his arms around her.

Zoe rested her head on his shoulder, aware of the solidness of his chest against her breasts, the tautness of his thighs against hers, the complete warmth of his arms.

He slowly rested his cheek against her head, and she felt him sigh.

"You all right?" she whispered.

"Yeah." He pulled back, away from her, forcing a smile. "Thank you. This was a...smart idea. Because I *am* a little tense, aren't I?"

"You should probably kiss me."

He looked as if she'd suggested he use the neighbor's cat for target practice. "Oh, I don't think—"

"Jake, I'm sorry, but you are not a *little* tense, you are *so* tense. If you come into that bar and hold me so politely like that, as if I'm your *grandmother*..."

He couldn't argue, because he knew it was true. "I'm not sure I'm ready to—"

"Then maybe we better come up with another plan. Maybe we should be trying to figure out a way to get Cowboy or Lucky into the CRO compound. If you can't handle this—"

Something sparked in his eyes. "I didn't say I couldn't handle this. I meant that I wasn't ready to deal with this *right now.*"

"If you can't do it now, how're you going to do it in a week or two?" she asked. "Come on, Jake. Try again. And this time hold me like you want to be inside me."

The something that had sparked in his eyes flared into fire. "Well, hell, that shouldn't be too hard to do."

He pulled her to him almost roughly and held her tightly, his thigh between her legs, her body anchored against him by his hand on her rear end.

She felt almost faint. "Much better," she said weakly. "Now kiss me."

He didn't move. He just gazed at her, that hypnotizing heat smoldering in his eyes.

After several long moments, he still didn't move, so she kissed him.

It was a small kiss, a delicate caress of his beautiful mouth with her lips. And he *still* didn't move.

But he was breathing hard as she pulled back to look at him, as if he'd just run a five-mile race. His eyes were the most brilliant shade of blue she'd ever seen in her life.

She kissed him again, and this time he finally moved.

He lowered his head and caught her mouth with his and then, God, he was kissing her. *Really* kissing her. *Soul* kissing her.

She angled her head to kiss him even more deeply, pulling his tongue hard into her mouth, wanting more, *more.*

He tasted like sweetened coffee, like everything she'd ever wanted, like a lifetime of fantasies finally coming true.

He pressed her even more tightly against him as she

clung to him, as still he kissed her, harder, deeper, endlessly, his passion—like hers—skyrocketing completely off the scale, his hands skimming her body as she strained to get closer, closer....

And then Jake finally tore his mouth away from hers. ''My God.'' He looked completely shocked, thoroughly stunned.

Zoe still held onto him tightly, her knees too weak to support her weight. ''That was...very believable.''

''Yeah,'' he agreed, breathing hard. ''Very believable.''

''Good to know we can make that seem...so believable.''

He pulled free from her embrace and turned away. ''Yeah. That's good to know.''

She had to lean against the counter.

''Look,'' he said, his back to her, ''it's really late and I have some things I need to do before morning, so...''

He wanted her to leave. Zoe moved carefully toward the door. ''I hope sleep is on that list.'' She tried to sound lighthearted, tried to sound as if her entire world hadn't just tilted on its axis.

He laughed quietly. ''Yeah, well, sleep's pretty low priority these days. If I don't get to it tonight, there's always tomorrow.''

She paused with her hand on the doorknob. ''Jake, that kiss—it wasn't real. We just made it *look* real.''

He turned and gazed at her then, the expression in his eyes completely unreadable.

''Yeah,'' he said quietly. ''I know that.''

Chapter 4

"Let's do it!" Harvard said, but stopped short as he caught sight of Jake. "Admiral. You're joining us for a run this morning, sir?"

"Do you have a problem with that, Senior Chief?"

"Well…no, of course not, sir." Harvard didn't say the word *but*. He didn't have to. It was implied.

Jake held onto the side of the team's beat-up station wagon for balance as he stretched the muscles in first one thigh and then the other. He kept his expression pleasant, his voice easygoing. "Say what you're thinking, H. If we're going to be a team, we can't keep secrets from each other."

"I guess I was thinking, sir, that if *I* were an Admiral, you wouldn't find me volunteering for PT at oh-seven-hundred on a morning after I'd been out on a sneak and peek until oh-*three*-hundred."

Jake looked at the faces of his men. And woman. Zoe was there, dressed in running gear that might as well have been painted onto her. He looked away from her, refusing to let himself think about last night. Refusing to think about that incredible kiss.

"Cowboy here was out as late as I was," he pointed out. "Lucky and Wes, too. In fact, who here closed their eyes last night before oh-three-thirty?"

No one.

Jake smiled. "So like you said, Senior, let's do it. I'm as ready as you are."

Harvard looked at Cowboy, and Cowboy nodded, very slightly.

The message couldn't have been more clear if he'd signaled with flags.

Don't let the old man hurt himself.

Jeez.

Harvard set the pace, taking the road that led in a two-mile loop around the campground at an unchallenging jog.

And no one complained. In fact, they hung way back, letting Jake be way out ahead, up with Harvard.

Not a single one of 'em thought Jake could keep up with them. Not even Billy or Mitch.

It would have been funny if it weren't so damned sobering. If his team didn't think he could keep up with them on a morning run, there wouldn't be much they'd trust him to do.

But then Zoe broke free from where she'd been blocked in, in the back, kicking her pace until she'd moved up alongside Jake. She didn't say a word. She just made a face, clearly scornful of the slow and steady pace. And then she lifted one eyebrow, her message again quite clear. *Shall we?*

Stop thinking of that kiss. God, he had to stop thinking about that kiss. Shall we *run?* she'd meant. As in run *faster.*

Jake nodded. Yeah. He turned and gave the senior chief his best-buddy smile. "Hey, H, how many times around this loop do you figure you'll go?"

Harvard smiled back. He clearly liked Jake. But this wasn't about being liked. "Oh, I figure twice'll do it, sir."

"And at this pace, that'll take you, what? About forty minutes?"

"A little less, I think."

"Dr. Lange and I are going to push it a little bit faster," Jake said, "and a little bit farther. We're going to do three loops in about two-thirds the time. Just let us know when you get back to camp."

Zoe was ready, and as Jake jammed it into higher gear, she was right beside him.

"Hey!" he heard Harvard say as they left him in their dust. He put on a burst of speed, hustling to catch up. "Admiral, this isn't necessary. You don't need to prove anything here."

"Obviously, I do."

"We're all tired this morning—"

"Speak for yourself. I'm an old man—I don't need much sleep."

Harvard looked pained. "I assure you, sir—"

"Save your breath, Senior. You're going to need it if you want to keep up." And Jake ran even faster.

Zoe stood under the campground shower and let the water stream onto her head.

She hadn't run a race like that in a long time. And it *had* been a race. Three times around the KOA campground driveway. At least six miles. At top speed.

It had been some kind of macho showdown, and Jake had come out on top. He was a good runner—he held something back, something in reserve for the end of the race. While everyone else was working overtime to keep up the pace for that last quarter mile, Jake had pulled a sprint out of his back pocket.

She shut off the shower and toweled herself dry.

The other SEALs had tried valiantly to keep up with the admiral, but Harvard was the only one who'd stayed neck and neck.

And when it was over, Jake had been able to carry on a

conversation. Bobby and Wes had been gasping for oxygen like fish on the deck of a boat, yet Jake had calmly given out orders, flashing that incredible smile of his at the pack of them.

At everyone but Zoe.

She slipped on her robe and wrapped her towel around her shoulders, using it to reach up and rub her wet hair as she headed toward the trailers.

The smile he'd sent in her direction had been self-conscious, and she knew he couldn't so much as look at her without thinking about that kiss they'd shared last night.

He was obviously embarrassed. It was clear he didn't know what to say to her, obvious that she'd overstepped the boundaries of propriety.

That was just perfect. She'd been trying to help, but all she'd done was make things awkward between them and...

Zoe had to laugh at herself—at her self-righteous attempt to justify what she'd done last night.

The truth was that she'd kissed Jake Robinson because she'd *wanted* to kiss Jake Robinson. Badly. She'd wanted to kiss him since she'd first found out about kissing, back in seventh grade.

She'd pushed too hard too fast, and now she was paying for it.

As she went up the steps to her private RV, she saw Jake standing with Bobby and Wes at the door to the main trailer.

He was watching her, but instead of holding her gaze, he looked away.

His message couldn't have been more clear. This assignment was going to be neither easy nor fun for him. He'd prefer to keep whatever it was that had made him kiss her the way he had locked deep inside of him forever.

He was still in love with his wife, and a man like Jake Robinson would never cheat, not even on a memory.

Lieutenant Lucky O'Donlon burst into the surveillance trailer as if his pants were on fire.

He skidded to a stop next to Bob Taylor and furiously whispered into the big enlisted man's ear. Lucky was gone as quickly as he came in, and now it was Bobby's turn to stand up.

Moving with the agile speed and grace of a ballet dancer, the six-feet-five-inch tall, seemingly six-feet-wide SEAL pirouetted elegantly over to his swim buddy, Wes Skelly, and, glancing almost nervously at Jake, he leaned over and whispered something into Wes's ear.

Another graceful leap and Bobby, too, was out the door.

Wes knocked all the papers from his file onto the floor in his haste to get to his feet. He scooped them up, tossed them on the table in random order, and scurried toward Cowboy, Crash and Mitch.

As he spoke to them, his voice was too low for Jake to hear, but he gestured with his thumb toward the door, then scrambled after Bobby.

Jake looked at Harvard, who was fine-tuning the programming for their satellite access computers. The big senior chief frowned as he watched Mitch rise to his feet and saunter out the door. He turned and met Jake's eyes and shook his head, anticipating the admiral's question.

"What the hell is going on?" Jake stood up for the first time in what seemed like hours, stretching his legs and heading toward the door.

Cowboy had crossed to the window and stood looking out.

Crash glanced out the door. "Apparently Dr. Lange has returned from her pool party."

"Yes," Cowboy said from the window. "She's definitely wearing a bikini. And she's definitely...wearing a bikini."

Jake opened the door, and stepped outside, intending to go out there and kick some ass. The male members of his team had no right to ogle Zoe, bikini or...

No bikini.

What she was wearing was, in fact, almost no bikini.

Two very small triangles of black fabric stretched across her full breasts, attached with a string that tied around her neck and around her back.

Oh, God, he was staring. Just like Lucky and Bobby and Wes and even unflappable Mitch Shaw, Jake was standing there and staring. He forced his eyes from her breasts and encountered her perfect rear end.

She was wearing some kind of a sarong-style cover-up around her hips, but it was white and completely wet and did little in the way of covering her.

In fact, it clung to her, outlining every detail of her black bikini bottoms, which weren't much in the way of bottoms at all. They were cut high on her legs, high on her rear. Oh, yeah, there was no doubt about it. Zoe Lange had a world-class rear end.

But Jake already knew that. He'd had his hands all over it just a few nights ago.

And he'd been avoiding her ever since.

"Isn't anyone going to get me a towel?" she asked.

Jake realized with a jolt that her hair was soaking wet. She was carrying a towel, but it was drenched and dripping, as was her bag and a pair of jeans she had over her arm. She still had beads of water on her shoulders and chest and…

The late afternoon air had an autumn chill. It was blatantly obvious that she was freezing.

He quickly lifted his gaze to her face. "What happened?"

"I got pushed into the pool on my way out of the party. Hal didn't want me to leave. But things were getting a little…too friendly." She was trying to be flip, trying to be tough and matter-of-fact. "It's no big deal. I got a little wet."

Lucky bounded over, a dry white towel in his hands, as Mitch reached to take her wet things.

"I'll hang these up for you," Mitch said.

It was amazing. Jake knew that after only three days of working together as a team, Lucky O'Donlon was hot for Zoe. But *Mitch?* Lieutenant Mitchell Shaw was not human when it came to distractions. He was the only man Jake had ever met who was completely nondistractable. Or so Jake had believed.

Lucky wrapped his towel around Zoe's shoulders, gently rubbing her arms, but she quickly backed away.

"Don't touch me!" Zoe's outburst surprised them all—herself included. She forced a smile. "Whoa. Where'd *that* come from? Sorry, Luke. I guess my whole afternoon was just a little too intense."

"Yo," Harvard said from the trailer door. "How come you guys don't throw *me* a welcome home party every time I come back to camp? We've got two months of work to do in two days and I see people standing around. Check the pay stubs in your wallets, please, and unless your pay grade is admiral, get your butts back inside."

"I need a shower, Senior Chief," Zoe said. "Give me twenty minutes to get cleaned up." She glanced at Jake as she wrapped her towel more tightly around her. "If that's okay, Admiral, I'll give you a full report then."

Admiral. It was her acknowledgment of his attempt to put a little space, a little formality between them since that night they'd kissed.

Hold me like you want to be inside me.

He wanted. Despite Daisy's memory, despite his and Zoe's age difference, despite the fact that she was at least partly under his command, a member of his team, he wanted her.

Keeping his distance seemed the smartest option under the circumstances. They were going to be forced into close quarters soon enough.

"A full report after you shower would be fine, Doctor."

Jake watched her turn away, watched her head toward

the small RV that held her private quarters. But then he saw it. Bright red on the white of the towel.

He caught up with her quickly. "Zoe, you're bleeding."

She looked at the towel, pulling it back to reveal a nasty-looking scrape on her right elbow. Jake lifted the towel to reveal a lesser abrasion on her other arm. They were the kind of scrapes a woman might get from being pushed down, hard, onto her back. "Wow," she said. "I didn't even realize...."

"I think I need at least some of that report now," he said tightly.

She lifted her chin. "It wasn't anything I couldn't handle."

He still held her wrist. "And that's why you're shaking?"

"I'm freezing," she lied. He knew she was lying. Whatever had happened *had* shaken her up.

"'Too friendly,'" Jake remembered. He gestured to her elbow. "Is this the result of someone being too friendly?"

She gently pulled herself free. "It was Monica's boyfriend. I think he was coked up. I handled it, Jake. His family jewels are now lodged somewhere between his tonsils and his sinuses."

"Note to myself," Jake said. "Don't ever get Zoe angry."

She laughed as he'd hoped she would, but then abruptly turned away—but not before he saw the sudden welling of tears in her eyes.

"I'll tell you everything," she said, "but *after* I shower, okay?"

"Yeah," Jake said, fighting to hide the sudden rush of anger and protectiveness that made him want to seek out and destroy this Monica's boyfriend. "I'll get you something hot to drink. And meet you back in your trailer."

"Thanks, Jake," she whispered. "That would be very nice."

Chapter 5

Zoe kicked off her shower slippers as she came inside her RV. She'd cranked the heat before she'd left for the bath house, and it was now close to roasting in the small trailer. But that was nice. She hadn't been truly warm in what felt like hours.

And she felt warmer still when she saw that Jake was, indeed, waiting for her in the small living area. He sat somewhat stiffly on the cheap foam seats of the built-in couch, three mugs of coffee on the table in front of him, and...

Three?

Mitch Shaw was sitting across the room, his medical kit on his lap.

Jake had brought a chaperon. He was probably going to pretend he'd only brought Mitch along as a medic, to make sure Zoe's elbows were cleaned and bandaged properly, but she knew better. He was afraid to put himself in a position in which he might kiss her again.

She smiled at Jake to make sure he knew that she knew better.

But he was in heavy team-leader mode, frowning slightly and very intense as he handed her one of the mugs and gestured toward Mitch. "I've asked Lieutenant Shaw to take a look at your elbows, Doctor."

Zoe gave the darkly handsome lieutenant a smile as she sat down next to him. "Mitch and I are on a first-name basis, Admiral."

That one actually got her the ghost of a smile. "Any time you're ready," Jake said, "I'm ready to hear your report."

She took a sip of her coffee and pushed back the sleeves of her robe.

"First things first—I accomplished my mission this afternoon," she said as Mitch looked closely at her left elbow and then her right. His hands were warm, his touch gentle, almost soothing. "Hal Francke offered me the job."

"Great," Jake said. "When do you start?"

"I didn't take it."

As she watched, Jake struggled to understand. "Why not? Because of what happened at the party? I mean, don't get me wrong, if you don't think it's safe for you to be there, or—"

"I didn't take the job because I didn't want to seem overeager," she explained. "I told Hal I'd think about it. I'll go into Mel's in a day or so and let him ask me again. I'll make sure a ton of people overhear, and I'll make him beg. Ouch." She involuntarily jerked her arm free from Mitch. Holy Mike, that had hurt!

"Sorry," he murmured, his dark hazel eyes apologetic. "There're still a few pieces of dirt—something that looks like very fine gravel—that I should remove. I don't think I can do it without hurting you at least a little. But if I don't get it out…"

"Just…try to do it quickly." She gave him her arm, aware that she was perspiring from the anticipated pain, sweat beading on her upper lip. "Admiral, can you do me a favor and shut off the heat?"

"What, you changed your mind? You no longer want to simulate the conditions on Mars?"

"Ha, ha. *You* try getting dumped into a fifty-degree swimming pool and then driving fifteen miles in some trash heap of a car that doesn't have a working heater." She clenched her teeth against the pain.

Jake smiled as he turned down the heat. "Someday we'll have to tell her about BUD/S Training, huh, Mitch?"

Mitch was completely focused on cleaning her arm. "If you can't handle cold, don't become a SEAL."

"A major portion of Hell Week—the fifth week of SEAL training—is spent freezing your butt off," Jake told her. "You get wet early on and stay wet for the entire week."

"Yeah, I've heard about that." Zoe closed her eyes. Damn, whatever Mitch was doing hurt like hell. "I read in some magazine article about Hell Week that you guys pee on yourselves to stay warm while you're in the water."

"Yeah, sure." Jake snorted. "*That's* what reporters find important. That we pee on ourselves. Forget about the hours and hours of training we go through, the endurance tests, the underwater demolition, the HALO training. That's not half as interesting as peeing on ourselves. Jeez."

Zoe sensed more than felt Jake sit down beside her. But she opened her eyes when he took her other hand.

"Squeeze," he told her. "And keep your eyes open. If you close your eyes and shut everything else out, it's just you and the pain. And that's never good."

"I'm really sorry," Mitch murmured. "You must've landed on this arm pretty hard to get this stuff embedded so deeply."

Zoe took a deep breath and let it out in a whoosh. Jake's eyes were so blue and so steady. She held his gaze as if it were a lifeline.

"What happened at this party?" he asked. "Keep talking."

"I arrived a little after noon," she told him, gripping his hand more tightly and biting back the urge to shriek as Mitch probed particularly deeply. "Everyone was drinking pretty hard. Mostly just beer. But about five people went into the house, and when they came out, it was pretty obvious they'd done a few lines of cocaine. Hal Francke was one of them. This other guy, Wayne, Monica's boyfriend—God, what a jerk! He's one of those former high-school football-star types—he used to be big man on campus, but now he's just big and fat and mean. He went inside, too. A few different times."

She squeezed Jake's hand harder. "Ow. Ow, ow, *ow!*"

And just like that, the pain let up.

"Got it." Mitch was done. He was perspiring nearly as much as she was, his eyes filled with apology and an echo of her pain.

"I just have to put some antibacterial ointment on it and bandage it up. The other one looks clean."

Zoe tried to hide that she was shaking. "Well, that was fun. Thanks so much."

"So how'd this happen?" Jake asked. She had to give him credit. He was obviously trying really hard not to look as if he wanted to go out and hunt down Monica's boyfriend, Wayne.

The stupid thing was, she liked it. She liked the idea of this man being her hero. God knows there was a point this afternoon where she would have been plenty thrilled to see Jake parachuting down from the sky, coming to save the day.

She wasn't used to working in a team, like the SEALs. In her job, she often had herself, and only herself, to rely on.

She gently pulled her hand free from his grasp. "I went further out in the back of the yard," she told him as Mitch bandaged her arm, "looking for Monica. There was a path that led down to a stream, and some of the party had moved in that direction. I was getting ready to leave—I wanted to tell her I was taking off. But she must've been inside the house—everyone else who'd gone down to the stream was gone, too. Except for Wayne, who'd followed me. Like I said, he was on something nasty, and he got a little rough.'' It was an understatement, and she could tell from his eyes that he knew it. "But it was no big deal," she continued. "I handled it, I handled him."

She was stretching the truth pretty thin there. Because it *had* been a big deal. Zoe could still feel the man's hands on her breasts, still smell the alcohol on his putrid breath. He'd been a behemoth of a man, and when he'd tackled her, when the weight of his body had crushed her against the grass and gravel, for one awful moment she'd been afraid he'd actually be able to overpower her.

It was an awful feeling, that helplessness.

But he was stoned and stupid, and she'd used her brain and her ability to aim with a solid knee kick and she'd gotten away.

Hal Francke had been with a group of men by the pool, and they, too, had had far too much to drink. Zoe had picked up her towel and her bag, extremely shaken and ready to leave without even saying goodbye to the hostess, when one of the men grabbed her and tossed her into the pool.

Hal had jumped in after her, rescuing her even though she damn well hadn't wanted or needed it. He'd put his hands all over her as he pulled her to the side of the pool. It had taken every ounce of restraint she had not to kick *him* in the family jewels, as well.

The water had been freezing. Her towel and clothes had been soaked.

Hal had thought that was funny as hell. He'd invited her to dinner, invited her to stay at his fishing cabin for the rest of the weekend, subtly insinuated that he'd all but pay her to have sex with him. She'd told him she'd consider the *waitressing* job, thanks, but that she'd have to get back to him.

And then, elbows stinging and dripping wet, Zoe had gotten the hell out of there.

"It was no big deal," she said again. She was lying.

And Jake knew she was lying. But he didn't press her for more details.

"As far as what the locals think about the CRO—" she continued with her report "—most of the people at the party don't know anything about them. All they know is the old Frosty Cakes factory's finally been sold, and that the people who bought it mostly keep to themselves. They wish it had been bought by someone wanting to get back into production—they'd hoped for more jobs in this area. They know about the electric fence around the compound, but not much about the rest of Vincent's high-tech security system. And that's about it."

"That's it for me, too," Mitch said, finishing bandaging her arm. He held onto her hand several moments longer than he had to. "Again, I'm sorry I hurt you, Zoe."

"It's all right." She smiled at him. "I forgive you."

Mitch's eyes were warm as he packed up his medical kit. "Good."

Jake cleared his throat.

Mitch stood up. "If you don't need me any further, Admiral…"

"Thanks, Mitch. I'll be along in just a minute."

Zoe watched the lieutenant let himself out, then glanced at Jake, wondering what he could possibly have to say to her that needed privacy. Why lose the chaperon now?

"Are you really okay?" he asked. He touched her with just one finger beneath her chin, turning her head so that she was forced to meet his eyes.

Silently, she nodded.

"Why do I get the feeling that you're not being completely honest?" he asked. "Look, let's make a deal. Right now. You don't lie to me, and I won't try to tell you what you should or shouldn't do. I won't make judgments about what might be too dangerous for you because you're a woman. But in return, you have to be brutally honest with me. You have to be able to pull your own plug, to pull yourself off some assignment that might get too uncomfortable for you for any assortment of reasons. Does that sound fair?''

Zoe nodded. Provided he could really do it. His instincts were to protect—anyone, really, but probably women in particular. He would need to be a truly exceptional leader to overcome his inherent prejudices in that regard.

But if anyone could be that kind of leader, Jake Robinson could.

''You've got a deal,'' she said.

''So. Honestly. Are you really okay?'' His gaze was so intense, she could have sworn he was trying to read her mind. ''What really happened, Zoe? Did this guy do more than just push you down?''

''Have you ever had your chute fail—you know, skydiving?'' Zoe asked.

He gazed at her for several long moments, but then apparently decided to let her answer his question in her own way. It was a tough question, and if she had to go in circles to answer it, that was okay with him.

''Skydiving, huh?'' Jake laughed softly. ''Funny you should mention that. Jumping is one of those things I've always hated. I mean, I've *had* to do it as a SEAL. It's part of the package. But some guys'll jump every chance they get. I've always had to force myself to do it.'' He paused. ''And yes, I've had to cut myself free from the main chute more than once. It was pretty damn terrifying.''

''You know that feeling you get right before you pull the backup chute—that sense of complete helplessness? Like, if *this* doesn't work, it's all over?''

Jake nodded. ''Oh, yeah. Personally, I like being in control, which is why I probably don't like jumping.''

''That's what it felt like today,'' she told him. ''When Wayne was…'' She closed her eyes. ''When he was on top of me, tearing at my bathing suit.''

Jake swore softly.

"You want honesty, Jake? For one awful moment, I thought I was going to be raped and that I wasn't going to be able to do anything to stop it. That kind of helplessness is not a really nice feeling, so you're right, I'm still a little shaken. But I'll be fine."

She opened her eyes to find Jake watching her, a mixture of emotions on his face. Anger. Remorse. Regret. Attraction. The power of his other feelings made him unable to hide his attraction. "Zoe, I'm so sorry this happened."

"It's really no biggie. I mean, I was the one who wasn't being careful. I should have known this particular guy would be trouble. And then I made a second mistake by letting him get too close. I definitely underestimated the situation. If I'm paying the right amount of attention, I'm completely capable of taking care of someone that size. But I messed up. And I almost paid for it."

"What's his last name?" Jake asked. "Wayne what?"

"No," Zoe said. "Sir. No disrespect intended, but I'm not going to tell you."

"You were sexually assaulted." His voice broke. "This is not something to just say oh, well about and let go."

"What are you going to do, Jake? Find him and beat him up? And maybe blow our cover when he recognizes you in a few weeks when you walk into Mel's bar with Christopher Vincent? Or maybe you think I should press charges? I'm supposed to be a drifter, right? My cover is that I've had my share of trouble with the law, that I'm jaded with the system—ready to be enlightened by the CRO's doctrine. Somehow it doesn't fit for me to go running to the police and shouting for justice."

He knew she was right. She could see it all over his face. He had such an expressive, wonderful face.

She leaned closer. "Our job here is to regain possession of that Trip X. That takes priority over everything. Even this."

Jake exhaled in frustration. "I just... I know. I just hate not being able to *do* anything."

She gave him a shaky smile. "You want to do something? You could put your arms around me for a minute."

He didn't need more of an invitation than that. He reached for her, and she found herself wrapped in his arms.

He smelled so good and felt so familiar—as if she'd been in his arms far more than just that one other time.

His arms were warm and so solid as he held her tightly, as he stroked her hair. It was funny how much better that made her feel.

It didn't mean she was weak. It didn't mean she wasn't strong. She didn't need him to hold her, but it sure was nice that he was there.

Zoe closed her eyes, not wanting this minute she'd asked for to end.

She felt him sigh and braced herself, waiting for him to pull away. But he didn't. And he didn't.

"God," he finally said on another sigh, still holding her tightly. "This just feels too good."

Zoe lifted her head and found herself gazing directly into his eyes. "You say that as if it's a bad thing."

He pushed her damp hair from her face. "It feels inappropriate," he whispered. "Doesn't it?"

She gazed at the graceful shape of his mouth. "Not to me."

"I'm not going to kiss you again," he said hoarsely, pulling away, pushing himself off the built-in couch and all the way across the tiny room. "Not until I have to."

Zoe tried to smile, tried to make a joke as he slipped on his brown leather flight jacket and prepared to leave. "Gee, I didn't realize kissing me would be such a negative."

He turned to give her a long look. "You know damn well that I liked it. I know it wasn't real, but nevertheless, I liked it too much. I'm leaving tonight," he added.

Zoe stood up. "*Tonight?* But..."

"I'm ready as I'll ever be and this...this is getting crazy.

You be careful working at Mel's," he ordered. "With luck, I'll see you in the bar in a few weeks."

"Jake."

He stopped with his hand on the doorknob and looked back.

Zoe's heart was in her throat. He'd liked kissing her. Too much. "I liked it, too," she said, adding, "kissing you." As if he'd needed her explanation.

Another man might've stepped toward her, pulled her into his arms and kissed her until the room spun. But Jake just gave her a crooked smile that was overshadowed by the sadness in his eyes.

"Be safe," he said, and walked out the door.

Jake knew from the way Harvard cleared his throat that the moment of truth had arrived.

It was time for him to leave. So if anyone was going to try to make him change his mind, it was now or never.

Jake had kind of hoped it would be never.

So much for hoping.

"Permission to speak freely, sir."

Jake looked from Harvard to all four of the lieutenants, and then at the enlisted men. They were all there but Zoe. She wasn't part of this. Or maybe the men had intentionally excluded her.

"This isn't a democracy, Senior," Jake said mildly.

"At least hear us out, Admiral." Admiral. When Billy called him admiral, it meant he was dead serious.

Jake sighed. "I don't need to hear you out," he said. "You don't think I'm up for this. You think it's been too long since I've seen action, since I've been out in the real world. You don't think I can keep up, despite the fact that every time we've run together, *you've* had to fight to keep up with *me*."

"This is different than running, and you know it," Billy said. "Yes, you're physically fit for—" He broke off.

Jake bristled. "Go on, say it. For an old man. Right?"

"Jake, I love you, and I'm worried about you," Billy said, cutting through to the bottom line, the way he always did so well. "I don't know why you're doing this when any one of us could find a way to get inside the CRO—"

"Because I can walk through those gates in the morning," Jake told Billy, told them all, "and have dinner at Christopher Vincent's private dining table by night. If you or Cowboy or Lucky were to go in there, God knows how many months it would take you to work your way up to just being able to stand guard outside the dining room door."

He looked them all directly in the eyes, one at a time. Billy. Cowboy. Mitch. Lucky. Harvard. Bobby. Wes. "We don't have months, gentlemen. The CRO could decide to do a test run of the Triple X at any time, in any city." They all had family, friends living all over the country, and his unspoken message cut through, loud and clear. Until they regained possession of the T-X, no one was safe.

Jake shouldered his bag of gear. "Now, who's taking Mitch and me to the airport?"

The Air Force flight to South Dakota seemed to take forever.

Mitch slept for most of it, only waking as they began their descent.

Jake was sick and tired of thinking about the way his team had questioned his plan. He'd worked hard over the past week to gain their respect. He'd thought his physical stamina, his ability to run hard and fast, had won them over. Obviously, he'd been wrong.

His team thought of him as an old man.

He wished Billy was with him instead of Mitch. He'd wanted to talk to the kid about Zoe, find out if he was shocked by Jake's intention to pretend he and the young doctor were romantically involved.

But Jake's plan had called for one of the SEALs to wind up arrested, thrown into jail for conspiracy and charges of

aiding and abetting the escape of a suspected felo
Mitch and Billy had volunteered, but Jake knew that playing this role would be hitting a little too close to home for
the kid. It hadn't been that long since Billy had spent time
in prison, facing very similar charges for real.

So Jake was here on the plane with Mitchell Shaw. A
man he'd always thought of as a friend.

A man who—just a few hours ago—had lined up with
the rest of the team and questioned Jake's command.

Right now, CNN was announcing a late-breaking story
of conspiracy and intrigue in the U.S. military. As the story
went, Admiral Jake Robinson had escaped from house arrest. He'd been confined to his quarters after being charged
with conspiracy, allegedly leaking top-secret military information to several extreme right-wing state militia
groups. Those militia groups had been lobbying for fewer
federal regulations, less control by the federal government.
Allegedly there were tapes, and the words Jake had spoken
could be interpreted as treasonous.

The military had been attempting to keep the entire affair
from the public eye, since as an Admiral in the U.S. Navy,
Robinson *should* have been among the staunchest defenders
of the federal government. But four days ago, as the story
went, Robinson had escaped his guards with the help of
three unidentified men, and now the incident was national
news.

All four of the men were currently at large.

To help this cover story along, Mitch and Jake were going to be spotted in South Dakota, and Mitch was going to
be apprehended while Jake once again made an escape.

Jake was then going to proceed, by car and on foot, to
Montana, leaving a trail that the CRO could trace if they
tried. And they would try—particularly after he showed up
on their doorstep, seeking asylum.

Within a few days, CNN would stop carrying the story—
Admiral Mac Forrest would see to that. And after several

weeks of hiding in the CRO compound, Jake would be able to leave hiding and venture into town.

And then he'd see Zoe again.

Zoe. Who'd liked the way he'd kissed her.

Mitch shifted his jaw, expertly popping his ears as the plane continued its descent.

"Hey, Mitch," Jake said.

"Yes, sir?"

"No," he said, "not sir. I've got something I need to discuss, and I need you to talk to me as a friend."

Mitch nodded, completely serene. "I'll do my best."

"It's about—"

"Zoe." Mitch nodded. "I figured you were going to say something. I'm sorry if I got in your way. I honestly didn't think you were interested in her—you've been avoiding her all week." He smiled slightly. "You know, Jake, I've found it's far easier to get a woman into your bed if you actually interact with her."

"I don't want to get her into my..." He couldn't finish the sentence—it wasn't true. He exhaled noisily in exasperation. "God, she's too young for me. How could I even be thinking about that?"

"She doesn't think she's too young." Mitch smiled again. "I've been hanging out with her. Telling her stories about *you.* She's yours if you want her, Admiral. And if you don't, I'm hoping I might be next in line."

Jake had to know. "She's beautiful and she's smart and she's *very* sexy, but...you've had the opportunity to meet plenty of beautiful, smart, sexy women, and as far as I've seen, you've never given any of them a second glance. So why Zoe? What is it about her?"

Mitch gazed thoughtfully out the window at the approaching runway for several long moments. "She's one of us," he said simply, turning to look at Jake. "I get the sense that she wants the things I want from a relationship— no strings, no promises, no regrets. Just good, clean, healthy fun. Sex that's just that—sex. No more, no less."

He laughed softly. "To be painfully honest, Jake, I tend to stay away from most women because I'm afraid of hurting them when I leave. And you know in our line of work, we always leave. We disappear on some assignment, and who knows when we'll be back. But Zoe..." He laughed again. "Zoe would never expect anything long term. Because she leaves, too. And she'd probably leave first."

The plane touched down on the runway with a jolt.

"I know you miss Daisy," Mitch said quietly. "I know how you felt about her. But you're not dead. And Zoe might be just what you need. It won't have anything to do with what you and Daisy had. It doesn't have to go too deep."

Jake sighed. "Just thinking about it makes me feel unfaithful."

"To whom, Jake?" Mitch asked gently. "Daisy's gone."

Chapter 6

Weeknights were the worst. Weekends were no picnic, but at least on Friday and Saturday nights, Mel's was crowded and Zoe was kept busy.

But on a Tuesday night like this one, Zoe sat at the bar with old Roy, who sat nursing a beer on the same stool every night and could have been anywhere from eighty to a hundred and eight, and Lonnie, who owned the service station on the corner of Page Street and Hicks Lane and was probably older than old Roy.

On Tuesday nights, Hal Francke had his bowling league, so even he wasn't around, trying his damnedest to brush up against her.

And Wayne Keating—Monica's boyfriend, the one who'd nearly overpowered Zoe—had been arrested for DUI. It was his third offense, and he was being held without bail. So there was no chance of him staggering into the bar and livening things up.

No, it was just another deadly boring Tuesday night in Belle, Montana.

Zoe was definitely going to go mad.

Two weeks had come and gone and come and gone and here she was, well into week five in her new career as barmaid, with no sign of Jake.

He'd gotten into the CRO compound. She knew that. She'd seen surveillance tapes of him being let inside. Even taken from a distance, she'd clearly recognized him. The way he walked, the way he stood.

According to the team, he'd been spotted from time to time within the confines of the electric fence.

But he hadn't come out.

Each time a car or van left the CRO gates and headed toward town, Harvard or Lucky or Cowboy would call, and Zoe's silent pager would go off. And she would know to be ready.

Maybe Jake would show up *this* time. Maybe...

But even though Christopher Vincent himself had come into Mel's a number of times, and always with an entourage, Jake had been nowhere in sight.

Zoe was completely frustrated. And getting a little worried.

Had something gone wrong? She called Harvard every night on the pretense of checking in, but in truth to find out if Jake had been spotted again during the course of the day.

What if he'd gotten sick? Or injured? What if Vincent knew he was only there to find the Triple X? What if Jake were locked in the factory basement, beaten and bleeding and...

Oh, dammit, and the really *stupid* thing was that beneath her worries and her frustration at this endless inactivity was the unavoidable fact that she missed him.

She *missed* the man.

She missed his smile, his solid presence, his calm certainty, the sweet sensation of his arms around her.

Zoe groaned, resting her forehead on the bar atop her folded arms. He'd only kissed her once, but she missed that, too. Holy Mike, when had she become such a hopeless romantic? And hopeless was the key word here.

This foolish schoolgirl crush she was experiencing was definitely one-sided.

Yes, the man had kissed her. Once. And afterward, he'd run screaming as hard and as fast as he could in the opposite direction. And when he kissed her again, it was going to be because he *had* to. He'd told her as much.

"Ya gonna do that singing thing tonight?" Lonnie leaned over and asked.

He was talking about the karaoke. Last Friday, Hal had bought a karaoke system secondhand and very cheap from a guy going out of business over in Butte. Zoe had been the only member of the wait staff brave enough to give it a try. The songs were mostly all retro dance hits, with a bunch of old country songs thrown in.

Zoe lifted her head to look in the mirror on the wall behind the bar. Besides Lonnie, old Roy, Gus the bartender and herself, there were only three other people in the place.

"I don't think so," she told Lonnie. "There's not much of a crowd."

Old Roy was already leafing through the plastic-covered pages that listed the song titles available on this karaoke system. "I love this old Patsy Cline song." He blinked at her hopefully. "Will you sing it? Please?"

It was the same song he played over and over on the jukebox at least three times every single night. "The record sounds much better than I do," she told him. "Here, I'll even front you a quarter."

"But we like it when *you* sing it." Now Lonnie was giving her *his* best kicked-puppy look. "I'd like to hear the other songs you did on Saturday night, too."

Zoe sighed.

"Please?" they said in unison.

She should really clean the bathrooms. God, she hated cleaning the bathrooms.

"Sure. Why not?" She went behind the bar to the stereo

system and powered up the karaoke player. "But if I'm going to do this, I'm going to do it right." She untied the short apron that held her ordering pad and change. She set it down, picked up the karaoke microphone and switched it on. "Ready for this, boys?"

Both Roy and Lonnie nodded.

She used the remote to turn on the TV behind the bar, setting it to receive the signal from the karaoke system. She put in the right CD and programmed the machine and...

Thunderous strains of pedal steel guitar came pounding out of the speakers. Old Roy and Lonnie both clapped their hands over their ears.

"Sorry!" she shouted, turning the volume down by a full half.

The words on the screen turned color, and she sang them into the mike. "Crazy..."

Old Roy and Lonnie sat paying rapt attention—the president and vice-president of her personal fan club—as Zoe did her best country diva imitation, singing to an imaginary crowd of thousands.

One song became two, then three and four. Each time it ended Roy and Lonnie gave her a standing ovation.

"Sing mine again," Old Roy requested.

When Zoe looked to the bartender for help, Gus just smiled. "I like that one, too."

"Last one," Zoe said. "Last time."

She didn't need the words on the screen this time as she sang. "Crazy..."

It was her finale, and she went all out this time, exaggerating all the moves. Roy and Lonnie grinned at her like a couple of two-year-olds.

And during the instrumental break and the subsequent key change, she climbed up to sing while standing atop the sturdy wooden bar, and they gave her a two-man wave.

Zoe knew it wasn't so much her voice that got them going. Her voice was pleasant enough, and she could certainly carry a tune, but she was no Patsy Cline. No, Roy and Lonnie were fans of her tight blue jeans and her low-necked tank tops.

She closed her eyes, threw her head back and struck a pose for the last chorus of the song, letting a very country-sounding cry come into her voice as she sang about being crazy for crying, crazy for trying, crazy for loving you.

As the last strains of music faded away, the room was filled with applause. Way too much applause for just Old Roy and Lonnie.

Zoe opened her eyes.

And looked directly down at Christopher Vincent.

The CRO leader was standing near the door, surrounded by about fifteen of his disciples.

She'd had no warning, no time to prepare, but then again, she'd taken off her apron—and in it, her pager—at least five songs ago.

"That was just beautiful," Vincent said. "Just beautiful."

She gave a sweeping bow. "Thank you."

"Someone want to give her a hand down from there?"

"Yeah, I'd love to."

Jake.

He pushed his way out of the crowd and stood smiling at her.

She didn't faint with relief, didn't gasp, didn't reveal in any way that she recognized him. Instead she looked at him very deliberately, as if she were checking out the new man, the handsome stranger in town.

He was dressed the same as the rest of the men, in blue jeans and a worn denim work shirt. But the faded jeans hugged his thighs, and the shirt fit perfectly over his very broad shoulders. He was heart-stoppingly, impossibly beautiful, his eyes an incredible shade of molten hot blue.

During the past four and a half weeks, she'd forgotten just how amazingly blue his eyes were.

He'd been looking her over as thoroughly as she had been looking at him, and now he smiled.

Jake Robinson had a vast collection of smiles in his repertoire, but this one was very different from any she'd seen in the past. This one was as confident and self-assured as all the rest, but instead of promising friendship or protection, this smile promised complete, mind-blowing ecstasy. This smile promised heaven.

Damn, he was good. He almost had *her* believing that she'd lit some kind of fire inside of him.

Christopher Vincent noticed it, too. Noticed it, and recognized it. And wasn't entirely thrilled by it.

Zoe held Jake's gaze, lifting an eyebrow in acknowledgment of the attraction that simmered between them and giving him an answering smile that promised maybe. A very *definite* maybe.

"Zoe." Gus was completely overwhelmed behind the bar.

Jake reached for her, and she leaned down to give the microphone to Lonnie before bracing her hands on Jake's shoulders. He held her by the waist and swung her lightly to the floor, making sure that before her feet touched the ground, every possible inch of her that could touch every possible inch of him was, indeed, doing so.

And oh, God, it felt so incredibly good. She wanted to hold him tightly, to close her eyes and press her cheek against his shoulder, hear the steady beating of his heart beneath the soft cotton of his shirt. He was safe, he was whole, he was finally here. Thank God, thank God, thank *God.*

She wanted to hold on to him for at least an hour. Maybe two. Instead she touched the side of his face and held his gaze for just a second longer, hoping he could read her mind and know how very glad she was to see him.

His arms tightened around her for just a second in an answering embrace before he, too, let her go.

"I'm Jake," he told her, with another of those killer smiles.

"And I'm Zoe," she said as she went behind the bar.

"Welcome to Mel's. I'll be your waitress tonight." She slipped her apron around her waist, and sure enough—inside the pocket, her pager was silently shaking. She quickly shut it off. "What can I get you?"

He sat on the bar stool directly in front of her. "What kind of beer do you have on tap, Zoe?"

He said her name in a way that called up all kinds of erotic images, in a way that made her mouth go dry.

She leaned toward him, gesturing for him to come closer, and she felt his gaze slip down her shirt, nearly as palpable as a touch. "I recommend bottled beer," she told him. They had a little problem with roaches. She didn't know how they got into the tap hoses, but they did, and…yuck.

"Then definitely make it bottled," Jake said. He was close enough so his breath moved her hair. "Whatever you bring me will be fine."

As she turned around and reached into the cooler, she could feel him watching her. Make-believe, she told herself. It was all part of an act. Jake Robinson wasn't really drooling over her rear end. He was just pretending to.

She opened the beer—a Canadian import—and set it down in front of him. "Glass?"

"I don't need one, no."

"Zoe, two pitchers, one light, one regular!" Gus called.

"Don't go anywhere," Zoe told Jake.

She could feel his eyes on her as she filled both pitchers. He was still watching as she carried them with a stack of plastic cups to the tables where Christopher Vincent and most of his men were sitting.

"What brings you boys out on a Tuesday night?" she asked.

"My friend Jake's been going a little stir-crazy," Christopher told her. "He's been…keeping a low profile. You don't recognize him from anywhere, do you?"

Zoe glanced at the bar where Jake was sitting, still watching her. "He looks like a movie star. Is he a movie star?"

"Not exactly." Chris looked around. "Where's Carol? I wanted to introduce him to Carol. I thought they would hit it off."

"She's off tonight," Zoe said. "Some kind of program going on over at her daughter's school."

"Maybe tomorrow then."

"Tomorrow will definitely be too late," Zoe told him. "Finders keepers, and all that—because *I* definitely saw him first. He's adorable."

Chris didn't look happy. But Chris rarely looked happy.

Considering he was the leader of the so-called chosen race, Christopher Vincent was not a particularly attractive man, mostly due to the grim expression he wore on his face nearly all the time, and partly due to his thick, dark eyebrows, which grew almost completely together in the middle. He was tall and beefy with long dark hair, which he wore pulled back into a ponytail. He kept his face hidden behind a thick, graying beard, and he usually wore tinted glasses over his dark brown eyes. He looked over the tops of them as he gazed at Zoe.

They were definitely the eyes of a fanatic—the eyes of a man who wouldn't hesitate to use the Triple X he'd stolen if he thought it would further his cause.

He was volatile, with a very short fuse.

"I saw *you* first," he pointed out.

Oh, brother, this was a complication she hadn't anticipated. Somehow over the past few weeks, she'd managed to catch Christopher Vincent's eye. "You're married," she told him, trying to sound apologetic and even regretful. "I have a personal rule about married men. I don't touch 'em. See, I want to get married myself, and since married men are already married…" She shrugged.

"I've been thinking about taking another wife."

"*Another…?*"

"The federal government has no right to force us to follow its restrictive rules about marriage and family. A man of power and wealth should take as many wives as he pleases.''

Oh, yeah? ''What does your wife think about that?'' Zoe asked.

''All three of my wives are kept very satisfied.''

Holy Mike. If they ever got desperate, they could bust this guy for polygamy. ''Wow,'' she said. ''Well. It's hard enough being a second wife when the first one's not around. I don't think I could handle the competition.''

''Think about it.''

''I don't need to, hon,'' she said. ''I'm the jealous type. I wouldn't want to share.''

''You could have my baby.''

And that was supposed to entice her? A baby with a single eyebrow with a complete lunatic for a father? ''Well, it's tempting,'' she said. ''But I really want to be someone's number-one wife.''

He gestured for her to lean closer. ''We sometimes share wives in the CRO,'' he said in a low voice. ''You could marry someone like Jake and still have my baby.''

Ooo-kay. ''Jake doesn't strike me as the kind of man who'd want to, you know, *share*.''

''He's very generous,'' Christopher Vincent told her. He looked up, past her, and smiled. He had a smile like a wolf—lots of teeth, more vicious than happy. ''Hey, buddy, we were just talking about you. Zoe here wants to marry you.''

Zoe held up her hands. ''Chris. Wait. I never said that.'' She turned to Jake. ''He's just teasing. He's crazy, you know—''

It was the dead wrong thing to say.

Christopher exploded, reaching out with one hand and grabbing the front of her shirt, pulling her down so that they were nose to nose, so that she was practically lying on the table in front of him, so that her tray clattered onto the floor. ''Don't *ever* call me crazy!''

"Hey," Jake said. "Whoa. Take it easy, Chris. Come on, pal, I'm sure she didn't mean to offend you."

Zoe felt him right behind her, his arms around her as he tried to pry the other man's fingers from her shirt.

Vincent released her, pushing her away from him, and she would have fallen over had Jake not been there.

"Dammit, Chris," Zoe said, refusing to let him see how badly he'd frightened her, how completely he'd freaked her out. "You ruined my shirt." She had to hold the front against her, he'd stretched it out so badly. He'd bruised her, too, by grabbing more than just her shirt. Way to woo a new wife, baby.

Gus had come out from behind the bar, and he was hovering nearby. "Everything okay over here?"

"I don't know," Zoe said. "Chris, are you done grabbing me?"

Jake's hands tightened on her in warning, but she didn't give him time to answer. "I've got to go change my shirt." Pulling free from Jake, she picked up her tray and handed it to Gus, then headed for the back room.

She sensed more than saw Jake follow her. And she wasn't surprised, after she fished a T-shirt from her backpack, to turn around and see him standing there, door tightly shut behind him.

He looked really upset.

Zoe wasn't sure who moved first, and it didn't matter. As she reached for him, he lunged for her, and then, God, she was in his arms, just holding him as close as she possibly could.

"Are you all right?" He didn't release her to ask, he just kept holding her as tightly as she was holding him. "When he grabbed you like that..."

"I'm okay," she told him. And she was. Despite the bruises Christopher Vincent had just given her, she was more okay than she'd been in a long time. She pulled back to look at him. "Are *you?*"

"This isn't going to work." The tone of Jake's voice

matched the intensity in his eyes. They'd turned into steel—hard and cold, with a razor-sharp edge. "The plan. I've got to come up with something else because I'm *not* letting you go in there."

"But—"

"He's dangerous, Zoe. He's completely unhinged. The whole organization's seriously off balance. Getting you inside as my wife is no longer an option. I don't want you anywhere near there. Besides, it's just not feasible, from what I've found out."

"Dammit, Jake—"

He kissed her. One moment, he was glaring at her, and the next his mouth was hard against hers, his tongue sweeping past her gasp of surprise.

Zoe felt herself sway, caught off balance for the briefest moment, before she clung to him, kissing him back with as much passion, angling her head to grant him deeper access.

He was kissing her. Jake Robinson was kissing her because he wanted to, not because he had to. Tears stung the inside of her eyelids, and for the first time she let herself acknowledge that she wanted Jake Robinson more than she'd ever wanted any man. He was her hero, her commander and in many ways her deity. She worshiped him, on every possible level.

He pushed her back so she bumped against the concrete block of the storage-room wall as still he kissed her. His hands were all over her as he pressed himself hard between her legs, pulling her thigh up along his as he strained to get closer, even closer, playing out her wildest fantasy. But when he cupped her breast far more roughly than she would have expected, she opened her eyes in surprise.

And saw Christopher Vincent standing at the half-open storage-room door, his hand on the knob as he looked in at them.

He pulled the door shut behind him, and when he did, Jake stopped kissing her. He took his hand from her breast but otherwise just stood there, eyes closed, breathing hard, forehead resting against the wall beside her.

She'd been wrong. Jake hadn't really been kissing her. Somehow he must've heard the door open. Somehow he'd known that Christopher was there.

It wasn't a want-to kiss, after all. It was a had-to kiss.

Zoe drew in a very shaky breath. "Oh, *God.*"

Jake pulled away from her, his eyes dark with apology. "I'm sorry—did I hurt you?"

She tried to joke. "Are you kidding? That was more fun than I've had in weeks."

He turned slightly away from her, and she realized that her shirt was hanging open in the front where Chris had stretched it, revealing the entire top edge of her very low-cut bra. She picked her T-shirt up from the floor, and turning her back to Jake, she quickly changed.

"We've got too much to talk about, too much to decide," Jake told her. "So I'm going to go home with you tonight."

She turned to face him, her heart in her throat despite the fact that she knew nothing would happen between them even if he *did* spend the night in her trailer. He'd *had* to kiss her. God, she was such a fool for thinking otherwise.

"I don't think that's a good idea. Why would you marry me if you can just get some whenever you want? Besides, I've set up my cover so that everyone out there in that bar *knows* that I'm looking to get married. What are they going to think if I just suddenly settle for casual sex?"

"I'm sorry," he said. "But I've changed my mind about the whole marriage thing. Zoe, this guy is *nuts*. The entire organization is screwy. The way they treat women is criminal. I can't let you do this."

"Jake, you *promised* that you'd let *me* decide—"

"That was before I knew how bad it would be. On top of that, Vincent's got security cameras everywhere. I found at least three in my bedroom. How the hell can I bring you there? Don't you think it would look a little suspicious when I don't make love to my gorgeous young wife?''

''So bring me there and make love to me.'' Zoe couldn't believe she was actually bold enough to say the words aloud.

Jake was silent, looking at her, looking hard into her eyes as if trying to see if she'd really meant what she'd just said.

She held his gaze, pretending she was as flip and blasé about the idea of being intimate with him, pretending she could shrug it off as just another job requirement, pretending it would mean no more to her than a way to find that missing Trip X.

It's no big deal, she told him with her smile, even as her heart was pounding.

''Even if you would do that,'' he finally said, ''I wouldn't. I *couldn't*.'' He turned away. ''That's not an option.''

Zoe felt like crying. He honestly didn't want her. Even with necessity as a solid excuse, he couldn't acknowledge that any of the passion that sparked between them when they kissed was genuine. And maybe it wasn't. Maybe he was the best actor she'd ever met, and all of the real passion was her own.

God, she was pathetic.

But that was just too bad. Because she had a job to do and no time to feel sorry for herself.

She took a deep breath. ''So you're just going to do this by yourself—find the Triple X on your own? All alone?''

''I need to get a message to Harvard. I think there's a way to intercept the images from the security cameras— but I'll need some equipment from him. If I can do that, you'll be able to see inside the CRO compound from the safety of the surveillance trailer.''

''What if that's not enough? Jake, you *know* it's going to be easier for me to help you find the Trip X if I'm there with you. I think we've got to leave our options open. So I'm not going to let you pretend to come home with me,

in case we need to use the marriage thing in the future.''
And wouldn't *that* be fun? Living with him twenty-four
seven, pretending to be lovers, all the while knowing that
she was about the farthest thing possible from the woman
he truly wanted?

She handed him her ordering pad and pen. ''Write Harvard a message,'' she continued. ''Write down whatever
equipment you need. Whatever *he* needs to know. I'll see
that he gets it.''

There was a knock on the door and old Roy stuck his
head in. ''Zoe, Gus is looking for you. Hal's bowling team
just showed up.'' He frowned at Jake. ''Say, young fellow,
you're not supposed to be back here.'' He stepped farther
into the room. ''Everything all right, Zoe?''

Zoe gave the old man a reassuring smile. ''Everything's
fine, Roy. Tell Gus I'll be right there.''

She looked at Jake as the door closed behind Roy. ''I
better get out there.''

He couldn't hide his frustration. ''There's more we need
to discuss.''

Zoe started for the door. ''Load the jukebox with quarters, then buy another round for your friends. As soon as
there's a lull, ask me to dance. Hal doesn't mind if the
waitresses dance with the paying customers. We can talk
more on the dance floor. Just make sure the songs you pick
are ballads.'' She paused, her hand on the door. ''I know
this is distasteful for you, but I can't think of any other
way for us to have a private conversation.''

''Zoe—''

She closed the door behind her and hurried to the bar.

Chapter 7

Jake made a quick sweep of the room as he headed for the jukebox. The bar wasn't filled to capacity, but compared to when he'd first come in, it was hopping.

A tall man with long, greasy salt-and-pepper hair and a droopy mustache was behind the bar with Zoe and the bartender. He had to be Hal Francke. Sure enough, he didn't move past Zoe in the crowded space without touching her in some way.

So bring me there and make love to me.

Jake shook his head to exorcise Zoe's husky voice. She'd been serious. He'd seen it in her eyes. She would have had sex with him, in front of those cameras, to boot, in order to get this job done.

He stared sightlessly at the listing of songs on the old-fashioned jukebox, wishing he had some of her recklessness, her impetuousness, her careless youth. Wishing he could break away from everything that held him to the past, but knowing that even if he could forget for one night, for one *hour,* even if he could lose himself completely in this woman's sweet arms, he'd wake up and be right back where he'd started in the morning.

Or maybe even in a worse place.

I know this is distasteful for you.... Zoe had said that as she walked out the door. He had to set her straight. He couldn't have her continue to believe that. There was a lot about this assignment that was distasteful, but being with her was not.

Like he'd told her nearly five weeks ago—he liked kissing her. Too much. And even after all this time apart, he still liked it. Still much too much. He'd thought the distance would be good, that it would give him some perspective, some sense of reality. But all those weeks he'd dreamed about her in ways that were outrageously inappropriate.

He'd started out dreaming of Daisy, erotic, sensuous dreams of lovemaking filled with heat and light and such vivid sensations. But his dream would shift and change, the way dreams often do, and then Zoe would become the woman in his arms, her body wrapped around him.

He'd wake up, dizzy and out of breath and achingly, painfully alone.

Jake forced himself to focus and fed the jukebox dollar bills, punching in all the slow romantic ballads he could identify. He'd just picked a Leann Rimes song when he saw Christopher Vincent approach, his image shimmery but unmistakable in the curved glass.

He felt himself tense and worked hard to keep the smile on his face a pleasant one. God, when Christopher had grabbed Zoe, Jake had had to physically restrain himself. He'd come damn close to picking the man up and throwing him across the room.

"I guess our new little waitress likes you," Christopher said.

Jake pushed the buttons for a Garth Brooks song, not even looking up. "Oh, is she new here?"

"She came into town a few weeks ago. Hal met her at

some party. Don't worry. I've checked her out. She's exactly what she says she is.''

"Well, that's good to know." Jake smiled at Chris. "But no real surprise. I mean, she doesn't come across as some kind of rocket scientist or—I don't know—some kind of biochemical engineer. Can you imagine her in a lab coat?''

Christopher laughed, and Jake laughed, too, knowing that the real joke was on the CRO leader. God, it was going to be so good to nail this guy....

"Yeah," Chris said, "I can imagine her wearing *only* a lab coat." He laughed again. "She is some hot ticket.''

Jake turned to the jukebox, uncomfortable with Christopher's openly lascivious appraisal of Zoe, not wanting to be a part of it in any way.

"I've seen her counting on her fingers," Chris continued, "but with a body like that, it's almost better that she's not too bright." He looked at the bar, watching Zoe as she poured another pitcher of beer. "Oh, yeah. She's choice.''

As if she were a cut of meat. Jake felt his smile turning even more brittle and he stared at the jukebox, reminding himself why he couldn't simply beat the hell out of Christopher Vincent right here and right now.

"Just so you know not to get your hopes up too high," Christopher told him before he walked away, "she's holding out for marriage, our little Zoe is. You'd have better luck with Carol.''

Jake glanced at the bar, but Zoe was gone. He quickly scanned the room, found her making the rounds of tables, double-checking that everyone had all the beer and liquor they needed to get them through the next few minutes.

She looked up, caught him gazing at her, and for a fraction of a second, he saw a glimmer of uncertainty in her eyes. Distasteful. Did she honestly think he found this part of the set up *distasteful?*

But just like that the uncertainty was gone and she smiled.

It was a very inviting, very warm smile, complete with

a very slow, very appreciative up-and-down look that was totally lacking in subtlety. It was a look he might've gotten back in high school, and his body responded in a way far more appropriate for a seventeen-year-old than a fifty-something grown man.

Jake moved toward her as surely as she made her way toward him. It was as if they both were magnetized, as if they couldn't have stayed apart from one another even if they'd tried.

Zoe set her tray on top of an empty table.

He slipped his hands into the back pockets of his jeans, afraid if he didn't he wouldn't be able to keep himself from reaching for her.

"I didn't buy another round yet," he told her. "When I came out, someone else had just—"

"It's okay." She looked away, as if suddenly shy. "You know, if you don't want to dance, we could try sitting at a table toward the back. But Gus and Hal might—"

He took his hands out of his back pockets, and just like that, he had her by her hand and was pulling her toward the dimly lit dance floor next to the jukebox. Just like that she was in his arms and swaying gently in time to the music.

"You should talk fast," she told him. "I don't know how long I'll have before Gus needs me."

He pulled her closer. "This is not distasteful," he murmured into her ear. "Let's start with that, all right?"

Zoe shook her head. "Jake, you don't have to—"

"It's just…" He searched to find the words that would explain. "It's very…weird for me. I was with only one woman for nearly thirty years—nearly your entire lifetime. Can you even imagine that?"

Silently, she shook her head.

"I'm going to make everyone in this bar believe that I've got a major thing for you," he told her. "And doing that will *not* be distasteful. I'd be lying if I told you I haven't spent the past weeks looking forward to this. Look-

ing forward to it, and dreading it, all at the same time.
You're a great kid, Zoe, and a beautiful woman and… And
I'm sorry if I can't be as blasé about any of this as you,
and I'm sorry in advance if I somehow make you feel bad.
Holding you, even dancing like this, hurts a little bit. But
it feels good, too. Really good. Which in turns hurts a little
bit more. Does that make any sense at all?''

She nodded. ''I'm sorry if I—''

''Let's not apologize to each other anymore. We've got
to do what we've got to do, right?''

She lifted her chin. ''*I* think one of the things *I've* got
to do is to get into the CRO compound.''

''Now, *that* idea *is* distasteful.''

''Jake, no, I've been thinking about it.'' She rested her
head against his shoulder, and when she spoke, he could
feel her breath against his throat. ''The best way for me to
help you find the Trip X is for me to be in there.'' She
lifted her head and looked into his eyes. ''Remember our
deal? Remember what you promised?''

''I didn't know what it would be like in there for a
woman. Zoe, whatever you've heard about the CRO—''

''I knew exactly what I was getting myself into when I
agreed to be a part of your team. I can handle it.''

''But *I'm* the team leader, and I need you to try it my
way first.'' And if his way didn't work… Jake wasn't sure
how they'd handle the cameras in the bedroom. Maybe they
could cover some, disable the others. Maybe they could
pretend to make love, under the covers….

He changed the subject, trying to banish the image of
Zoe in his bed, her body soft beneath his.

No. He refused to give up on the idea that they could
find the Triple X *and* keep Zoe safely out of harm's way.
And out of his bed.

''I'm sorry it took me so long to get here,'' he said.
''Christopher tends toward delusions of grandeur, and he
imagined this terrible altercation the moment I stepped outside of the CRO gate. I think he was a little disappointed

when I made it all the way into town without being chased by federal agents.''

The song ended and they stopped for a moment, waiting for the next song to start. It had almost exactly the same slow, pulsating beat. He'd picked the songs well.

As they began dancing again, she shifted her body even closer and rested her head against his shoulder. How could she fit so perfectly in his arms?

''So how *did* you convince him to let you come to town?'' she murmured.

''Well, I, um, I thanked him for his hospitality and sanctuary, but I told him that I wouldn't be able to stay with him any longer unless I at least had the opportunity to, um…'' He laughed, embarrassed. ''Well, to, you know….''

''Ah.''

''And since there are no single women in the CRO over age thirteen…''

She lifted her head. ''He didn't offer you one of his many wives?''

''Are you kidding? The man's almost obsessively possessive.''

''Hmm. The sharing doesn't go both ways, huh?''

''Sharing?''

''Just more CRO unpleasantness. Women as chattel. You know, it's a good thing you made it into town today,'' Zoe interrupted herself. ''The team was starting to make plans to liberate you. You had us all worried.''

Jake swore softly. ''Why can't they just sit tight and trust me?''

''They care about you.''

''They think I'm too old.''

''*You* think you're too old.''

Jake pulled back slightly. ''What the hell is *that* supposed to mean?''

Zoe shook her head. ''Nothing. Look, Jake, I've been—''

''Nothing, my ass! You wouldn't've said it if it meant nothing.''

''Okay, it meant something, but it's a personal something, and if we've got limited time to talk here, the personal stuff should be the last thing we get to.''

He couldn't argue with that. Unfortunately it didn't make him wonder exactly what she'd meant any less. *He* thought he was too old. Jeez.

''I've been thinking about alternatives to this whole setup,'' she said. She pulled him close, breathing into his ear as if her words were seductive promises rather than a plan for an alternative operation.

God, he'd forgotten for a moment—he'd been standing there arguing with her. They were supposed to be just short of making out on the dance floor. He held her closer, and she moved toward him willingly, her breasts soft against him. He buried his face in her sweet-smelling hair. Oh, God.

''What's your take on the hierarchy of power inside the CRO?'' she murmured, her breath hot against his ear. ''I've always gotten the impression that Christopher Vincent's it. That without him, the organization would fall apart. And if that's the case, why don't we just grab Vincent on one of his trips outside of his compound? Hold him hostage in exchange for the Trip X?''

''I've thought about that, too,'' Jake admitted. He kissed her neck, ran his hands down her back to cup her rear end. Oh, *God.* Bad mistake. But once his hands were there, it would've looked odd for him to move them right away, wouldn't it? What were they talking about? Hostage. Vincent. Right.

''It's not an option,'' he told her, hoping she wouldn't notice the huskiness of his voice. He cleared his throat. ''Vincent's got contingency plans for all kinds of disaster scenarios. Everyone in the CRO compound has a battle station to go to if the Feds suddenly launch an attack. He's stockpiled enough food to withstand a two-year siege. He's got an escape route charted out of this bar, in case he suddenly finds himself a target while he's here.''

She slipped her hands into the back pockets of his jeans, pressing his hips tightly against hers. ''With or without an escape route, we could get him.''

''I know that. But what I don't know is what his contingency plan is in regards to the Triple X. His lieutenants might not know what it is they've got. His orders might be for them to use it if he's taken. So, no, we're not going to grab him. Not without finding out more.''

Jake tried to shift back, extremely aware of the fact that when she pulled him that close, there were no secrets between them—including the secret he'd been trying to keep about the enthusiastic way his body was responding to her nearness.

He tried to make his voice sound casual, conversational. As if he weren't affected by the sensation of her breasts against his chest, as if he couldn't feel her heat as she pressed herself against his thigh. ''Hey, have you heard from Mitch?''

''Not since he's been arrested.'' Zoe smiled, her hands traveling up his back. ''We almost didn't recognize him when we saw the news report on CNN.''

''Yeah, he's good with disguises. I looked twice at that little old man sitting at the bar just to be sure it wasn't him.''

''It's not. Mitch is still in custody,'' Zoe told him. She ran her fingers through the hair at the nape of his neck and it felt impossibly, sinfully good. ''He's being held at the same federal penitentiary where Christopher Vincent's stepbrother is doing ten to twenty for armed robbery.''

Jake laughed. ''Well, jeez, that's pure genius. I mean, I knew Christopher had a stepbrother who'd been in trouble with the law, but... Whose idea was it to send Mitch to the same prison?''

''I'm a fan of doing just that little extra bit of research,'' she told him modestly. "We lucked out that the stepbrother was in a federal jail and—"

"It was *your* idea. Good job, Lange. So you're the genius, huh?"

"Whoa," she said, laughing. Her eyes sparkled and danced with amusement. She was so pretty, so full of life. The longing that hit him was so strong, it took his breath away. "Don't go overboard. Yes, it was a good idea, but—"

She stopped short, her smile fading at the look he knew was in his eyes. He couldn't hide it, and he prayed she would think it was only part of the game they were playing.

They'd both stopped moving, and they stood on the dance floor just holding each other. She gazed at him, her beautiful lips slightly parted, and when he didn't move, she stood on her toes and kissed him.

It was the smallest of kisses, light and delicate, a feathery brushing of her lips across his. She searched his eyes again, then stood on her toes once more. This time she kissed him a little bit harder. This time she tasted him, gently touching the curve of his lips with the very tip of her tongue. And this time he kissed her, too, just as delicately, just as softly.

Jake's heart was pounding, and he was dizzy from wanting more. But he took his cues from her, letting her lead, refusing to push her into harder, deeper, longer kisses, no matter how badly he wanted just that.

She delicately swept her tongue into his mouth and he groaned aloud. She took him right to the point where he *knew* they were on the verge of crushing their mouths together and positively inhaling each other, but instead, she pulled back.

"We're both good actors," she whispered, "but we're not *this* good. Part of this is real, Jake, whether we want to believe it or not. That's what I was trying to say when I told you I'd make love to you. That I also *want* to make love to you."

Jake didn't know what to say.

She kissed him again, hot and sweet and long. "That's me kissing you, no games, no pretense. We can have it both ways, you know. We can do our jobs *and* get naked—if you can get past everything you need to get past, if you can come to the conclusion that you're not too old for this sort of thing."

"Ah," Jake said, finally finding his voice as she pulled free from his arms. "We've finally come to the personal stuff."

"I bet you look good naked," Zoe told him as she picked up her tray and headed to the bar.

Jake wanted both to laugh and cry. He'd never met anyone as completely in-your-face honest as Zoe Lange. She knew what she wanted, and she wasn't shy about asking for it.

She wanted him.

And his big problem was that he wanted her, too.

Even though he knew that wanting her was wrong.

Chapter 8

"Oh, hell, he's naked!"

Bobby Taylor thrust his big hands in front of the video monitor. But because there was more than one camera, there was more than one screen to cover. Wes Skelly grabbed Zoe's chair and spun her so she was facing the other direction.

She just laughed at them. "Oh, come on, you guys. Like I haven't seen a naked man before? I grew up in a very small house with four brothers. I'm sorry to disappoint you, but the male anatomy has just never been a mystery to me."

"Yeah, but he's an admiral," the bigger SEAL told her. Bobby Taylor could have made a fortune playing professional football. At six feet seven inches, he weighed at least two sixty, maybe even more. When he sat down, he took up two chairs, but very little of his bulk was fat. He was simply enormous. Yet despite that, he was one of the most graceful men Zoe had ever met. He was part Native American—part Navajo, he'd told her. He had the darkest, most serene brown eyes she'd ever seen. "He's earned the right to towel off after his shower without an audience."

"Besides," Wes added, "you don't want to be looking at him naked. He's an old man."

"He is *not*—"

"Okay," Bobby said. "He's got his shorts on. Although it still seems a little disrespectful for us to be staring at an admiral when he's in his underwear."

Zoe spun her chair to face the row of video monitors. Jake stood, displayed from three different angles, combing his hair out of his face. One of the cameras must've been positioned directly behind the mirror, because he gazed straight into it, his eyes a vivid blue. His arms were over his head, his biceps and triceps flexing.

"I'm sorry, Skelly," Zoe said, tapping that screen. "But that is *not* an old man. I don't know where you get off calling him that. He's in better shape than you are."

His stomach was rock solid and his chest was muscular, despite being badly scarred.

"Wow," Bobby said, subdued by the sight of all those scars. "He's seen some action, huh?"

"Two years ago he was the target of an assassination attempt," Zoe said. God, if those scars were any indication, he'd been nearly mortally wounded. It was a miracle he was still alive. He'd miraculously escaped death many times while in Vietnam, too. Some people said he'd led a charmed life. Without a doubt, luck had always been his constant companion.

Zoe hoped that same good fortune was riding copilot with Jake right now. If Christopher Vincent even *suspected* Jake was there as a spy...

On the screen, Jake threw his comb on top of the dresser. He took his jeans from the closet. Too bad. He had very nice legs. As Zoe watched from three different angles, he pulled on his jeans and covered them up.

His bedroom was a former executive office for the old factory, the walls still covered with cheap, tacky paneling, ancient orange-shag carpeting on the floor, blessedly faded. The furniture was cream-colored, with gold ornamentation—directly from a low-rent motel liquidation sale. She'd have thought a group declaring themselves to be the chosen race would have a little more taste.

"Besides behind the mirror," Zoe mused, "the other cameras are, where? Over by this window…" She pointed to the screen. "And…here near the door?"

Wes spread the floor plan of the CRO compound—the former Belle Frosty Cakes factory—out on the counter behind her and she swiveled her chair to face him.

"In Admiral Robinson's quarters, the cameras are here, here and here." He highlighted the locations in pink.

"Any in Jake's bathroom?" she asked, leaning over for a closer look.

"At least one," he told her. "Here."

"Show me that one," she said, turning to the video screens.

Bobby keyed a command into the computer, and the image on the far left screen changed.

The camera in the white-tiled bathroom had a clear shot of the door, the sink and the toilet. But not the tub. The tub, with the shower, was off to the side, out of camera range. Interesting.

On the other two video screens, Jake buttoned up his shirt, pocketed his wallet and keys and left the room.

"Can you follow him?" Zoe asked.

"Yeah, as long as he doesn't go too fast." Bobby had fingers the size of hot dogs, yet they flew over the computer keyboard. "But even if we do lose him, it won't take long to find him again. As soon as he speaks, we can use the computer and trace him by his voice."

On screen, Jake walked purposefully along the corridor. He had a cocky walk, with a spring in his step more befitting a twenty-five-year-old. It was self-confidence, Zoe realized. Jake Robinson walked the way he did because he trusted himself completely. He liked himself, too.

It was powerfully attractive.

It had been two whole days since she'd seen him last, and Zoe felt a sharp tug of longing. She missed him.

They'd been together every evening at the bar for two and a half weeks before that. During that time Zoe had smuggled to Jake the equipment he'd needed to enable the SEALs to tap into the CRO security cameras. *And* during that time, they'd established a very hot, very high-visibility romance.

Zoe had made it clear to all the patrons of Mel's Bar that she was holding out for marriage. Despite the sparks she and Jake made on the dance floor, she publicly refused to bring him home with her. And Jake, he'd made it clear that he wasn't ready for any kind of commitment.

It was kind of funny, actually. In truth, the man was Mr. Commitment. He would still be married to his first wife right now if she hadn't died. And Zoe didn't doubt for one nanosecond that he'd still be *happily* married.

Conversely she, Zoe, had never even imagined herself married. She'd never seen the need, considering that she'd never truly been in love. She'd always purposely sought out and let herself fall halfway in love with men she knew would never be right for her. Halfway in love was all she'd wanted, though. It was safe. She knew exactly what she'd get, knew she'd never be in too deep, never out of control.

She was doing the exact same thing with Jake, too. Even if she could convince him to make their relationship more physical, more intimate, she knew damn well it would never go beyond that. He still loved his wife, and he wasn't looking to replace her.

Zoe could love Jake—just a little—and still be safe.

So she did. And she used her feelings to bring a certain authenticity to her role. No, she would not sleep with him, not until they were married. Well, okay, pretending *that* was a stretch. A long stretch.

And at times, when Jake held her in his arms on the dance floor, or when she kissed him goodbye each night, she thought the sheer irony would drive her completely insane. Here Jake always pretended that he wanted to spend the night with her, and Zoe always pushed him away.

She could think of only one thing she wanted more than to spend these long, cold autumn nights with Jake Robinson in her bed. She wanted to find the Trip X. But that was the *only* thing she wanted more.

Still she sent Jake back to the CRO fort each night. And each night she slept alone.

Each day, she locked herself in the team's surveillance trailer, using the computers to access the CRO cameras, electronically searching for the missing canisters of Triple X.

She was exhausted, bleary-eyed and completely frustrated on many, *many* levels. She wasn't going to find anything this way. She had to get in there, inside that electric fence. She needed to search with more than just her eyes, restricted by the lens of a camera.

She had to get inside Christopher Vincent's private quarters, into those few rooms where there were no security cameras. The more she came into contact with Vincent, the more she was convinced that he was the type of man who'd get off on keeping a crate of deadly poison—enough to wipe out the capital city of this country—on the sideboard of his private dining room.

She'd had it. She'd played it Jake's way for long enough. She was going to get inside the CRO walls whether he liked it or not.

On the video monitor, Jake turned a corner, and with a flick of his fingers, Bobby made him appear on a different screen. The enormous SEAL didn't consult any list, didn't look at the factory schematic. He just somehow knew the camera codes.

"You've already memorized both the layout of this part of the factory and the location of the cameras?" she asked.

"I've got the whole factory up here." He tapped on his forehead. "I'm pretty good with maps."

Pretty good?

"Morning, John," Jake said in greeting to a man heading in the same direction. Bobby made another adjustment, and their conversation about the current dreary weather came in crisp and clear over the speakers, fading slightly as they moved away from one microphone, getting louder as they walked past another.

"Tell me about the audio signal," Zoe said. "Do all the cameras have microphones, or is there a different miking system?"

"There's a combination," Wes told her. "The dedicated mikes are higher quality, but they're also more expensive so there're fewer of 'em."

"Is it possible to speak quietly enough so's not to be heard?" Zoe asked. "I guess what I need to know is, once I'm in there, is there any way I'll be able to talk to Jake *without* the mikes picking up our conversation?"

"Mid to high-range frequency overload will block low-volume conversation," Bobby said. He typed in a new command, and on the right-hand screen, the CRO kitchen appeared. About a dozen women were in the big room, about half of them washing dishes. "See?"

"Run water," Wes interpreted. "And speak softly. But don't whisper. A whisper could cut through."

Sure enough, in the kitchen, water was running from the faucet, and Zoe could only make out the words of the women who raised their voices significantly when they spoke.

"We also found a spot where the security cameras were set up a little carelessly," Wes told her. He pointed to the floor plan again, and she stood to get a better look, stretching her legs. "Up here there's access to the roof. There must've been some kind of recreation deck there at some time. And the entire northwest corner of that area is completely out of camera range. It overlooks the millstream— an added bonus, running water. Again, speak softly, and your conversation will be covered by the sound of the water. You won't be overheard."

Bobby turned in his chair to face her, his dark eyes very serious. "Zoe, are you sure you want to go in there?"

"Yes."

"Don't take this the wrong way," he said, "but I'm not sure the admiral's got this under control."

"Admirals can lose touch," Wes agreed. Since Bobby was so tall and broad and always with him, Wes always seemed short and wiry in comparison. But Zoe had to lift her chin to look at him as he straightened up. He had a pack of cigarettes rolled up in his T-shirt sleeve, revealing a stylized barbed-wire tattoo that ran completely around an extremely well-developed bicep. He may have been wiry compared to Bobby, but only compared to Bobby. Wes Skelly was no lightweight, that was for sure.

"Since when did you start smoking again?" she asked him.

"Since I've been nervous as hell about this op," he countered. "Since we've been sitting here for weeks, relying *only* on Robinson, getting no closer to finding that Triple X crap."

"Human beings slow down," Bobby pointed out.

"After you hit a certain age, your reaction time really starts to suck," Wes agreed.

"It's a fact of life."

"Don't get me wrong," Wes said, "the admiral's a good guy—"

"For an admiral—" added Bobby.

"And we know he used to be a SEAL—"

"A long time ago—"

"But it *has* been about a million years and—"

"You know how on 'Star Trek,'" Bobby started earnestly.

"On *classic* Trek," Wes interjected with a grin.

"Whenever a commodore's on board the *Enterprise*—"

''And the intergalactic antimatter's about to hit the fan—''

''And this old, out-of-touch commodore takes command of the ship because he thinks he's got all the answers, and Captain Kirk's got to fight both the bad guys *and* the good guys to save the day?'' Bobby continued.

''Bob and I are alarmed at the remarkable parallels we've found between those episodes and this current mission,'' Wes told her. ''We're sitting out here in the woods with this old rusty commodore, and our captain's back in California. It doesn't bode well for the Federation.''

Zoe started to laugh. ''You guys are too much.''

''Actually, Zoe…'' Wes's grin faded. ''We *were* kind of hoping you'd talk to the admiral, you know, convince him that it's time to try to get more of the team inside those walls.''

They were kidding, but only halfway.

''You guys need to read a book called *Laughing in the Face of Fire* because you obviously have no idea who you're dealing with here,'' she told them. ''You have no idea what Jake did in Vietnam, do you?'' She knew they didn't. Their expressions were blank. ''I can't believe you wouldn't at least try to find out *something* about your team leader.'' She laughed again, but this time in disbelief. ''Jake's not the commodore, boys. He's the captain. And if you're not careful, *you'll* be the good guys he's got to fight so he can save the day. He needs you standing beside him—not standing in his way.''

''At the risk of annoying you,'' Wes said, ''I have a theory that your loyalty to the admiral isn't really loyalty, but instead has something to do with the fact that you've been sucking face with him for the past few weeks. Sex confuses things. Particularly for women.''

''*Excuse* me?''

''I think you annoyed her,'' Bobby commented, turning away to hide his smile.

''It's some kind of hormonal thing,'' Wes said, amuse-

ment dancing in his eyes. He *knew* he was completely piss-
ing her off, damn him. "You *think* it's loyalty, but it's
really just your hormones responding to the power of an
alpha male, even if he is a little on the ancient side."

Zoe stood up. "Well, it's been fun, but it's time for me
to leave this den of total ignorance. You know, I bet you
could find the book-on-tape copy of *Laughing in the Face
of Fire.* I realize now that reading might be too big of a
challenge for someone as pea-brained as you, Skelly."

Bobby laughed. "What are the odds they've come out
with a comic book edition? You might get him to read
that."

Wes pretended to be offended, but he couldn't keep a
smile from slipping out.

"You know, if this was 'Star Trek,' wiseass," Zoe heard
him say to Bobby as she went out the door, "you'd be
Lieutenant Uhura, sitting there in high heels, keeping hail-
ing frequencies open. How does *that* make you feel?"

"Like I'm in damn good company," Bobby said.

Zoe wasn't in Mel's when Jake arrived.

He knew it was only a matter of time before she showed
up—she would've been paged as the surveillance team saw
him leaving the CRO gates.

He nursed a beer as he stood by the jukebox, filled with
the same sense of anticipation and dread he felt every night
before he saw Zoe.

She would tell him hello—she always did—with a deep,
searing, burning kiss. God, he loved kissing her. Loved *and*
hated it.

Hated it because her kisses so completely overwhelmed
him. When Zoe kissed him, nothing else existed. His world
narrowed down to him and her, his mouth, her mouth, his
arms around her, her body against him.

When Zoe kissed him, he could barely even remember
his own name, let alone the taste of Daisy's kisses.

Zoe had completely invaded his dreams, as well. More

than once he'd woken up reaching for her, so certain that his impossibly detailed, incredibly erotic dreams had been real.

Lately in his dreams, he only saw Daisy from a distance. He'd spot her from the bedroom window of his Washington apartment and go out the French doors onto the deck to call to her. Halfway there, he'd realize he was naked, that he'd just been in bed with Zoe. His voice would catch in his throat, and Daisy would disappear.

He didn't need Joseph and his dreamcoat to figure out what *that* meant.

He'd wake up, aching from guilt and need. It was not a good combination.

Jake glanced at his watch. Dammit, where *was* she?

Tonight he wasn't just anticipating her arrival because he wanted to kiss her. Tonight he had some vital information he needed to pass along.

"If you're looking for Zoe—" Carol, one of the other waitresses, the pretty, dark-haired, forty-something one, stood behind him, holding her tray "—she called in sick again tonight."

Sick. Again? Oh, damn, he'd purposely stayed away for a few days. What if she'd been sick all that time? What if she'd needed him? "Is she all right?"

Carol shrugged. "Gus thinks it's the flu. Personally, I just think she's pouting."

"Thanks for letting me know." Jake finished the rest of his beer and carried the empty bottle toward the bar.

"Before you go racing out to her place," Carol said, following him, "you should probably be ready for her to hand down an ultimatum. That girl wants some kind of commitment, Jake. She told Monica you've been dragging your feet so hard, she was starting to give second thoughts to becoming Christopher Vincent's fourth wife."

Jake nearly dropped the bottle. "What?"

Carol smiled. "Yeah, I figured you didn't know about that. Apparently your friend Christopher has been hitting on Zoe, too. He wants to add her to that sick little harem he's got going up there at the old Frosty Cakes place.''

"She never said a word about that to me.''

"I'm going to give you some unsolicited advice, Jake. Zoe's a little wild, a little out of control. That's her nature. But she wants a ring. This is probably the first time in her life she's held out for something like this, and I'm certain that she's serious. I know you haven't known her for that long, but she wants to get married before she turns thirty, and she's getting close to the point where she doesn't particularly give a damn *who* she marries. But she *is* in love with you. You should hear her talk about you—it'd make you blush.''

"She *does* go on and on and *on* about you, Jake.'' Somehow the bartender had become a part of this conversation. The two old men who were permanent fixtures in the bar were also unabashedly listening in.

"If you feel anything for her at all, buy her a ring,'' Carol advised him. "Have Christopher Vincent do that mumbo-jumbo wedding ceremony that he does. It's not real, anyway. He has no more authority to officiate at a wedding than my pet poodle. But it'll make Zoe happy, you'll get what you want for as long as you want it, and it'll keep her away from Christopher. He's just a little too rough with women, if you ask me.''

"You'd be a damn fool not to marry Zoe for real,'' one of the old men said. Roy. Zoe had told him that Roy was ninety-two years old. "If I were just twenty years younger, I'da asked her myself the first time she came in here.''

Zoe's trailer was parked just down the block, in the empty lot alongside Lonnie's gas station. The light was on as Jake approached.

She opened the door before he even reached the steps— she'd been watching and waiting for him.

She was wearing her jeans and that little flowered T-shirt she'd had on in Washington the first time they'd met. Her hair was down, long and silky around her shoulders. She wore almost no makeup, and her skin seemed to glow with good health.

"I guess you don't have the flu," he said as she closed the door behind him.

"Gee, you sound almost disappointed."

Her gym bag was packed, her backpack, too. They lay on the floor of the tiny hall that led to the trailer's single bedroom.

Dammit, she *was* actually trying to force his hand. She wanted him to marry her and bring her to the CRO compound.

"Going somewhere?" he asked. He tried to keep his voice and his smile pleasant, but he knew they were both a little too tight.

She met his gaze and didn't try to pretend either one of them didn't know exactly what was going on. "It's time, Jake."

"What if I say no, it's not time? What if I tell you no, you're not getting inside the CRO fort? Is that when you blatantly defy me—and sign on to be the fourth Mrs. Vincent?"

He was furious with her, but his anger wasn't entirely because she was attempting to override his authority. He was mad as hell that she could consider sex to be so insignificant, that she could hold her own self in such low esteem. He was livid at the idea of her giving herself to Christopher Vincent. Her motivation might be selfless, but dammit, it was *wrong*.

And it drove home the fact that she was willing to be with Jake, too, for the same wrong reasons.

And in a flash of insight that was a little too glaringly clear, Jake knew that he didn't want Zoe to want him, *too*—in addition to her desire to make this mission a success. He wanted Zoe to want him, period. In spite of the mission. Outside of the mission.

The way he wanted her.

She didn't blink. "You know that I'd prefer doing it this way. Going in there with you."

He let himself glare at her, let his words crackle with his displeasure. "Yeah, and *I'd* prefer doing it *my* way. I *am* the team leader, or have you forgotten?"

Zoe flinched at his high volume, but then lifted her chin in that way she had that could infuriate him and make him admire her, all at once. "*Are* you the team leader, Admiral? If so, why are you letting Jake the protective man interfere with what's best for this op? The plan was to get me inside that factory so I could help you find that Trip X. It was a good plan—until you stopped thinking like an admiral. You *promised* me that as far as my safety and comfort went, you'd let me draw the line. We had a deal—until you turned around and reneged."

"You want me to let *you* draw the line?" Jake couldn't believe it. "Where's your line, Zoe? As far as I can tell, it doesn't exist. You're not drawing any line at all, if you're willing to *marry* Christopher Vincent to get inside the CRO fence!"

Chapter 9

Jake was beyond upset.

For the first time since Zoe had met him, he didn't have a smile ready to pull out to help diffuse or relax the situation.

His eyes were cold and as hard as blue steel, and he looked at her as if she were a stranger, as if he didn't recognize her.

Zoe didn't know what to tell him. She opted for the truth. "I wouldn't really have married Christopher Vincent," she admitted. "I just thought.... I don't know. Maybe it would give you the incentive you needed to get me in there this other...this *safer* way."

He clearly didn't believe her. Why should he? She'd worked hard to make him think she was tough and ruthless. "Things weren't progressing at a speed that satisfied you, so you decided to resort to emotional blackmail, is that what you're saying?"

She couldn't deny it, but she could try to justify it. "I'm the expert, Jake. I should be in there."

His eyes were as cold and as empty as the darkness of outer space, his voice flat. "I should send you home."

Her chin went up. "You could do that, Admiral, but you couldn't stop me from going to Pat Sullivan and getting reassigned right back here."

"And then you'd use the fact that Christopher Vincent wants to sleep with you to get through the CRO gates, right?" He laughed, but there wasn't any humor in it. "Funny, I thought I heard you just say you wouldn't do that."

Zoe felt like crying. She'd worked overtime to make Jake believe that she was blasé about sex. She'd pretended so hard that it was no big deal. She was not demure, she was not shy. She could use her looks and her body as just another tool of her trade.

She'd started out wanting to shock him, wanting to shake him up and, yes, wanting to impress him. She was a modern woman, a Gen X-er. She might be young, she might be a woman, but she was an expert in dealing with weapons of mass destruction, an authority in a field that was more frightening than the most terrifying horror movie. Yet despite that, she had the ability to remain detached and in control while sheer chaos raged around her. She was cool, she was tough, she could get the job done—see, look? She could remain as emotionally unattached as James Bond when it came to matters of the heart. That proved she had what it took to be good at her job, didn't it?

She *was* good at her job.

But none of the rest of it was true.

Except now he believed it was. And he was not impressed.

She'd painted herself into this unfortunate corner, there was no doubt about it.

Jake sat tiredly on the built-in sofa. "You know what the really stupid thing is, Zoe?"

She was. *She* was the stupid thing.

"I came into town tonight to tell you that we're out of

time.'' Jake looked at her and gave her a crooked smile. ''I came to find out if you still wanted to marry your way into the CRO compound.''

Zoe sat across from him, suddenly sharply focused. ''Out of time? How?''

''I found out when Christopher's planning to use the Triple X,'' Jake told her. ''He's celebrating his fiftieth birthday in three weeks. He and his lieutenants have been talking about the big party they're having in New York City. How the big party's going to get covered by CNN. I figure we've only got about a week and a half before they'll try to move the T-X. We need to find it before then, for obvious reasons.''

The CRO could carry it out of state in plastic baggies, in small amounts. And then the team would have a hell of a time tracking it down. They could recover most of the Triple X and thousands of people could *still* die.

They had to find it. Now.

''Yes,'' Zoe said. ''Yes, I'll marry you.''

Someone had found Zoe a white dress.

It wasn't a wedding dress, but with her hair up, she looked angelic.

Jake stood in the front of Mel's Bar, watching as she proceeded toward him, down an aisle they'd made by moving the tables and chairs. He didn't know the name of the song that was playing on the jukebox, but the melody was haunting.

Zoe was so beautiful, his throat ached.

But this wasn't real. None of this was real.

The CRO didn't believe in marriage licenses. They opposed state intervention in something as personal as marriage. And thus, according to their rules, Jake could propose marriage at 8:37 p.m. and be watching his bride walking down the aisle toward him by eleven that same night.

Beside him, Christopher Vincent cleared his throat. He smiled as Jake glanced at him. Jake smiled back. And felt a small surge of triumph. There was a lot that was really, *really* wrong about this mock wedding ceremony, but at least Jake knew one good thing that would come of it. After tonight, Christopher Vincent would have no chance of getting his hands on Zoe.

He could see apprehension in her eyes as she got closer. Her smile was tentative, and he knew he hadn't completely managed to hide his sense of dread.

Jake didn't want to marry her. He didn't want to pretend to marry her. And he *really* didn't want to bring her back to his bedroom at the CRO compound. It was hard enough resisting her here, in a public bar. How was he going to handle sharing quarters with her?

Somehow, he was going to do it. He was going to pretend to make love to her, and he was going to sleep in the same bed with her night after night. If anything could cool his body's eager response to her nearness, it would be those three security cameras positioned around his room.

Zoe handed the flowers she carried to Carol and took his hand. Her fingers were cold. Her dress was lovely, with no sleeves and a sweeping low neckline that exposed the tops of her full breasts, but it was a summer dress, and fall was cold and crisp and far more suited to turtlenecks here in Belle, Montana.

He took both of her hands in his, trying to warm them. She was wearing perfume—just the slightest, subtlest scent.

"Kneel," Christopher Vincent commanded.

Jake helped Zoe down onto the floor, then prepared to join her. But Chris stopped him.

"Just Zoe," he said.

She looked up at them, frowning slightly. "Just me?"

"You have to show the proper respect to your husband and to the other men of the CRO," Christopher told her. "On your knees, head down, eyes averted."

This was it, Jake thought. This was where Zoe would stand up and laugh in Christopher's face.

But she didn't. She stayed there on the floor, and she

bowed her head. And he knew again how high she thought these stakes were. If she would do this, she would do *any-thing* to find that missing T-X.

Anything.

The thought made his stomach hurt.

The ceremony was short, filled with words like "obey" and "submit," "abide by" and "yield." It was a step back toward the Dark Ages for women everywhere.

Yet throughout it all, Zoe murmured her acquiescence.

It was nothing like his wedding to Daisy, and yet Jake found himself hesitating as he reached down to take Zoe's hand. It was time to slip a plain gold ring on her finger, but the depth and meaning of the powerful symbolism was tarnished by the loss of equality. The ring seemed far more imprisoning as she knelt slightly behind him, as he tagged her as if she were some kind of pet or possession.

Taking a deep breath, he pushed the ring onto her finger. If she could kneel and bow her head, he could do this.

There was no ring for his finger—he was grateful at least for that.

Finally, at last, Zoe was allowed to rise.

It was time to kiss the bride.

She looked at him then, and there were tears in her eyes. And he knew that as hard as this had been for him, it had been a million times harder for Zoe—Zoe, who'd probably never knelt for anyone before in her entire life.

He kissed her softly, gently, trying to reassure himself as well as her that none of this was real.

She clung to him then, and he closed his eyes and held her close. Wishing...what? He didn't even know.

"I'm sorry," she breathed into his ear, barely loud enough for him to hear. "I'm so sorry, Jake. I know how hard this must be for you."

He pulled back to look at her in surprise as he realized that the tears in her eyes were for *him*.

The crowd in the bar was applauding. Carol and her

friend Monica threw rice. And Jake stood there watching a tear escape from Zoe's eyes and slide down her cheek.

And he couldn't help himself.

He kissed her.

Not because he had to.

But because he wanted to.

Her lips were so soft, and she tasted impossibly sweet. How could someone as tough and strong as Zoe taste that sweet?

He gently coaxed her mouth open, taking his time, kissing her slowly, completely, deeply. Very, very deeply.

Time ground to a halt and the noise in the room faded to a dull roar. Nothing mattered, nothing existed but the woman in his arms.

He wanted to kiss her forever. He wanted this moment to go on and on, endlessly.

He felt her melt against him, felt heat pool in the pit of his stomach, felt his knees grow weak.

God, if a single kiss could be this good...

He pulled back, breathing hard.

Zoe's eyes were wide as she looked at him.

And then Chris and some of the other men from the CRO were slapping him on the back, shaking his hand, buying him a drink.

He looked at Zoe, surrounded now by Carol and Monica, old Roy and Lonnie, and she was still gazing at him, a question in her eyes.

He nodded. Yes. But she still didn't get it. Or maybe she didn't believe him.

"That was me kissing you," he told her silently, knowing she could read his lips.

She smiled, but her eyes welled with fresh tears. And this time he wasn't surprised.

Chapter 10

It was definitely weird.

Walking into the CRO fort was like walking onto the set of her favorite television show.

Zoe had seen it, in complete detail, on the surveillance video screens many times before.

She'd studied the entire former factory while in the team trailer. She knew the layout nearly as well as Bobby Taylor now.

She could find the main kitchen in a blackout with her eyes closed if she had to. She knew where all the cameras and microphones were located in the compound yard. She knew the shortest route to Jake's quarters from any given point in the place.

But she hung back, letting Jake lead the way.

She would have to remember to let him walk several paces in front of her. A CRO rule.

He'd left his room unlocked—apparently everyone did. He opened the door, holding it politely, the way her father might have done for her mother, to let her go in first.

She knew this room well, too. The colors were slightly different than they'd appeared on the video monitors, though, the red-orange of the shag carpeting a little more brassy, the paneling a little more nicked and worn.

She looked into the mirror, wondering who was watching them right now. Were Bobby and Wes pulling a shift? Or Harvard? Or was it Luke O'Donlon? The entire team knew that everything said and done in this room was purely for the benefit of the cameras. They knew that nothing was real, but still…

She turned to face Jake. "Well. This is…. At least it's nicer than my trailer."

Jake set her bags down on the long, low dresser top. He forced a smile. "It'll do for now."

Holy Mike, could they sound any more uptight? They were supposed to be newlyweds, on their wedding night. They'd both been pretending they were eager to get back here, that they were hot to be alone, but now what?

Jake had definitely been right—this was not going to be any fun. Not while knowing three cameras and God knows how many people would be watching them.

He came toward her, slipping off the jacket he'd put over her shoulders during the ride to the factory. He carefully hung it on the back of a chair, then smiled at her again.

"Mind if I…?" He reached for her hairpins, starting to take them out without really waiting for her reply.

"No, I don't mind." She helped him, and her hair tumbled around her shoulders.

"I love your hair," he said.

Zoe closed her eyes as Jake ran his fingers through it.

"It's so soft," he murmured. "Like a baby's."

He was touching more than her hair, touching her neck, her throat, her shoulders, her arms.

She opened her eyes, and the sight of herself in the mirror caught her off guard. She looked completely enthralled, her eyes half closed, her lips slightly parted, each breath she took making her breasts press even farther out of this two-sizes-too-small dress Carol had pulled out of the back of her daughter's closet.

"Are you cold?" Jake whispered, his hands warm against her arms.

"No, I'm—"

"Yes, you are," he said, silently ordering her to agree. "Your arms feel a little cold."

What was he doing? "I am," she said. "A little."

He kissed her jaw, her throat, the tops of her breasts. The sensation nearly made her burst into flames. Cold was the complete last thing that she was.

"Why don't you climb into bed—under the covers?" He smiled. "We'll see what we can do to get you warmed up."

Ah. *That* was what he was doing. Once they were beneath the covers, no one would be able to tell if they were making love or simply trying on each other's underwear. Especially if they turned off the lights.

Zoe turned her back to him. "Will you unzip me?"

He hesitated slightly, and she knew that he'd been hoping she'd just keep the dress on. But that would seem odd—too odd. She glanced over her shoulder at him. "Please?"

He touched her then, fumbling slightly with the tiny zipper pull. She felt his fingers trail down the entire expanse of her back as she held the dress on in front.

He kissed her neck, his voice suddenly husky. "I'll be right out."

Jake turned out one of the lights as he went into the attached bathroom and closed the door behind him.

God, his heart was pounding. Without a doubt, this was going to be the longest night of his life. He washed his hands, stalling, trying to get his heart rate down to near normal, splashed water onto his face.

But when he closed his eyes, he could see only Zoe's smooth, bare back. All that perfect skin beneath his fingers.

She wasn't wearing a bra.

He laughed aloud.

He was going to have to climb into that bed with her

and pretend to make love to her—oh, and while he did that, she would be half-naked in his arms.

He gazed at his dripping wet face in the bathroom mirror. Maybe he could keep *his* clothes on.

Yeah, right. That would look very unsuspicious. After he'd been drooling after her for weeks, *he's* suddenly Mr. Shy?

God, maybe he should just give up and make love to her.

Jake looked hard into his own eyes, recognizing the truth, recognizing that *that* was what he really, *really* wanted tonight. Sex purely for the sake of sex. No strings. No responsibilities. Just Zoe's legs locked around him as he lost himself inside of her.

As he lost himself.

Lost. Himself.

And he *would* lose himself. He'd wake up in the morning, and everything he valued most would be gone. His integrity. His honor. His profound sense of what was good and right.

And how would he be able to look himself in this mirror then?

He wasn't ready for that. Not now. God, maybe not ever.

Jake took off his shirt, stepped out of his shoes and his pants and turned on the shower.

He knew what he had to do.

But he wasn't done stalling.

Zoe heard the shower go off as she lay in the dark, waiting for Jake.

She heard the rattle of the shower curtain being pulled back, and then silence.

God, her heart was pounding.

She waited and…

The bathroom door finally opened, flooding the room with light. And there was Jake, a dark silhouette with broad shoulders, a towel slung casually around his waist.

She couldn't tell if he was smiling. She kind of suspected

he wasn't. But God, if there were ever a time she could have used one of his reassuring smiles, it was now.

He flipped the switch for the bathroom light, and the room again was dark. But not completely dark. The search-lights that illuminated the grounds of the compound shone in through the ancient blinds.

She could see Jake as he walked toward her, as he sat down on the edge of the bed.

"Sorry I took so long," he said. "It's been kind of a long day, and I thought you might appreciate it if I had a quick shower."

"I'm a little nervous," she whispered. Honestly. Not just for the benefit of the microphones.

Her eyes had adjusted to the dark, and she could see his face clearly. "I am, too, Zoe," he said quietly. Also honestly.

He smiled at her then. It was a smile that held an apology, a smile that was charmingly embarrassed, yet still self-assured enough to broadcast his awareness of the dark humor of this completely bizarre situation.

Zoe smiled back at him. "I think you're sitting out there because you want to hear me beg."

Something sparked in his eyes. "Begging usually works nicely for me. But tonight it's not necessary."

He dropped his towel on the floor as he slipped beneath the covers.

His skin was cool and smooth as he reached for her, as he kissed her. He pulled her close, his legs deliciously solid against hers as he intertwined them, his chest exquisitely solid against her breasts as his hands slid along the satiny back of her nightgown.

She could sense his surprise and then his relief. Oh, brother, had he really thought she would just be naked beneath these covers?

He had. He pulled back slightly to look at her, to check out the clingy black satin and lace that barely covered her breasts and swept all the way down to her thighs.

"Nice." His voice was husky; his eyes were warm. "Very nice. Very, very, *very* nice."

Zoe giggled. She couldn't help it.

Then Jake started laughing, too, and she laughed harder.

And once she started, she couldn't stop. This was just too absurd. She was finally in bed with this man that she wanted more than anyone in the world. She finally had him exactly where she wanted him, only she couldn't do anything about it because everyone and their right-wing, racist twin brothers were watching on their surveillance video screens.

Welcome to the Jake and Zoe Show.

It was completely insane. They were pretending to be lovers who'd waited to be married before making love, except they weren't really married, at least not in the eyes of the law, *and* they weren't really going to make love. Reality and pretense were all twisted in an enormously untangleable, ridiculous knot.

Jake was fighting it. He was trying not to laugh, but that just made it worse.

Zoe clung to him giddily. Their sudden unexplained laughter would be considered extremely strange, but there was nothing either of them could do to stop.

Jake tried to kiss her, but couldn't do it. He buried his face in her hair, laughing so hard he was crying.

They had to do *something* to make it look as if they were getting it on. Zoe pulled him more completely on top of her, cradling him with her body, linking her legs around him and—

Jake tried to pull back, but he couldn't move quickly enough.

He was completely aroused. He'd been lying beside her in such a way that had kept her from knowing that, but now the hard truth—as it were—was unavoidable.

And just like that, they both froze, both stopped laughing.

"Oh, God, I'm sorry," he breathed. He was beyond embarrassed. He was mortified.

"No," she said. "No, Jake, because I want—"

"Don't," he rasped, and kissed her to keep her from saying it.

Zoe kissed him hungrily, telling him without words what he already knew.

I want you, too.

He groaned as she pressed herself up against him, groaned as she kissed him harder, sweeping her tongue more deeply into his mouth.

But then he pulled back. He stopped kissing her and started rocking the bed, his movements obvious from the squeaks of the springs, the way the mattress bumped the wall. But it so lacked finesse, Zoe struggled not to laugh again. Or cry. She was so overwhelmed with emotion and desire, she wasn't sure what would come out if she opened her mouth.

He collapsed on top of her with a shout, pretending it was over far too quickly, pretending he'd found release. They lay there, both breathing hard for many long seconds.

Jake was still rock solid against her thigh, and Zoe wondered if, like her, he was ready to weep from sheer frustration.

But then he rolled off her, swearing softly, and she turned to look at him.

He lay on his back, one arm thrown up and over his eyes. "I'm sorry," he said. His words were for the microphones—they were back in pretend mode. "It's been a long time for me and—"

"Sh." Zoe didn't dare reach for him, didn't dare touch him. "It's okay. We've got the entire rest of our lives to get it right."

"I'm just...embarrassed." He looked at her, lowering his voice. "I *am* sorry."

"It's okay." There was nothing else she could say, not

without fear of blowing their cover, not without making Jake even more tense.

He'd kissed her this evening, for real, back in Mel's bar, but clearly he wasn't ready yet for anything more, despite his body's obvious betrayal.

She ached for him to hold her, ached for them to finish what they'd started, ached because she knew it wasn't going to happen. Maybe not ever.

She lay beside him, far too warm beneath the blanket, afraid to move for fear she might brush against him.

"Thank you for marrying me," she whispered, knowing how terribly hard all of this was for him.

Jake just laughed. "Yeah," he said. "Sure."

Chapter 11

Jake stood in the shower with his eyes closed, letting the water drum down onto his head.

He'd gotten maybe an hour of sleep last night.

He'd lain awake for hours, hyperaware of Zoe lying next to him in that bed.

It was only a double, not as big as the queen-size mattress he was used to, *and* it had a big, broken-down valley right in the center, to boot. Every time he tried to get comfortable, he sank toward the middle of the bed and ended up brushing against Zoe.

The smoothness of her legs.

The softness of her shoulder.

The cool satin of her barely there black nightgown.

Dear God. He'd been so glad at first that she'd put *something* on. But as the night had dragged on, he'd found himself thinking about the way that slinky texture had felt beneath his fingers, the warm firmness of her body beneath that, the black lace against the creamy fullness of her breasts....

Dear God.

Dear God.

She'd slept about as well as he had.

He'd sensed her, lying awake, tensely clinging to her side of the bed.

At one point, he'd heard her breathing deepen, heard her finally fall asleep. But as she'd relaxed, she'd turned toward him, nestling against him, her hand on his chest, her legs against his.

He'd tried gently to push her legs back, knowing he'd never sleep with her there like that, afraid of what might happen if he pushed his way between her thighs while they both slept. But as gentle as he'd tried to be, he'd woken her up. She'd stared at him, stared at her hand placed so possessively on him, and she'd retreated to her side of the bed with a murmured apology.

He'd finally slept fitfully, waking himself up every few minutes with a start, trying to police himself.

This last time, exhaustion had overtaken him. He'd slept for at least an hour.

And had woken up with Zoe wrapped tightly in his arms. Her soft rear end pressed against him, his face buried in her sweet-smelling hair, his right hand securely cupping her breast.

He'd extracted himself from her this time without waking her. Morning light was finally streaming in through the cracks in the blinds, and he'd gotten out of bed, aching in every way imaginable.

He'd gone for a run, pushing himself far beyond his usual five miles, and by the time he'd come back to the room, the bed was neatly made and Zoe was gone.

With luck, she was as good as Pat Sullivan had said she was, and she'd return to the room with the six missing canisters of Triple X in hand.

Jake laughed aloud, knowing how completely ridiculous it was to think Zoe could simply find the Trip X by walking the halls of the CRO compound on her first morning here, but irrationally hoping just the same. It was about time *something* in this op came easily.

"Hey," Zoe said, pulling back the shower curtain and stepping into the tub. "What are you laughing about in here all by yourself?"

Jake hit his head on the showerhead, quickly turning so that his back was to her. "Zoe! *Jeez!*"

He still had shampoo in his hair but he shut the water off, reaching for the towel that was hanging on the back of the bathroom door.

But she reached past him and turned the water back on.

Soap ran into his eyes and he swore sharply as he wrapped the towel around his waist despite the water streaming down on him. "What the *hell?*"

She leaned against him, close enough to speak directly into his ear, her voice low. "We can talk quietly in here. With the water running, our words won't be picked up by the microphones if we speak softly enough. And the camera is over the window. This is the only place in your entire suite where we can't be seen."

Jake nodded. "Well," he whispered, rinsing the soap out of his eyes. "Isn't this convenient?"

"Don't whisper," she warned him. "Use your regular voice—just keep it really low." She laughed softly. "You can open your eyes and turn around. I've got clothes on."

Thank God.

He turned around—and realized he'd offered up his prayer of thanks just a little too soon. Zoe was in her underwear—a running bra and an entirely too skimpy pair of panties.

"We have a little problem," she told him seriously, as if she always held important meetings in the shower, half naked.

Her running bra left little to the imagination to start with, but wet, it molded itself to her breasts. Breasts that he knew more than filled the palm of his hand. And he had big hands.

He focused on her eyes. Water beaded on her long eye-lashes, making her look even more freshly beautiful than ever.

"Problem?" he repeated stupidly.

"As a new member of the CRO through marriage," she said, her voice so low he had to lean closer to hear her, "I apparently only have probationary status here. I'm not allowed to leave this room unless you're with me."

Jake swore loudly, and she put her finger against his lips.

She pulled her hand back quickly, as if touching him had burned her, and he knew that despite her efforts to pretend otherwise, she was not unaffected by the fact they were standing together, barely dressed, in the shower.

I want you, too. The words he hadn't let her say out loud last night seemed to echo against the tile as the steam from the shower swirled around them.

Zoe cleared her throat. "The guard who escorted me back here wasn't completely up on the exact rules." She continued quietly, sounding far more businesslike and matter-of-fact than he could have managed given the circumstances. "But as far as I could gather, there's some sort of special vacation deal for newlyweds. As a woman, I'm supposed to work, but I'm not allowed to join a work party for at least four glorious days. Unfortunately, we don't *have* four glorious days to waste."

In order to hear her, Jake had to stand so close he could count the drops of water on her face. One of the drops ran down her cheek like a tear and landed on her collarbone. As he watched, it meandered down her chest, slowly gathering speed as it disappeared between her breasts.

Jake closed his eyes. The towel around his waist was completely soaked. It weighed about ten pounds and hung low on his hips. He had to hold it up with one hand as he kept the soap from his hair out of his eyes with the other.

"So now what?" he asked.

"So we temporarily ditch my intended plan to flit about, dodging cameras and guards like an invisible little ghost, and we march boldly—together, holding hands because, hell, it's our four-day honeymoon—into Christopher's private quarters.''

She was starting to shiver, and he turned them both around so that she was standing directly under the stream of warm water. She tipped her head back, letting the water flow on her face and all the way down her smooth, flat stomach. She squeezed her hair back with her hands and smiled at him. "Thanks."

Jake hiked his towel up higher and moved closer so he could speak directly into her ear, careful not to touch her. "I know you think Christopher's keeping the Trip X somewhere in his suite, but I can't get past the fact that if the CRO's going to take out all of New York City in a matter of weeks, *someone, somewhere* has to be working on some kind of delivery system."

He slipped slightly on the slick bottom of the tub and caught himself on the tile wall, his other hand still firmly holding the towel. By some miracle, he'd managed not to touch her, but just barely. He held on to the wall, bracing himself, his arm extended past her head, about a quarter inch from her cheek.

"There's got to be a bomb or missile being made to carry the Triple X." He tried to continue as if nothing had happened, but his voice was raspy and he had to stop and clear his throat. "It's got to go off at the right altitude above the city, at a time when wind conditions are acceptable. The CRO's got to have a lab to—"

"It's not here," Zoe said definitely. She turned her head to speak into his ear, and her cheek grazed his.

Jake had never had to have his heart started again by a jolt of electricity through paddles in a hospital's ER, but he now knew what it would feel like.

"Sorry," she breathed. "God, this is…"

"Awkward," he said, trying to laugh. "Again."

"Maybe we should just…" She looked at him, and the flash of uncertainty in her eyes took his breath away. Zoe?

Uncertain? But then she laughed, too, and whatever he had seen was gone. "If only we'd known, we could have packed our wet suits."

Zoe in a wet suit… "Do you scuba dive?" he asked.

"I'm learning. Or, rather, I was learning. It was mostly my friend Peter's idea, and when, well…" She shook her head and rolled her eyes. "Let's not go there."

Peter, huh?

"We've gone off track," she said briskly. "Where were we?"

"Discussing the lab," he said. Whoever Peter was, he was completely insane to have had Zoe and left her. "There's got to be a lab. Somewhere."

"Not here," she told him with complete confidence, instantly back on track. "Not in this facility. Just the quick look around I had this morning verified what I've seen from the surveillance cameras. And you said yourself you've been over this place with a fine-tooth comb. Maybe there's an outside source—"

"No. No way." Jake was just as convinced. "Vincent would *never* go outside of this little kingdom he's made."

Zoe released all the air in her lungs in a burst of exasperation. But then she froze, gazing into his eyes, ignoring the water that was hitting the back of her head. "Jake, what if…"

He could practically see her brain smoking, she was thinking so hard. She laughed aloud, the expression on her face morphing from disbelief to amazement to real excitement.

"Holy Mike, what if Chris doesn't know what he's got?" She gripped Jake's arm. "My God! He may think his birthday surprise will take out a few dozen racially inferior types in the New York subway system—kind of like that horrible incident in Japan a few years ago. He may not know he's got enough Triple X to turn the entire tristate area into a graveyard." She shook him slightly. "You've got to convince Chris that it's time to share secrets. Do whatever you have to do, Jake, but get him to tell you what the hell his plan is.''

"Oh," Jake said. "Gee. Is that all?" He took her arm and shook *her* slightly. "What do you think I've been trying to do all this time, Zoe?"

She had the decency to look embarrassed. "I'm sorry."

Awareness dawned in her eyes the exact moment Jake realized it, too. They were holding on to each other, her hand on the taut muscles of his forearm, his palm against the smoothness of her shoulder.

Jake would only have to move his head about an inch and a half, and he would be able to kiss her.

She moved her hand. "Sorry. I'm...sorry."

He spun them both around so that he was standing once again under the force of the water. He released her so he could use that hand to rub the last of the shampoo from his hair. His other hand was still holding the towel for dear life. "Just let me rinse off," he said. "And then you can...do what you need to, and after, we can take a walk, see if Christopher's in."

"And after *that,* I have something I want to show you," she told him. "A place we can go to talk without being overheard. It's outside, though, so dress warmly."

Dress was the key word. It would be very nice to have a private conversation in which they both had on all of their clothes.

Jake maneuvered his way to the other side of the narrow tub, reaching to open the curtain and step out.

But Zoe stopped him, holding on to the edge of his completely soaked towel. "Better leave this behind," she said. "And try to look happy."

Happy. Instead of impossibly, intensely, overwhelmingly, painfully, achingly frustrated and upset.

Jake laughed. No problem.

"There were at least three rooms he didn't show us." Zoe lay on her back in the warm autumn sun on what had probably at one time been the Frosty Cakes employees' recreation deck.

Christopher Vincent had welcomed them effusively into his private quarters. When Jake had told him Zoe was eager for a look around, the CRO leader had given her what could only be described as a significant glance when Jake's back was turned.

Zoe had given him a loaded smile in return, hoping that he'd give them a more thorough tour if he thought she was interested in whatever tawdriness he had in mind.

Whether he'd given them a more thorough tour or not, there was no way of knowing.

All Zoe knew was that the missing canisters of Trip X weren't anywhere in sight in his private dining room, his bedroom, his enormous private bath or the three suites his wives and their young children occupied.

Jake and Zoe hadn't been allowed into his private office. According to the layout of the factory that she'd studied in the SEALs surveillance trailer, she had to guess there were somewhere between two and four additional rooms in the area they hadn't seen. But a lab? She *still* didn't think so.

She turned to look at Jake, who was stretched out on his stomach, his arms folded underneath his head. His face was upside down from her perspective. He'd moved close enough to talk softly and still be heard beneath the rather bucolic sound of the nearby waterfall, but only their heads were together. His body and legs were a full one hundred and eighty degrees away from hers. Still, even that way, they were uncomfortably close. Too close.

She laughed. Two miles would've been too close, given the power of her attraction to him.

"What's so funny?" he murmured, his eyes half shut.

"You look tired," she said.

"You do, too."

"I didn't sleep much last night."

The half-lowered lids were only a ruse. His brilliant blue

eyes were as sharp as ever. "Yeah," he finally said. "I know."

"May I say something that I feel needs to be said—even at the risk of embarrassing you?"

Jake closed his eyes. "No."

"Jake."

He opened his eyes and sighed as he looked at her. "What's the point?"

"For starters, we're going to be in bed again together tonight," she told him. "Have you thought about that?"

"The thought has crossed my mind one or two million times already today," he said dryly.

"The fact that you had a—"

Jake closed his eyes. "Don't say it."

Zoe rolled onto her stomach, pushing herself onto her elbows, supporting her chin with the palm of her hand. "You know, I probably would've been offended if you *hadn't* been so turned on. The past few weeks have been *extremely* intense, and correct me if I'm wrong, but I've got to believe you haven't made love since—"

"No," he said, cutting her off. "You're not wrong."

Since Daisy died. Zoe swallowed, aware that Jake hadn't wanted her even to say Daisy's name. Her heart broke for him. And for herself. "You must miss her so much."

"She was irreplaceable," Jake said quietly.

Zoe had known that. She just hadn't thought it would sting quite so much hearing Jake speak the words aloud.

"You know I find you very attractive," Jake said. He laughed. "And if you didn't know that, well, after last night you certainly knew it, huh?"

"I knew," Zoe said. "Before last night."

"Forget about the part where I'm old enough to be your father, okay?"

"I have."

Jake laughed. "Yeah, well, I haven't. But let's pretend for the sake of argument that I have. This thing between us, babe, it's still going nowhere fast. I can't get past the act that Daisy's still the woman I love. I just don't see myself—'' He broke off, unable to continue.

Zoe nodded, gazing at the waterfall, trying to convince herself that the tears in her eyes were the result of the too-bright sun. She couldn't look at him. But she had to ask. 'And those times when you really kissed me?''

He was silent for several long moments. ''Contrary to what you believe, I don't always do the right thing.''

She did turn to look at him then.

He smiled crookedly, tiredly. ''I know you see me as that all-powerful hero from Scooter's book, but honey, in truth, I'm just a man. Lead me not into temptation and all that. Sometimes temptation is just a little too tempting, and then I make mistakes. And sometimes I just make mistakes—completely on my own. No help from any outside force. I don't want you—but I want you. Sometimes the part of me that wants you shouts down the other part.''

Zoe studied his face. Jake. The man. He was right, in a way. For years he had been her hero. Invincible. Intrepid. Noble. Immortal. Yet beneath all that, he *was* just a man.

A very *good* man.

''So are you just planning to be celibate for the rest of our life?'' she asked.

Her question caught him off guard. ''I don't know,'' he said honestly.

''Well,'' Zoe said carefully. ''When you do know, if the answer to that question is no, I hope you'll come and find me.''

Jake put his head down on his arms and laughed. But when he lifted his head, propping himself up on his elbows the way she was, his eyes were filled with a curious mix of both sadness and heat. ''See, now, like right now is one of those times I really struggle with, because right now I have this completely overpowering urge to kiss you.''

Zoe wanted to touch his beautiful face, to push back that unruly lock of hair that fell down over his forehead. But he didn't.

"You have to tell me the best way I can be your friend, Jake," she said. "Do I move closer when you say that to me? Or should I back away?"

He was close enough to kiss her, and his eyes dropped to her mouth before he looked into her eyes. "Are you strong enough to back away?"

Was she? "Right now, yes. Tomorrow? I don't know."

"Then back away," he breathed. "Please."

Zoe didn't move. "Tell me about Daisy."

Jake blinked. And laughed. And backed away himself. "Well," he said. "She was absolutely nothing like you."

Zoe quickly looked away, but apparently not quickly enough.

"Whoa," Jake said, catching her hand. "I didn't mean that the way it sounded. I mean, I meant it in a good way. You're so strong, so certain. You're a scientist, and Daisy…" He laughed. "She didn't have a lot of use for science or math."

Zoe gently pulled her hand free. Backing away. "She was an artist, right?"

"Yeah, mostly a painter, both oils and watercolor, although she did go through a charcoal phase, too. She was…" He forced a smile. "Pretty amazingly brilliant." He was quiet for a moment. "She never came out and said it, but she hated what I did—what I do—for a living. And when Billy decided he wanted to be a SEAL, too…" He shook his head. "She didn't like to talk about it. She just locked herself in her studio and painted." He rolled over onto his back and stared at the sky. "I think I managed to make her incredibly unhappy at times, but she loved me enough to pretend it was all right. And I loved her too much even to consider that she might be happier without me. And yet, you know, in our own way, we did okay. We had so much more than most couples I've known."

He turned his head and looked at her. "Okay, Lange. Your turn. 'Fess up. Who's this Peter?"

Zoe tried to smile, but she couldn't. "No one," she said

quietly. "He was nothing. Not compared to what you had with Daisy."

"It's not fair to make comparisons."

"Yeah," Zoe said. "It is. You talk about love in a way that I can't even comprehend." She took a deep breath. "You know, Jake, last night was the first time in my life I've ever slept all night in the same bed with a man."

He tried to hide his incredulousness and failed, sitting up to look at her. "Really?"

Zoe nodded and sat up, too, unable to meet his eyes. "I've had relationships—obviously—but it's always been, 'Well, gee, that was fun. See you in the morning.'" She braced herself and looked at him. "I've never lived with anybody. I've never gotten that close. I've never even wanted anyone to stay the night."

Jake had known a love the likes of which most people only dreamed. And she… She wasn't even one of the dreamers. She hadn't even dared to do that.

Jake sighed. His face was so serious without his usual hint of a smile lurking around his mouth. "This must be very hard for you. I'm so sorry. I've been thinking only of myself—"

"Look, it's no big deal. I just wish—" She broke off, unable to say it.

He touched her again, his fingers warm against the back of her hand. "What?"

She wanted to know what it would be like to sleep in Jake's arms, all night long, with his warmth and strength wrapped around her. But there was no way she could tell him that. Not after promising him she'd back away. She shook her head. "I wish a lot of things that are definitely better for you not to know."

Jake laughed as he stretched out on his back again, arms above his head.

He was silent for such a long time, Zoe turned to see if perhaps he'd fallen asleep.

But he was staring at the nearly painful blueness of the

Montana sky. He met her gaze, though, as if he'd caught her movement out of the corner of his eyes, and he smiled.

It was a smile that echoed everything she was feeling. Longing. Sadness. The knowledge that the price they'd both pay for the sweetness of a temporary joining was a high one.

Too high for Jake.

Chapter 12

"Oh, yes," Lucky O'Donlon said from his seat at the video monitors. "There *is* a god. Zoe's getting ready for bed."

On the other side of the trailer, Bobby and Wes didn't even glance up.

"Hey, Ren and Stimpy, didn't you hear what I said? Zoe. Moments. From being. Au naturel."

"Don't hold your breath," Wes said. "You're Lucky, but not *that* lucky. She knows exactly where the cameras are."

Sure enough, Zoe stood in the one place in the room where she had her back to all three cameras. And she undressed in segments, taking off her shirt and slipping on her nightgown while she still had on her jeans. She pulled both her jeans and her bra out from under the gown.

It was very disappointing.

On the other hand, the nightgown was black and short and very, *very* sexy. It highlighted her exceedingly generous upper body in a most pleasing way.

"Oh, man," Lucky murmured. "Imagine coming back to your quarters and finding *that* waiting for you."

Wes finally came to look over his shoulder. "Youch! Way to dress for bed, Dr. Lange!"

"Show a little respect," Bobby rumbled.

"I only said youch," Wes complained.

"Next time, say it with more respect." But even while Bobby said the words, he pulled his chair closer to the video screens.

"Who was on duty last night?" Wes asked.

"I was," Bobby said.

"Am I correct in assuming that she put that on last night, and you didn't tell me?"

"It didn't seem to warrant a phone call to the other trailer," Bob said. "So, no, Skelly. I didn't. Besides, I happen to respect Zoe, so…I didn't."

"That is one beautiful woman." Lucky glanced at Bobby. "And I say that with the utmost respect."

"So where's the admiral?" Wes asked. "He is a seriously dedicated team leader if he opted for a sneak and peek instead of playing honeymoon for the cameras with a babe in a black negligee. Sheesh, can you imagine *having* to do that? For Uncle Sam, Mom and apple pie, yes, I *will* suffer and kiss the beautiful blonde. What kind of training do you think I should go for next, so that I'll be given this kind of assignment?"

"Yeah," Lucky said. "Talk about a silver bullet…"

"I think it must be very difficult," Bobby said. "For both of them. He cares a great deal for her. And Zoe…" He sighed. "She's falling in love with Jake."

Lucky and Wes both turned to look at him.

"You're nuts," Wes said. "He's way too old for her."

"She can't fall in love with him," Lucky said, turning to watch her on the screen. She was lying on the bed, on her stomach, as she read a book. "She's supposed to fall in love with *me*. Beautiful women always fall in love with me."

Wes shook his head. "You think you're kidding, but it's true. You're a babe magnet. When Zoe first walked into that meeting at the Pentagon, I cursed you out, Lieutenant, sir, because it seemed inevitable she would take one look at you and not even talk to the rest of us."

"As soon as this assignment's over," Lucky said with a sigh as he watched Zoe on the screen, "she's mine." He smiled. "Hey, it might be fun to actually have to chase a woman for a change."

"It's not going to happen," Bobby said. "She's got a jones for Jake."

"Since when are you on a first-name basis with an admiral?" Wes asked.

The enormous SEAL shrugged. "Since I found a copy of that book Zoe was talking about. It was in the library. Jake's pretty amazing. The things he did with explosives… The man's an artist. You should read it."

"Yeah," Wes said. "Right. Read. Maybe in my next lifetime. So where exactly *is* Admiral Amazing?"

Bobby took over the command keyboard and started to type, and on one of the screens a rapid-fire sequence of empty corridors began to appear.

"He just had a private meeting with Christopher Vincent," Lucky reported. "He endured the slimeball's company for more than two hours just to get a chance to ask him about this bogus birthday celebration. And when he finally did get down to business, Vincent tells him he's got to pledge all he's got to the CRO if he wants to be privy to CRO secrets. The admiral says, great. I'm ready to do that. Right now. Let's go. But Vincent says no. Not till after the honeymoon, essentially ordering the admiral to go back to his quarters and get busy with his new wife for the next three days."

"Perfect," Wes said, scoffing. "Zoe goes to all this trouble to get inside the compound, thinking it'll speed up the search, but what it really does is slow things down."

"Got him," Bobby said.

On screen, the admiral was heading down the corridor that led to his room. His pace slowed as he approached the door, and he paused for a moment outside, just staring at the knob.

"Oh, man," Lucky said. "I'd be knocking the door down, I'd be in such a hurry to get inside that room."

On the two screens that still showed two different angles inside the room, Zoe put down her book and looked toward the door.

It didn't open, and she slowly sat and then stood up, staring at it.

Outside the room, the admiral took a deep breath and finally reached for the doorknob.

Bobby keyed in the third of the bedroom cameras, and from the new angle, as the door opened, Lucky could see the man's face.

On screen, Zoe visibly relaxed. "I didn't realize it was you. I heard footsteps stop right outside the door and…"

The admiral turned to close and lock the door behind him. "Sorry I took so long. Chris can really keep a conversation going. I was a little afraid you might've gone out looking for me."

"Why would I do that?" she asked. "I knew where you were. Besides, you told me I had to stay here."

He turned to look at her, smiling slightly. "I guess I just—"

That was when he noticed what she was wearing.

"Boing!" Wes said. "Hel-lo, Mrs. Robinson. How *are* you this evening, dear?"

Lucky didn't know how he did it, but the admiral managed to keep his tongue securely in his mouth as he gazed at Zoe and her incredible nightgown.

The tension in the room was palpable, though. It carried through the airwaves all the miles across the valley, through the receiver, through the wires that led to the video monitors in the trailer.

Zoe spoke so softly, Lucky had to turn the volume up.

"I was just…reading. I was tired so I…got ready for bed a little while ago and…"

"Are you going to be…" The admiral cleared his throat. "Warm enough in that?"

"I don't have anything else."

"No flannel pajamas?"

Zoe laughed, a nervous burst that she tried to squelch. "It's pretty warm in here."

Well, that was the understatement of the year. Lucky could practically feel the heat rising from the screens.

Jake took his wallet and a set of keys from his pockets and put them on top of the long, low dresser. "You know if you're tired, and I'm not here, you don't have to wait up for me."

"The idea of waiting up for you isn't a particularly appealing one," Zoe said. "Is it going to happen frequently?"

"Well, you know, I hope not—" Jake moved toward her "—but if evening is the only time Christopher can schedule to meet with me—"

She moved out of his reach. "What's the deal with this place, Jake? When am I going to be able to leave this room?" She lifted her chin, made her voice louder, sharper. "What exactly do people do here for fun? Someone told me today that CRO women aren't allowed to go into Mel's. Don't get me wrong, it's not like I want my old job back, but I'd like a chance to go grab a beer if I want to. And if I'm not allowed to do that, when *am* I supposed to get a chance to kick back?"

"She's picking a fight," Bobby said. "Way to go, Zoe."

"And is it true what I've heard?" she added. "That in three days I'm supposed to join some sort of chain-gang work detail and *clean* all day long?"

The admiral gave her one of his let's-keep-this-in-perspective smiles. "I'm sure it's not *all* day lo—"

"While you do what? Stand around and be good-looking?"

Jake laughed aloud, and Zoe's expression got even more fierce.

"You think this is funny?" she said. "Then *you* go clean. I'll sit around with the guys."

"I'm sure I'll get to do my share of the cleaning. It's just they've found this place runs a little better if the women are organized in teams and—"

"So it *is* true," she said.

"It's just the nature of the commune, babe. Everybody's got to chip in."

"I'm sorry, I didn't quite hear what it is *you're* going to be doing? Sitting around burping all day with the rest of the men?"

Wes laughed out loud.

"And what about those three princesses and their ugly little babies?" Zoe continued. "*They* got served at dinner just like the men."

"Those are Christopher's wives and kids. You know, he's a little eccentric, he's got—"

"Three wives. I know. I saw their rooms. *They* don't have peeling paneling on *their* walls."

Jake reached for her again, pulling her into his arms. But she stood there stiffly, angrily. He kissed her shoulder, her neck, but she didn't move. She just stood there, straight as a rod. He tried to kiss her lips, but she moved her head and his mouth glanced off her ear.

"I'm really tired," she said tightly, pulling free from him. "I'm going to sleep."

"Oh," Lucky said, making a face. "The freeze-out. The temperature in the room just dropped to a frightening fifteen below."

As Jake watched, Zoe climbed into bed, turned on her side and clutched the blankets to her chin.

"Come on, Admiral," Wes said to the screen. "No self-respecting man would just stand there and watch his plans to get it on go up in smoke."

"Any self-respecting man caught in this situation would

definitely drop to his knees and beg,'' Lucky agreed.
"Honey, I'm so sorry. Of *course* I want to go to your crazy
parents' house on the one weekend I have off this year...."

Wes nodded. "Of *course* I want to sell my racing boat
and buy a washer and dryer."

"Of *course* I want to poke myself in the eye with this
sharp stick. I don't know *what* I was thinking...."

"Zoe." On screen, the admiral sat down on the other
side of the bed.

Zoe was absolutely silent.

"I'm sorry, babe. I thought you knew what this place
was all about."

Nothing.

"Come on, Admiral Amazing. Down on your knees.
Climb under the covers and get to work. Do *something* or
this glacier's gonna freeze you to death."

Jake just sighed. "We can talk about this more in the
morning." He stood up and tiredly went into the bathroom,
closing the door behind him.

"He's just giving up," Lucky said.

"That's the point. He doesn't want to touch her," Bobby
said.

"He's nuts. Why the hell doesn't he want to touch her?"

"He doesn't want to touch her because he *wants* to touch
her," Bobby explained.

Lucky looked at Wes. "They're pretending to be married. So instead of pretending to get friendly, they pretend
to have a fight, because *he* doesn't want to touch one of
the ten most beautiful women in the world. That make any
sense to you?"

"Nope." Wes shook his head. He looked at Bobby.
"But you understand this, don't you? I am seriously worried about you, Robert Taylor."

Zoe clung to the edge of the bed, listening to Jake
breathe in the darkness, wondering if he'd fallen asleep yet.

She heard him draw in a deep breath and let it out in a sigh, and she knew he was as wide awake as she was.

She had a plan that she hoped would get her inside of Christopher Vincent's private office. As soon as the restrictions on her were lifted, she would go to him—alone—and request a private meeting. She would tell him she didn't realize the nature of the hard work involved in being a regular CRO wife. She would imply that she was much more suited to other tasks.

And if Jake knew she was planning to do this, he would have an absolute cow. No, not a cow, a full-grown stegosaurus.

Not that any of this would get that far. She would never put herself into a situation where she'd actually have to sleep with the CRO leader. She'd never compromise her sense of self that way, despite the fact she'd done everything but told Jake she would.

She sighed. This afternoon, she'd all but promised Jake she'd back away from him, and keep backing away. And she'd come up with that idea to stage a fight when he'd been out talking to Chris. Fight, and then go into a major pout. It had kept them from touching, kept him even from having to kiss her good-night.

Kept them from pretending to make love.

She'd seen the flare of intense relief in Jake's eyes when he'd realized what she had been doing—and why. He wasn't the only one who had been relieved. She wasn't sure how much more close contact she could take.

"Zoe."

His voice was so quiet in the darkness, at first she thought she'd imagined it.

But then Jake touched her. Reaching across the grand canyon in the middle of the bed, he touched her, his fingers light against her arm.

Zoe's heart nearly stopped.

"I think we should stop fighting," he said.

Were his words purely for the microphones, or did he actually intend them to have double meaning?

"Come here," he whispered. "We'll both sleep much better if you let me hold you."

She turned to look at him. His face was dimly lit, his eyes colorless in the darkness.

"Come on," he said, pulling her toward him, meeting her in the middle.

His arms felt so good around her, tears stung her eyes. He wore no shirt, and his skin was so warm, his chest so solid. She could smell just a hint of his delicious cologne and the mint of his toothpaste.

She held on to him tightly, knowing she should push him away, knowing she'd virtually promised him she would.

She could feel his legs against her and—

Zoe looked at him. He was still wearing his jeans. Denim. The ultimate in protection.

He smiled that crooked smile she'd come to know so well. "This'll be nice," he breathed. "We both really need to sleep, and…"

And he'd not only remembered what she'd told him this afternoon on the roof, but he'd also read between the lines. He'd figured out one of the things that she'd wanted so badly was for him to hold her in his arms all night long.

Zoe kissed him. She couldn't help it.

He sighed as he met her lips in a kiss that was impossibly sweet. It was filled with desire, but coated in something else, something wonderfully warm, something so much stronger than mere passion.

"Good night," she whispered.

His voice was like velvet in the darkness. "Night, babe."

Zoe closed her eyes and, with her head tucked safely beneath his chin, she fell asleep listening to the steady beating of Jake Robinson's heart.

Chapter 13

"Do you ever think about Vietnam?"

Jake leaned his head against the concrete block wall, lifting his face to catch the weak rays of the afternoon sunshine. "Nope. Never."

"Are you lying?"

Zoe was sitting next to him. They were sitting on the deck that overlooked the waterfall again. Killing time.

They'd spent the morning wandering around the CRO fort, searching for closed-off areas and locked doors that they might've missed. But they'd had to stop, afraid of being too conspicuous.

They'd then spent about an hour collecting as much information as they could about the CRO work teams—finding out what Zoe would have to do to be assigned to the team that cleaned Christopher Vincent's private rooms, including his office.

From what Jake could gather, the first thing she had to do was to be a part of the CRO for at least five years.

That meant they had to find another way in, another way

to get the information they needed. And that way was going to be through Jake pledging his loyalty to the CRO and Christopher Vincent.

And that brought them here, to the roof of the factory, where they sat out of range of the cameras, their voices covered by the rush of the water. Killing time until their "honeymoon" officially ended.

Zoe had her hair pulled into a ponytail, and without any makeup on, she looked about eighteen years old. "You *are* lying," she said. "Aren't you?"

Jake opened his eyes and looked at her. "Yep."

"You probably never talk about Vietnam, right?" She had taken off her boots and socks and sat with her bare feet stretched out in front of her, legs crossed at the ankles. She had small, elegant feet—quite possibly the nicest feet he'd ever seen.

He went back to looking at the sky. It was much safer.

"A lot of the guys who were over there don't want to talk about it," he told her. "And people who weren't there, well… It's not something that's easy to explain. But you know what that's like. You probably never talk about the assignments you've been on."

"Most of my assignments have been top-secret."

"Mine, too. But I meant the ones that weren't."

Zoe sighed. "Yeah, you're right. Peter could be pretty flip and, well, sarcastic. He was so jaded and cynical, I just never told him anything that really mattered." She glanced at him. "The bad stuff *or* the good stuff."

"I never wanted Daisy to get upset," Jake said. "I *did* talk to her about some of the really bad voodoo that went down in Nam. We both needed me to talk about that, just to get past it, you know? But it would really upset her when I talked about the reasons I'd kept going back—the reasons I stayed in the Navy. She didn't understand why I needed it. She didn't understand what I got out of it."

"That sense that you're actually *doing* something, you're actually taking action, instead of just being a bystander."

Zoe nodded. "There's so much hand-wringing that goes on in the world while nobody does a damn thing. I joined the Agency because I wanted to do more than compile frightening statistics about chemical and biological weapons. I wanted to track the suckers down and destroy them."

"And then there's the rush, too," Jake said. "She *really* didn't understand the adrenaline rush."

"I'm not sure I understand it myself." Zoe sat up, putting her socks and boots on as the late afternoon got colder. She pulled her legs underneath her to sit tailor style. "It's weird, isn't it? I was once…somewhere I shouldn't have been, in a country that would not have welcomed me with open arms under any circumstances. I was checking out reports that a pharmaceutical factory was cooking up anthrax. I went into the factory covertly, found what I needed to prove those reports were accurate and came back out— but not quite as covertly, after I nearly knocked over a security guard." She laughed, her eyes shining as she remembered. "It was insane. I was being chased by about twenty soldiers across the rooftops of the city in this amazing thunderstorm. Wind, lightning, hail—it should have been terrifying, but it wasn't. It was so exhilarating. So amazing. I can't explain it. I couldn't explain it then, either."

"You don't have to," Jake said, sitting up, too. "I know exactly what you mean. It's like, you're not just alive, you're *beyond* alive. It's…"

"Incredible," she finished for him, laughing. "It seems crazy. You look at a situation and there are all these risks, and you think, I should be running away from this as fast and as far as I can. You think, This time this could kill me."

"But then you think, But I bet I know how to beat this…"

"Yeah." She smiled. "I know how to win."

"So you do," Jake said. "You win, against all the odds, and it's so damn great."

"It's beyond great," she said.

She was sitting there, completely lit up, her eyes sparkling as she smiled at him.

Jake knew he was grinning at her, but he couldn't stop. "You must've been one of those kids who tried to parachute off the roof with a bedsheet."

"I had four brothers," she told him. "I had to learn to fight just so they'd let me tag along. And I had to prove—almost daily—that I was tough enough and daring enough to get inside the hallowed walls of their clubhouse. So, yeah, I did my share of roof walking. It drove my father nuts." She laughed. "I think I still drive my father nuts."

Her father had been in Nam. He was one of Jake's peers. A man whose life he'd helped save. A man who would definitely disapprove of the kind of thoughts Jake had been regularly having about his daughter.

Jake had woken up this morning with Zoe in his arms, and for about four very long seconds, his brain had played one hell of a trick on him. The extremely erotic dream he'd had about making love to her just moments before was still shockingly vivid in his mind, and he'd temporarily confused fantasy with reality, confused that dream with real memories. For a few endless seconds, he'd believed he truly had kissed her last night, her body arching eagerly up to meet his as he'd driven himself deeply inside of her.

But then reality intervened and he'd remembered what had really happened. Nothing. Nothing had happened.

Yet the thought of actually making love to Zoe had taken his breath away.

Yesterday, he'd told her that their relationship was going nowhere. He'd started to tell her that he couldn't imagine making love to any woman besides Daisy. He'd started to tell her he didn't see himself with anyone else—he just couldn't picture it.

But he hadn't been able to finish his sentence, because it wasn't the truth. Not only could he imagine making love to Zoe, but he could see it in his mind's eye in shockingly intimate detail.

"What made you decide to join the Navy?" she asked, pulling him back here, to the roof, where they both were fully dressed.

Her jacket was open and she was wearing a long-sleeved T-shirt tucked neatly into equally snug-fitting blue jeans. She seemed comfortable in her clothes, though, comfortable in her body. And why shouldn't she?

For most of his life, Jake had had the kind of good looks that most people made a big fuss over. But when he gazed into a mirror, he'd only seen himself. No big deal.

In the same way, Zoe had lived with *herself* all *her* life. She'd seen herself naked, washed that body every day in the shower, brushed her hair while looking into those liquid brown eyes in the mirror.

Like him, she was probably well aware that her package was wrapped in ultra-high quality paper, but—also like him—she had plenty of other, more important things to think about.

She was looking at him, waiting for him to answer her question about the Navy. Why had he joined the SEALs?

"My father was a UDT man in the Second World War," he told her. "He was part of the underwater demolition teams, the precursors to the SEALs."

"Was he career Navy, too?"

Jake had to laugh at that. "No. He was about as non-regular Navy as anyone I've ever met. He was a diver before the war, spent most of his time doing salvage ops in the Gulf of Mexico, living on a boat down in Key West, pretty much being a beach bum. He was tapped to join the teams after the disaster at Tarawa, when the Navy really started developing underwater navigation. He served in the Pacific until V-J day, and then he hunted down my mother in New York. He'd met her when she was a nurse in Hawaii. He went all the way to Peekskill and grabbed her out of the arms of her extremely boring fiancé, literally hours before the wedding, and pretty much immediately got her pregnant with me.'' He laughed again. ''Frank, my father, was something of an underachiever, but when he finally decided to take action, he was extremely thorough.''

''So you grew up in Peekskill, New York?''

Jake looked at her. ''You planning to write up an article on me for *Navy Life* magazine?''

She laughed. Damn, she was pretty when she laughed. ''Am I being too nosy?''

''Do I get to grill *you* after you're done with me?''

She smiled into his eyes. ''You've read my Agency profile—probably the Top Secret-eyes-only version. So you know pretty much all there is to know about me.''

''And you're telling me you didn't manage to get hold of *my* profile from the Agency?'' he asked.

''Your Agency profile contains your full name, your date of birth and only a very brief sketch of your naval career, my mysterious friend. Most of what I know about you is from Scott Jennings's book. And he doesn't say anything at all about your childhood. I'm just…'' She shrugged expansively. ''Curious.''

She was curious. But was it a professional or personal curiosity? Jake wasn't sure which alarmed him more.

He was silent so long, Zoe began to backpedal. ''We don't have to talk about this,'' she said. ''We don't have to talk at all. I just… I wanted…''

''We lived in New York until I was about three,'' Jake told her quietly. ''I don't really remember it, but apparently we were poor but happy.''

''Jake, you really don't have to—''

''I had an extremely unconventional—but incredibly happy—childhood,'' he said. ''You want to hear about it or not?''

''Yes,'' she said. ''I want to hear about it. Please.''

''This is completely off the record,'' he said. ''We're talking as Jake and Zoe. Not Admiral Robinson and Secret Agent Lange. Is that understood?''

"As Jake and Zoe," she said. "As friends. That's understood."

Friends. They *were* friends. That was why he felt so warm inside whenever she smiled at him. That was why he felt good just sitting here, next to her. It was why he could hold her in his arms all night long and wake up having slept better than he had in months. Years, even.

"Good," he said, letting himself get lost for a moment in her eyes. Friends. Yeah, they were friends.

"Are you waiting for a drumroll before you start?" she asked, eyebrows lifting slightly.

"Do you have a problem with me taking my time?" he countered.

Zoe smiled sheepishly. "Sorry. It's hard to break the habit of always being in a hurry. I'm not the most patient person in the world." She took a deep breath, letting it slowly out. "Please," she said. "Whenever you're ready."

Jake laughed. "I love it when impatient people think they can fool everyone and pretend that they're in control. Meanwhile, they're wound tighter than a yo-yo and ready to go off in twenty different directions from tension."

"I'm more than willing to discuss the causes of my tension—and potential ways to reduce a little of my stress. But something tells me you might want to stick to a safer topic right now."

Jake cleared his throat. "Yeah," he said. "Okay. Let's see. Where was I? Peekskill. Right. I was about three, and Helen and Frank—my parents—both had jobs teaching at a private school, that is, until my great-uncle Arthur died."

Jake could think of three or four really powerfully excellent ways to relieve a little of his own stress, and he desperately tried to push them far, far from his mind. *Friends.*

"Artie had just a little less money than God, and he left it all to Frank. Frank being Frank, both he and Helen handed in their resignations on the spot. Helen being Helen, they stayed until the end of the school year. But in May, we all packed our things, put our furniture in storage and spent the next fifteen years traveling. We went *all* over the world—London, Paris, Africa, Australia, Hong Kong, Peru. If we found a city we liked, we stayed for a few weeks. But if it had a beach, we stayed much longer. We spent about two years in the Greek Islands. Another two in Southeast Asia, not too far from Vietnam. It wasn't always safe, the places we went, but it was *always* exciting. Frank taught me to dive and Helen homeschooled me. Instead of being poor and happy, we were rich and happy—not that you could tell we were loaded from looking at us.''

Frank had been easygoing, almost to a fault, and Helen had been intensely driven, determined to completely finish every last little project she started. Jake had inherited her drive but had learned to disguise it with his father's laid-back attitude. He'd learned that in a command position, his men trusted him implicitly because of this—because of his relaxed air, his ability to exude the fact that everything was—or would be—okay.

"So you joined the SEAL units because you wanted to keep traveling?'' Zoe asked.

"I joined for a lot of reasons. One of them was because I had friends in Vietnam. I spoke the language, I…felt like I could make a difference, maybe help end the conflict.'' He smiled. "And of course, there's that age-old reason kids join the SEAL units—I had a fascination with explosives. I liked to blow stuff up. You know, SEALs can make a bomb from just about anything. Let me loose in a kitchen, and I can make a powerful explosive from the junk I can find under the sink.'' He grinned. "And I can have fun while I'm doing it.''

Zoe laughed. "That's interesting,'' she said, "because in *my* line of work, I tend to try to *keep* things from blowing up.''

"Maybe that's why we work well as a team,'' Jake said. "It's that yin and yang thing.''

Yin and yang. Female and male. He shouldn't have said

that, shouldn't have made the comparison. He held his breath, hoping she wouldn't go there again. Her last remark about stress had been about all he could take.

"I'm not used to working in a team," Zoe told him, neatly ignoring his potentially sexually loaded comment. "I'm used to going in someplace, completely on my own, and getting the job done without having to ask permission or wait for orders."

"Well, for someone who's not used to it, you're doing a damn fine job working on my team."

She chewed thoughtfully on her lower lip. "Does this mean you forgive me for trying to force your hand the other night?"

The night he'd gone to Mel's and had been told she was out sick. The night he showed up at her trailer to find her bags already packed, Zoe ready to go to the CRO compound one way or another. With Jake. Or with Christopher Vincent. The thought still made his stomach hurt.

"Zoe, I—"

She held up one hand. "No, don't answer that. I know I was way out of line, and that's not something that can be fixed by only an apology."

Jake had to smile. "It would help at least a little if you actually *did* apologize."

"Oops." Zoe's answering smile faded as she gazed into his eyes. "I *am* sorry, Jake."

"But not sorry enough not to do it again if you had to."

Her eyes were completely subdued, level and sober as she looked at him. "Sitting out here like this, it's easy to forget why we're in the CRO fort. But if we don't find that Trip X soon..."

"I have an appointment with Christopher Vincent on Tuesday morning," Jake told her. "And if I can't convince him to appoint me as one of his lieutenants and let me in on the birthday party plans, I'll take a trip into town. On my way out of the gates, I'll give the rest of the team a signal. Cowboy and Lucky will go into Mel's while I'm there, and they'll 'recognize' me as former Admiral Robinson—wanted by FInCOM. I'll make it back to the compound, but within an hour, the place will be surrounded. We'll be in siege mode, but *I'll* be the catalyst, not the Trip X. The CRO still won't know the Finks know about the nerve gas—they'll think this is only about catching me. It'll buy us more time, because no one—and nothing—will leave the fort until the situation's resolved.''

Zoe nodded. ''And you don't think being surrounded by FInCOM agents might make Chris decide to try out the Trip X?''

''I'm willing to bet he won't. Of course that's something we'll have to monitor carefully from inside. And as the FInCOM target, I'd hope I'd be privy to any plans Christopher has to resolve the issue.'' Jake paused. ''Again, this is the backup plan. First we wait and I go in and try to talk to Christopher.''

''But not until Tuesday.'' Zoe sighed. ''I feel as if this waiting is all my fault.''

''It could be worse,'' Jake pointed out. ''There could be a four-week honeymoon period instead of four days.''

''I'm not very good at waiting,'' she admitted. ''Sometimes even four minutes seems way too long.''

''Back in Nam,'' he told her, ''my team once got pinned down by these VC builders who came in and— It was the weirdest thing, Zoe. We were out in the middle of nowhere, and they started digging pits and building wooden flooring for tents literally feet from where we were hiding in the brush. We were pinned there until nightfall, and then, instead of getting the hell out of there and going back to civilization, we hung out for nearly four days. It drove the guys mad—we were just sitting there—but I had this hunch, and sure enough. The VC were building a POW camp. The tents were for their officers and guards. The pits were for the prisoners, mostly Americans. We just sat tight and watched as they brought in about seventy-five of our men.

"My SEALs started to hand signal me." Jake moved his hands, making the signals that enabled a SEAL team to communicate without speaking. "Now? Attack now? And I just kept signaling wait. *Wait*. We were way outnumbered. There were too many VC, *and* there was no way we could've taken them all out without killing some of the POWs in the crossfire. Besides, I had another hunch."

Zoe nodded. "God bless those hunches, huh?"

It was the funniest thing. He was telling this story—one of his stories about a triumph in a war that had far too few triumphs, and he knew that Zoe understood everything he was saying. He knew she understood everything he'd felt. He'd helped to kill dozens of enemy soldiers that day, but in doing so, he'd saved over seventy Americans who otherwise would never have come out of that jungle alive.

It was crazy. In a way, this twenty-nine-year-old child understood him completely. He looked into her eyes, and he knew that she knew his anguish *and* his exhilaration. Even though she'd never been in quite that same situation, she *knew*. They were so alike in so many ways. And because of that, Jake had an intimacy with Zoe that he'd never had before, not with any other woman.

Not even Daisy.

Especially not Daisy.

Daisy had loved him, Jake knew that without a doubt. And he'd loved her, too, with all his heart. But despite that, there were parts of himself he'd purposely kept hidden from her. There were parts of his life that he'd simply never shared.

"So we sat there," he told Zoe, "and we watched while they ordered the POWs into those pits and into the cages they'd made—these little, cramped god-awful…" He exhaled his revulsion. "One of the prisoners, a Brit, he spoke in Vietnamese about prisoners' rights—and they hung him from his feet and tortured him to death."

He closed his eyes, remembering, hating the powerless feeling of knowing there was nothing he could do. He knew now as well as he'd known then that if he'd let his men attack, dozens of the other prisoners would be mowed down by the VC's automatic weapons. With those kinds of odds, in a direct firefight, the SEALs wouldn't necessarily win. And if they didn't win, they'd be dead—or worse. They'd be locked in those cages, too, thrown in those pits.

Zoe took his hand, linking their fingers together, squeezing gently. "How many did you save?" she asked. "Seventy-four?"

He nodded, loving the sensation of their clasped hands far, *far* too much, hoping she'd pull her hand away, praying that she wouldn't.

"And still it's the one you couldn't save that you dream about, right?"

He forced a smile. "Funny you should know that."

"Tell me about the seventy-four," she said, still holding his hand.

Jake knew he should let go of her hand, maybe even move six inches or so away from her. Somehow they were now sitting close enough for their shoulders to touch, for their thighs to connect. How had that happened?

"How did you get them out?" she asked.

Jake drew in a deep breath. "Well, after they…did what they did to the Brit, they just left him hanging there. All the other prisoners went into the cages and pits without a fight, just completely beaten down both physically and psychologically." His voice shook. He couldn't help it, even now, all these years later. "God, Zoe, they were naked and starving—some of them skin and bones, some of them reduced to little more than animals and…"

He didn't know how it happened, but Zoe wasn't just holding his hand anymore. She was in his arms, holding him as tightly as he was holding her. Oh, dear God. He buried his face in her sweet-smelling hair, knowing for certain that if she kissed him, he'd be lost.

He had to keep talking, keep his mouth moving.

"After they were locked up, the camp commander sent

a half a dozen men out to stand guard.'' His voice was raspy, but he couldn't stop to clear his throat. As it was, his lips were brushing the side of her face. ''They'd built the camp in this sheltered area on the side of a mountain, and there was only one way in and out. So with the guards posted and the prisoners locked up tight—''

''Everyone else relaxed.'' She lifted her head to look into his eyes.

Her mouth was inches from his. Soft. Sweet. Paradise.

''We struck covertly after dark,'' he told her. ''And we dispatched the VC soldiers silently, tent by tent.''

She knew what that meant. Dispatched silently. She knew the price he'd paid for those seventy-four lives—he could see her complete awareness in her eyes.

''The six men standing guard went down just as easily. They never expected to be attacked from within their camp. We armed those POWs with the VC's weapons and walked down that mountain and out of that jungle.''

Zoe pulled away from him slightly to narrow her eyes at him. ''Why do I know it couldn't have been *that* easy?''

''We had a few firefights on the way back to our side of the line. But compared to some ops, it *was* very easy.''

''I would've loved to see your captain's face when you came walking in with seventy-four POWs and MIAs.''

He couldn't make himself let go of her. It felt too good holding her this way. She was so warm and soft against him.

''I didn't stick around to see anyone's face,'' Jake said. ''We just dropped 'em and went back out there.''

''Because you couldn't bear the fact that you'd only saved seventy-four instead of seventy-five?''

''We watched them cut him, Zoe. We watched the—'' He shook his head, swearing softly. He pulled back and would have let her go, but she wouldn't release him. And he was glad of that. ''Look, it wasn't something that I'm ever going to forget. But I swear, I played that scenario over and over and over in my mind—I still sometimes do.

And there was no feasible way we could have saved him. I made a choice to save the seventy-four.'' He laughed in disgust. "And in order to do that, I had to turn my back on that one very brave man.''

"But that's the way life works," Zoe told him. Her fingers combed through his hair at the nape of his neck, both soothing *and* nerve-jangling. "Every time you face someone, you turn your back on someone else. Your team saved my father's life, Jake. His platoon was nearly wiped out, and he and about a dozen other Marines were left for dead. You and your SEALs were the only ones brave enough to try to bring them out. You used explosives and with only seven men, you made the Vietcong believe we'd launched a counteroffensive. It provided enough of a diversion to get a chopper in there and get those men out."

"You know, I remember that," Jake said. "That was one of the long shots that actually paid off. Your dad was one of those men, huh?"

"Don't you realize, when you chose to go in after my father's platoon, you turned your back on dozens of other Marines who also needed rescuing that day?"

Jake didn't know what to say. "I guess I never thought of it that way."

"It's all a crapshoot," she told him seriously, gazing at him with those impossibly beautiful brown eyes. "Every decision, every choice. You go with your gut, and you've got to trust yourself. But after it's all said and done, you've got to celebrate life. Seventy-four men went home to their wives and mothers because of you. Seventy-four lives that you directly touched, and hundreds and *hundreds* that you indirectly touched. Mothers who didn't spend twenty years flying an MIA flag on their porch. Wives who didn't have to raise their children alone. Children who didn't have to grow up without a father—or children like me who would never even have been born."

"I know all that. I just wish…" He sighed. "It just never seemed to be enough. I always found myself wanting to save just one more man. And then just one more, and one more. But the truth is, I could've been bringing five hundred men out of that jungle each day, and it still wouldn't have been enough.''

"You told me you weren't that superhero from Scott Jennings's book, that you were just a man,'' Zoe said. "And if that's the case, you should try to keep your personal expectations down to the mere mortal level.'' She took a deep breath. "And as long as I'm criticizing, I've got to be honest and wonder why a man who's as alive as you would want to spend all his time keeping company with the dead.''

She wasn't just talking about Vietnam anymore. She was talking about Daisy.

"Grieve and let her go, Jake,'' she whispered.

How was it possible that he could be thinking about Daisy while gazing into Zoe's face and wanting desperately to kiss her?

Grieve and let her go....

"We should go back,'' Jake whispered. "It's getting dark. You must be cold.''

"I'm not cold,'' she told him, her gaze dropping to his mouth before she looked into his eyes. "Are you?''

He couldn't stand it anymore. "I really want to kiss you,'' he whispered. "It's killing me to sit here, holding you like this, and not kiss you.''

"Then kiss me,'' she said fiercely. "You're not the one who died, dammit!''

Jake didn't move. He didn't have to move, because she kissed him.

What he should do and what he wanted fought the shortest battle in the history of the world, and what he wanted won.

He kissed her almost roughly, completely on fire, sweeping his tongue possessively into her mouth, pulling her on top of him so that she was straddling his legs. The heat between her thighs pressed against him, her breasts soft against his chest as he lost himself in the hungry sweetness of her mouth.

He heard himself groan as he touched the smoothness of her back, as his hands slipped beneath the edge of her shirt.

He might've gone along with it. Might've? He knew damn well he would have. If Zoe had tugged at his clothes, if she'd reached for the buckle on his belt, he wouldn't've been able to fight both her and himself any longer. He would've made love to her, right there on the roof.

But she pulled back, pushing herself off his lap, nearly throwing herself a solid five feet away from him, breathing hard, and swearing softly under her breath. "I'm sorry." She dropped her head onto arms that were tightly hugging her folded knees, unable to look at him. Her voice was muffled. "I promised you I'd back away, not attack you."

"Hey, it's not like we both didn't—"

"No?" she said, looking at him, her eyes a gleaming flash in the rapidly falling darkness. "Then what are you doing sitting over there? Why didn't you follow me over here?" She answered her own question. "Because just letting it happen is a whole lot different from making it happen."

He couldn't deny it.

"You know I want you," she said softly. "But I want you to want me, too, Jake. I don't want to make love to you thinking that this is only happening because of some temporary insanity on your part, or some chink in the armor of your code of ethics. I don't want to have to feel guilty for seducing you, or overwhelming you, or tempting you, or anything. I want you to look me in the eye and tell me you want to make love to me. I want to meet you as an equal. I respect myself too much to accept anything less."

Zoe pulled herself to her feet, brushing off the seat of her pants. "So," she said. "Unless you want to come over here and take my clothes off, I think I'll head back inside."

Jake didn't move. "Zoe, I'm—"

"Sorry," she finished for him. "Don't be. I know I'm

asking for too much.'' She started for the stairs leading down off the roof. ''Give me a few seconds before you follow. It can't hurt to give Chris the impression that we're still fighting.''

A few seconds. Jake needed more than a few seconds to regain his equilibrium.

He stared at the sky and watched the first few stars of the evening begin to shine. The air had grown crisper colder, and his breath hung in front of him in a cloud.

Indisputable proof that, as Zoe had pointed out, he was *not* the one who'd died.

Chapter 14

Zoe hummed to herself as she got ready for bed. She hoped if she sounded calm and relaxed, she'd look calm and relaxed, as well—instead of completely, teeth-jarringly, heart-janglingly nervous.

Jake had watched her all through dinner. She'd sat at the table with the other women, and he'd sat next to Christopher Vincent. And every time she'd looked up, Jake was gazing at her.

She'd laid everything she was feeling out on the table this evening on the old recreation deck.

Well, nearly everything. She hadn't revealed this feeling of intense warmth she got every time the man smiled at her. She hadn't revealed the feeling of pulse-pounding, dizzying free fall she got from the desire she sometimes saw in his eyes.

She *had* told him how much she wanted him.

And Jake had turned her down. Again.

Yes, he was a man, and yes, he was attracted to her, but

he didn't want her. Not really. Not desperately. Not the way she wanted him.

Normally, she didn't require being hit over the head with a hammer to receive a rejection. She didn't know why with Jake she insisted upon embarrassing herself again and again.

She put on her nightgown, wishing desperately that she'd brought something a little less revealing, wishing she'd brought her bathrobe. She'd purposely left it in the trailer, thinking it didn't quite seem like something Zoe the waitress would own. It was a little too demure, a little too classy for the part she was playing right now.

Jake sat on the edge of the bed, untying his boots, the muscles in his powerful arms and shoulders flexing beneath the cotton of his T-shirt and standing out in sharp relief in the low-watt light.

He'd told her no in every possible way. He wasn't ready for a physical relationship. He'd made that clear. He'd told her he wanted to be friends. And up on the deck, they'd been doing really fine as far as friendship went—or at least they had been before she'd gotten all stupid and started holding his hand.

She knew *that* was a mistake right from the moment her fingers had touched his, but she'd tried to convince herself that friends sometimes held friends' hands. Same thing when she suddenly found herself holding him in her arms.

But then she'd lost it. And she'd kissed him. Again.

And then, stupider and stupider, she'd had the gall to feel hurt when he'd let her know—again—that he truly wasn't interested in their relationship going in that direction.

Oh, if she hadn't stopped them, he might've let his good intentions slip. He might've let himself be carried over the line, bulldozed by the intensity of her passion.

She watched Jake's reflection as he pulled his T-shirt over his head and unfastened his jeans. He glanced over, and Zoe quickly looked away, but not before he'd met her eyes in the mirror. Great. Now he'd caught her watching him undress.

But instead of turning away, he moved toward her, toward the mirror. "If this bothers you, I can wear a shirt to bed."

It took Zoe a few long seconds to realize that he was talking about the latticework of scars on his chest.

"No," she said. Was he nuts? Was that *really* why he thought she'd been staring at him? It would have been hysterically funny if her sense of humor hadn't been stretched so thin. "Really, Jake, that doesn't bother me at all."

He was looking critically at himself in the mirror. "Funny, isn't it, that I survived Vietnam virtually unscathed, only to have this happen when I was supposedly safe at home?"

"I look at those scars," Zoe said softly, "and I can't believe you survived. It was some kind of assassination attempt, right?"

The killers had come into his own home, past his security guards. They'd gained entry by pretending to be part of a team of Navy SEALs sent to protect the admiral from death threats he'd been receiving. After he'd been shot, the Navy had taken him to a hospital safe house and had publicly released news of his death, both to protect Jake and to catch the man who'd sent those killers.

Zoe had been in Kuwait when she'd heard the news on CNN, and she'd sat on the balcony of her hotel for hours that night, just looking at the lights of the city, deeply mourning the loss of a man she'd never met.

Jake met her eyes in the mirror. "It happened two years ago, Christmas. It took me a long time to get back to speed, physically." He turned and tossed his shirt into the laundry pile in the corner of the room, then took his wallet and keys and change from his jeans pockets, lining them neatly up on the dresser as he spoke. "You know, in a way getting shot wasn't so bad. I mean, with a physical injury, recovery goes in stages. It's all laid out for you. The doctors have done it before, there's no real mystery to the process.

"First the bullets are removed, and then the doctor stitches you up. Then the wound is bandaged and drained, and you lie in a hospital bed, and you focus on surviving, one day at a time—one *hour* at a time if you have to. Then the bandages get changed, and the injury is cleaned, and you fight infection and sleep a lot so your body can heal. Then finally after you're out of the ICU, you stop merely surviving and start rebuilding your strength, still through bed rest. Then, even though it hurts like hell, you get mobile. You get out of bed and take first one step, and then two until you can make it over to the bathroom and back without falling down. Then there's physical therapy, more restrengthening.

"Sure, no two injuries are ever exactly alike," Jake continued, "and I had individual challenges each step of the way, but even getting around those challenges was pretty clear-cut. If I do A, then I'll improve. If I do B, I'll improve that much faster. If I do C, I'll hurt myself, so don't do C."

Zoe understood. He was talking about far more than his physical trauma. He was trying to explain himself, explain what he was feeling and why exactly he had turned her down again this afternoon.

"Emotional recovery isn't as easy." All his coins were in perfect little stacks on the dresser, and he knocked them over with a sweep of his fingers and went to sit on the bed.

He glanced at her, one hand on the back of his neck, as if it ached. "You're not dealing with muscles and bones. You're dealing with something far more fragile and far less identifiable. Something that doesn't have as clearly a defined list of steps to do, you know, to go about fixing the problem. See, like, if *you* do A, *you* might improve, but if *I* do A, I might end up in a worse place than where I started. Do you understand what I'm saying?"

Zoe nodded, holding his gaze. He was talking about losing Daisy, about his dealing with his loss. "I do understand, and Jake, really, you don't have to—"

"On the other hand," he said with a crooked smile, "since it's all trial and error in terms of what works and what doesn't, it seems crazy to just never try A or B or even C, out of fear it's going to hurt worse. Because what if it doesn't hurt? What if it helps?"

What was he telling her?

"I'm tired of being afraid, and I'm tired of feeling so damn alone." His voice shook slightly, and he stood up swiftly, using both hands to push his hair from his face as he laughed in disbelief. "Jeez, this is perfect. Can I make myself sound any *more* pathetic?"

Zoe took a step toward him but stopped herself. Dammit, she wasn't going to do this again—offer comfort and then get horribly embarrassed and hurt when her deep-burning desire for this man overpowered her self-control.

But this time, Jake reached for her.

And as he drew her into his arms, she felt herself melt. Oh, God, she was the pathetic one.

His hands were against her back, her shoulders, her neck, running through her hair, the sensation enough to make her cling to him mindlessly. Dear God, what would happen if he kissed her?

He did, so sweetly, so gently, she had to close her eyes against the rush of tears that came. She knew she shouldn't, but she couldn't help it—she opened herself to him, and he kissed her harder, possessing her mouth with absolutely no uncertainty, completely and unquestionably in command.

This was all for the cameras. Zoe knew that their conversation must have been cryptic and confusing to anyone listening in, but this embrace was completely obvious. To anyone watching, anyone who didn't know better, it would look as if Jake wanted her. And as if she wanted him.

They'd be half right.

It was all she could do to stay on her feet, and she wasn't

aware that he'd pulled her with him into the bathroom until he closed the door behind them.

He broke their kiss to lift her up as he stepped into the bathtub. Zoe was slightly off balance, and he held her with one arm as he yanked the curtain closed and turned on the water with a rush.

Jake still wore his jeans and she had on her black night-gown and they both were instantly soaked. The water was cold, it hadn't yet heated up, but maybe that was a good thing. God knows she was way too hot.

She tried to pull back from Jake but then stopped, extremely self-conscious about the fact that her silk gown was glued to her body, extremely aware that she was still touching him and he was still touching her.

But instead of letting her go, he pulled her close and kissed her again.

It was a kiss that meant business, a kiss loaded with passion and need and a wildly burning hunger.

It was a kiss no one but Zoe and Jake could possibly know about.

She looked at him in surprise, unable to believe what he was telling her.

"I want to make love to you, Zoe," he said softly, touching her hair, her face. "But there are four billion reasons we shouldn't. The cameras—"

Her heart was pounding. He *wanted*. She was in his arms, her body pressed against the very solid length of his, her hands against the taut, slick muscles in his arms, his shoulders. It was finally okay to touch him. He *wanted* her to touch him. "No one can see or hear us in here."

"Our age difference—"

"I don't have a problem with that."

He smiled slightly at her vehemence, his fingers still in her hair. "How about the fact that I'm your team leader—"

"Technically, I'm here as a consultant for your team. You're not my boss. Pat Sullivan is. Believe me, I've already checked the rules. This isn't fraternizing. I'm a civilian.''

He exhaled a short burst of laughter. ''Well, it's good to know the shore patrol isn't going to rush in to arrest us.''

''I can think of only one reason we shouldn't make love right this second,'' Zoe said, ''and that's that all my condoms are in the other room, in my purse.''

Jake took a small square of foil from his back pocket and tossed it into the soap dish that was attached to the tile wall. ''I've got that part covered,'' he told her. He smiled crookedly, sweetly uncertain. ''Or at least I will, if this is still what you want.''

''It's what I want. Oh, God, it's what I want.'' Zoe pushed his wet hair from his face, her heart in her throat, completely aware of what he'd just told her by having that condom ready and in his pocket. He'd planned this. He'd come to terms with all of his reservations and he'd consciously made a choice. This wasn't accidental. It wasn't about reacting to high emotions and high passion. He wasn't being bulldozed. He truly wanted this to happen.

Still she had to be sure. ''About those other three million, nine hundred and ninety-nine thousand reasons we shouldn't—''

''The hell with them. They don't hold up to the one very solid reason we should,'' Jake told her, kissing her hard but much too briefly on the mouth. His voice was husky, his eyes filled with heat. ''Dammit, *I* want to, and *you* want to, and life's too bloody short. We're both grown-ups and—''

He kissed her again. Longer this time. Pulling her even closer and covering her breast with his hand. Touching, gently kneading, exploring the tautness of her nipple, his thumb rasping against the thin wet silk that covered her. The sensation was nearly unbearable, and she moaned aloud.

Jake did, too. ''God,'' he gasped pulling free from their

kiss. ''I've wanted to touch you like this since you walked into that meeting in the Pentagon.''

Zoe had to smile. She had him beat. She'd clocked many, *many* fantasy miles with Jake Robinson—starting all the way back when she was a young teenager. He'd been her hero nearly half her life as she'd thrilled to stories of his bravery, his ability to command and his loyalty to those men who followed him.

But it was his soul, his very humanness—his confessed imperfections—that moved her in ways she'd never dreamed she could be moved.

Time seemed to slow as he looked at her, as he touched her, still gently, through the black silk of her gown. The fire in his eyes was incredible as he caught one finger in the slender strap and tugged it down her arm. The clinging triangle of fabric peeled away from her breast infinitesimally slowly, and Zoe felt her desire-tautened nipples tighten under the heat of his gaze.

Jake sighed his approval, smiling into her eyes before he lowered his head and kissed her breast. His lips and tongue were so soft against her, she felt herself sway.

The shower was drumming down on them both, steam swirling around them as Zoe helped Jake peel off her gown. He was no longer taking his time, and as he looked at her, standing naked before him, she felt nearly burned by the desire in his eyes. And then his hands were everywhere, his mouth—hungry now—everywhere else.

Dizzy with need, she reached for the waistband of his jeans, and he helped her, pushing down the zipper, tugging at his pants.

But the wet denim was plastered to him, and it stuck to his skin. Jake slipped on the slick surface of the tub and caught himself, laughing as he desperately tried to rid himself of his jeans. Zoe tried to help, but she suspected she was making the entire process even more difficult.

She was giddy with laughter, too, as they wrestled with this final barrier that lay between them. The irony was incredible. Jake had finally given in, yet he couldn't have made it more difficult for them to make love if he'd tried.

He sat on the edge of the tub and, with Zoe pulling and Jake pushing, they peeled his jeans off, one leg at a time.

Zoe pushed her wet hair from her face as she knelt on one knee in the tub, laughing at him. She was even more beautiful than Jake had imagined, and God knows he'd spent quite a bit of time imagining.

He wanted nothing more than to look at her, and as he did just that, her laughter faded, leaving behind only heat. The desire in Zoe's eyes was incredible, and Jake knew that he was looking right back at her in exactly the same way.

She moved toward him, slowly, still on her hands and knees.

His mouth was dry. He was sitting there, soaking wet, water drumming down upon him, yet his mouth had gone bone dry.

She reached for him, and he lunged for her, pulling her with him, tightly against him as he stood up.

This was the right thing. Despite all his reservations, holding her like this, being with her like this felt so good, so *right*. His fears fell away, too. Silly fears like, that after three years, he might've forgotten how to do this, that after three years, he'd embarrass himself completely. More intensely complicated fears, like he wouldn't be able to go through with this, wouldn't be able to keep from thinking about—

But he could only think about Zoe. Zoe, who smiled into his eyes and made him feel hope again. Zoe, who held his hand and understood why he'd given his entire life to the Navy, to the SEALs, because she'd been, perhaps not precisely there, but to very similar places.

Zoe, naked in his arms, soft and wet and smooth. It was beyond heaven. He ran his hands across her body, unable to get enough of touching her, her skin like silk beneath his fingers. He groaned aloud as he cupped her rear end, pulling her closer to him, feeling her so soft against his hardness, dying—just a little—as she reached between them and closed her fingers around him.

He kissed her, and she gasped into his mouth as he touched her just as intimately. She was so warm, so ready, and she opened herself to him, sliding her leg up and around his.

Jake reached for the condom in the soap dish, and his hand closed around Zoe's fingers.

He had to laugh. Zoe was many things, but reserved wasn't one of them. Beads of water sparkled on her eyelashes as she smiled at him and gave him the wrapped condom.

She slid down his body, kissing her way down his chest and his stomach and… Jake nearly crushed the little package in his hand.

God, he wanted a bed. He wanted to take Zoe into the other room and love her all night long. He wanted to take his time. He wanted her to lie back for him just to look at, her beautiful hair spread out on the pillows. He wanted to spend a solid hour just kissing her breasts. He wanted to explore every inch of her body with his mouth and the very tips of his fingers. And he wanted her to look into his eyes as he filled her completely.

He laughed aloud. The things she was doing to him were taking him dangerously close to the edge.

But this wasn't really what he wanted. He pulled her up, into his arms, and kissed her hard as he fumbled with the foil wrapper. He stepped slightly out of the stream of the shower and covered himself.

Zoe slipped behind him, and he could feel her breasts against his back, her stomach against his rear end as she rubbed herself against him. She wrapped her arms around him, her hands cool against the slickness of his chest and stomach. And lower.

"Am I helping?" she asked.

Jake laughed. "Oh, yeah."

"You know, you are," Zoe breathed into his ear, "without a doubt, the sexiest man I've ever met."

Jake turned toward her, that half-embarrassed, half-sheepish look in his gorgeous blue eyes, and she had to laugh. "You honestly don't think of yourself that way, do you?" she asked him.

"What way?" He pulled her hips against him as he lowered his head to touch the tip of her breast lightly with his tongue.

Zoe closed her eyes, pushing herself against him, further into his mouth. He drew her in, harder, and then even harder, and she moaned her approval.

"As the complete hottie that you are," she told him when she finally could speak.

He lifted his head and laughed at her. "Wow, and all this time, I thought I was an admiral in the U.S. Navy."

"Admiral Hottie." Zoe laughed at the look he gave her.

His hands had taken up where his mouth left off. There was no doubt about it. Zoe knew he liked *her* body, too. She sighed as he caught her nipple between his thumb and fingers.

"I'm not even sure what that means," he said. "Hottie." He laughed. "Jeez."

"Check yourself out in the mirror sometime."

His eyes half closed as she pressed herself against him, as she started to move against him in a slow rhythm, and his hand tightened on her breast. "Is that all I am to you? A *hottie?*" His voice was still light, playful, but Zoe looked into his eyes and answered him honestly.

"The fact that you're a hottie is just a bonus," she told him, touching him, unable to keep herself from touching him. "I want you inside me, Jake, because I think that when I get you there, I'll have a little taste of everything really good and right that I've been missing all my life." She forced a smile. "Whoa. That was too intense, huh? I'm—"

"No," he said. "Don't apologize for being honest. I love

the way you look, too, but we're also friends. *Good* friends. And that's what's making this so damn good already. Even though I'm still not inside you.'' He lowered his voice. ''I'm dying to be inside you.''

Zoe couldn't breathe, couldn't speak. She couldn't do more than let herself be kissed.

Jake's kiss was proprietary. It was completely possessive, controlling and commanding, but for the first time in her life, Zoe truly didn't mind.

He lifted her up, breaking their kiss so he could look into her face, into her eyes, as he slowly, *slowly*—screamingly slowly—entered her. He pushed her against the slick, wet tile wall, but there was nothing to hold on to, nothing to do but let him keep control.

With her legs around his waist and her back against the slippery wall, her mobility was limited. But with Jake still holding her gaze, with all the pleasure he was feeling clearly written on his beautiful face, it was an incredible turn-on.

And for the first time since Zoe could remember, she placed the complete control of her immediate future into another person's hands.

Into Jake's very capable hands.

He pushed himself a little bit further inside of her, smiling slightly as she moaned just a little too loudly.

''Sh,'' he breathed, still holding her gaze as he took his sweet time.

His next thrust was just as slow but twice as deep, and Zoe caught her lower lip between her teeth to keep from crying out again.

Jake's smile widened. ''That looks like something I should be doing.'' He leaned forward and gently tugged on her lip with his teeth. She moaned again—she couldn't help it.

He laughed as he kissed her, filling her with his spirit as well as his body. The pleasure was so intense, Zoe couldn't do more than whisper his name.

With the shower raining down on her sensitized skin, with his mouth doing things to her breasts that she'd never imagined possible, with the cold tile against her back and Jake, hot and heavy, moving so infuriatingly, wonderfully slowly inside of her...

It was beyond perfect.

She breathed his name again, and even though she didn't say it in so many words, he somehow knew she was close to the edge.

"Come on, Zoe," he murmured, his lips on her ear, on her face, on her throat, her breasts. "You're gonna take me with you. I want to go right with you...."

Zoe kissed him. As wave upon wave of pleasure exploded around her, she kissed Jake so she wouldn't cry out. He inhaled her in return, driving himself even harder, even more deeply inside of her. She felt him explode, felt him shake with his release, just as he'd promised.

And still Jake kissed her.

He kissed her and kissed her and kissed her, holding her there pinned against the shower wall, still buried deeply inside of her.

His mouth was so sweet, his lips so gentle, Zoe should have been in complete and unquestionable heaven. But she couldn't stop thinking. *Now what?* Jake had done it. He'd made love to another woman for the first time since his wife had died. What was he thinking? What was he feeling?

Was he kissing her because he was trying to avoid facing himself another few minutes longer? Was he overwhelmed with regret? Did he hate himself? Did he hate *her?*

But then, "I wish I could kiss you all night," he murmured, his breath warm against her ear. "I wish we could make love again, tonight, in a bed, no covers, lights on...."

Relief made her laugh. He sounded all right. That was a good sign, wasn't it? "As much as I'd like that, too, I think the fact that our entire SEAL team would be watching might be a little distracting."

Jake laughed, too, as he gently lowered her to the tub

floor, as he turned away and efficiently cleaned himself up. "We're almost out of hot water," he said. "Want a shot at it before it's completely gone?"

"Thanks."

What had once been an awkward switching of positions in the crowded tub was now an opportunity for full body contact. Jake kissed her, and as she quickly lathered herself with the soap, he helped. He helped her rinse, too, his hands skimming her body, his touch so deliciously possessive. Who would've ever thought that would turn her on so completely?

He held her close, her back against his front, his arms wrapped around her, his hands caressing her breasts.

"I can't seem to get enough of you," he said softly. "I think I might need two solid weeks of leave, a hotel with room service, a heavy-duty lock on the door, a king-size bed and you."

Zoe closed her eyes as he weighed her breasts in the palms of his hands, as he kissed her neck, as she felt his body start to grow harder, already, against her rear end.

But then he caught her hand. Her fingers were waterlogged, the tips starting to wrinkle. "Uh-oh, we've been in here too long."

The water was starting to run cold, and Zoe turned to look at Jake. "Are you ready to get out?"

"No." But he reached past her to turn off the water. And then he stepped back from her, reaching outside the shower curtain for a towel. He opened it as he handed it to her, wrapping it around her shoulders.

"Thanks."

He started to step out of the shower, to get a towel and dry himself off in the bathroom—he didn't care who saw him naked—but Zoe caught his arm.

"Really," she said quietly, looking into his eyes. "Thanks."

He laughed slightly, shaking his head as he looked away

from her, at his feet, before he leaned forward to kiss her. "Thank *you*."

He stepped out of the shower, and Zoe realized he hadn't quite managed to look her completely in the eye.

He'd had no problem holding her gaze while they were making love, but afterward... She realized that after, he'd done everything possible to keep from having to let her look deeply into his eyes.

It was all an act. The sweet words, all of it. He wasn't okay with any of this—he was just pretending to be so as not to hurt her feelings. He was kissing her so he wouldn't really have to face the truth.

Zoe shook herself. That was absurd. Jake was quite possibly the most honest man she'd ever met. Why would he start hiding the truth from her now?

Unless maybe he was hiding that truth from himself, as well.

But now that the water was off, there was no way she could confront him.

The shower curtain opened slightly, and Jake leaned in. He held something out to her—one of his T-shirts. "I figured you wouldn't want to put that nightgown back on."

It was impossibly sweet and completely considerate, but Jake definitely didn't hold her gaze. He quickly backed away, letting the shower curtain drop.

"Thanks," Zoe whispered.

Okay, so he *wasn't* completely happy about this. She'd expected that, hadn't she? She had absolutely no right to feel upset, no cause for this sudden ridiculous rush of tears that pressed against her eyelids and threatened to escape.

What did she expect? That Jake would make love to her once and fall instantly in love with her? That he'd forget all about his life with Daisy?

Zoe scrubbed her face with her towel, fiercely willing her tears away.

But as she slipped Jake's T-shirt over her head, as she

breathed in his familiar clean, warm scent, the tears returned.

And she knew with a clarity that was unquestionable that although Jake hadn't fallen head over heels for her, she was completely, indisputably, impossibly in love with him.

Chapter 15

Zoe's heart broke into a thousand pieces as she stood in the doorway that led to the recreation deck, watching Jake as he sat alone in the cold morning air.

His back was against the concrete wall, his knees up and his head down on his folded arms.

It was entirely possible that he was crying.

Zoe had woken up this morning alone in their bed. It had been barely oh-six-hundred, and Jake was already gone.

She'd washed quickly, shutting her mind to the memories of all that she and Jake had done in that very shower just hours earlier. But after she'd dressed, Jake still hadn't returned.

She didn't need to be a rocket scientist to know where he'd gone. And even though she wasn't supposed to walk the halls of the former Frosty Cakes factory alone, she slipped out of their room and headed for the recreation deck.

"So are you just going to stand there, or are you going

to come out here and talk to me?'' Jake lifted his head to look at her.

How had he known she was here? She hadn't made a single sound as she'd approached. And she was positive that when her heart had broken, it had broken silently.

She moved toward him slowly, warily, certain that she didn't want to see evidence of tears on his face. But his eyes were dry, and he managed to smile.

Zoe sat next to him, careful not to sit too close. ''Are you all right?''

This morning he could meet her gaze. His eyes looked tired. ''I expected to feel really bad.'' He didn't try to pretend her question applied to anything else. ''I thought I'd feel, you know, as if I'd cheated on Daisy.'' He shook his head. ''But I don't. I feel…''

He reached down and took her hand, lacing her fingers with his, squeezing her hand. Zoe just waited, praying he'd tell her how he felt. Praying he'd say the words she was dying to hear. It was ridiculous, really. In just a matter of seconds, she'd gone from brokenhearted to wildly hopeful. Holy Mike, if love could make a levelheaded person experience emotional shifts more often associated with mental illnesses, she wasn't sure she wanted to be in love.

Unfortunately, it wasn't something she could shut off.

She'd tried *that* this morning, too. It wasn't going to happen.

''I feel alive,'' Jake told her. ''For the first time in years, I…honestly feel alive. It's…'' He squinted at the overcast sky before glancing at her and smiling crookedly. ''It's actually a little scary.''

Alive. Alive was good.

Wasn't it?

''You're amazing, you know,'' Jake told her. He put his arm around her, pulling her close. ''Last night was… amazing.'' He kissed her, and Zoe's hope grew about a mile and a half high, like that magic bean stalk in that fairy tale. ''You're exactly what I needed.'' He kissed her

again, longer this time, his fingers lightly tracing her collarbone at the open neckline of her shirt. *"Exactly."*

Zoe closed her eyes, dizzy from everything she was feeling. Desire—always desire, whenever Jake was concerned.
He was, and would always be, the most desirable man in
the world to her. Need, hope, she felt that, too, and pleasure—such sweet pleasure from his kisses and his touch.

Love. Oh, God, as terrifying as it was, she wanted him
to love her, too. Just a little bit. She wouldn't need much
to be satisfied—maybe just a tenth of the amount he'd
given to Daisy....

He kissed her again, and she shifted closer to him, moving his hand so it covered her breast.

He sighed and laughed. "I guess it wasn't hard for you
to figure out what I like, huh?"

Zoe kissed him, pushing herself more fully into his hand.
"I'm glad I've got what you like."

"I like everything about you, Zoe," he said, pulling back
to look into her eyes. "Not just your body."

Like. Not love. Still, his words were sweet.

"We're in tune," he told her, "you and me. I can be
completely honest with you—about everything. You know
as well as I do how important this mission is. You know
exactly what the dangers and the risks are. I don't have to
hold things back to keep you from being upset." He
paused. "And I don't have to worry about hurting you
when this op is over and we go our separate ways."

Oh, God. Zoe closed her eyes as she leaned against him.
Now *she* was the one afraid to let him look into *her* eyes.

"Maybe that's why I'm so okay about this," he murmured, running his fingers through her hair. "I know you're
not looking for anything permanent. I know you don't want
anything more than sex—I mean, friendship, sure, but...
What we did last night was intensely powerful, but...it was
mostly physical. I mean..." He laughed. "You don't want
to marry me, right?"

He didn't let her answer. She wasn't sure she *could* have

answered. "But that's okay," he continued. "It's okay with me, and it's okay with you. And, see, that's what I think makes this work. I know that *you* know that I can't give you my heart."

Jake's heart.

In just a short amount of time, it had become the one thing in the world Zoe wanted more than anything. She wanted to walk out of the CRO compound in possession of the six missing canisters of Triple X, and Jake's heart.

Jake kissed her, and she sat there, with his arms around her, watching the first few flakes of snow drift from the overcast sky, praying he wouldn't see the truth when he looked into her eyes.

He was wrong.

Somehow she'd broken all of her rules. Somehow she'd let herself cross that line. She was crazy in love with him.

And she wanted his heart.

Desperately.

"He's not getting it done," Lucky said. "We're almost out of time."

Harvard was giving him that stone-cold look that implied not only was Lucky a kindergartener, but he was a *misbehaving* kindergartener. "What do you suggest we do, Lieutenant? Mutiny?"

"No." Lucky took a deep breath. "Look. I just think it's been long enough. Let's try to get at least a few more men inside." He swore. "What we *should* do is get the entire *team* inside."

"That's not going to happen," Harvard said. "Because even with my blond wig, my complexion is a little too far from fair."

"So let's get in whoever we *can* get in. Me and Cowboy. Wes. We can give him one of those skinhead haircuts—"

"Notice how he doesn't volunteer to shave his own head," Wes said.

Lucky was completely exasperated. "Dammit, what difference does it make?"

"If it didn't make a difference, you'd've volunteered to shave your own—"

"Fine, I'll shave my damn head! Let's just get the hell in there! I'm so damn tired of sitting here doing nothing!"

As soon as the words were out of his mouth, Lucky realized that the problem here wasn't necessarily with Admiral Robinson. The problem was *his.*

He swore again. And then he apologized. To all of them. Especially Wes Skelly and the senior chief. "I've got a little sister in San Diego. Ellen. She's still in college." He rubbed his forehead. God, his sinuses were killing him. "I keep thinking San Diego would be the perfect city for these clowns to test the Trip X, and it's making me crazy."

"I've got a little sister, too," Wes said.

"Yeah, I know that it's no excuse," Lucky said quietly. "We've all got family. I just… No offense, Crash, I know you're tight with the man, but admirals should stay behind desks."

"Even admirals who used to be SEALs who specialized in demolition?" Crash spoke so rarely that when he *did* open his mouth, the entire team paid attention. "Even admirals who became so proficient with C-4 explosives that they literally wrote the book we all trained from—as well as the book that might be just a little too advanced for a few of us here?"

"I didn't know that," Harvard admitted. "How come I didn't know that?"

"You wouldn't. As the leader of the Gray Group, Jake's worked hard to keep a low profile," Crash said. "That's why that book by Scooter Jennings irks him so much. I know some of you have read it."

"I have," Bobby said in his basso profundo. "It's good stuff."

Cowboy lifted the book out of his lap, flashing a sheepish grin. No wonder he'd been so quiet during all this. He was reading, and he was just a few pages from the end. "This reads better than fiction."

"I'm reading it after Junior," Harvard said.

"It's all true, you know," Crash said. "And it chronicles just one of Jake's tours in Vietnam. He's seen more action than all of us in this room combined."

Lucky couldn't keep his mouth shut. "But that was thirty years ago."

"He's been out from his desk and in the real world often enough since then," Crash told him. "You guys want to hear a story?"

"Oh, yeah," Wes said. "Uncle Crash, tell us kids a story."

"S squared, wiseass," Bobby intoned. "*I* want to hear."

Cowboy, even fewer pages from the end, put down his book.

Crash had their full attention. He smiled. "Jake was in Saudi Arabia during Desert Storm, and his team was assigned to take out this one Iraqi Scud missile launcher that kept evading us. The Iraqis would fire the Scud at our troops, then move that sucker to a new location. Jake's SEAL team was working off of satellite pictures and getting nowhere, so Jake—he wasn't an admiral yet, but he was close—he tells whatever commodore was in charge that he and his men were going to try to check things out a little closer to the source. What he *didn't* say was that a little closer turned out to be downtown Baghdad, deep inside enemy lines. When they got into the city, Jake and his team split up. They had the locations where the Scud launcher had been set and fired from over the past few weeks, so they searched those neighborhoods for a place where something that size might be hidden.

"Jake's team finds not one, but *two* Scud missile launchers, *and* they uncover the location of a chemical weapons storage facility. So there Jake is, in the middle of Baghdad, with more than enough explosives to take out a single Scud launcher but not quite enough to do all three targets. He knew he could try to stretch it thin, but that way he risked destroying nothing.''

"Damn, what did he do?" Harvard asked.

"I'd've blown the Scud launchers and given the location of the chemical site to intelligence," Wes said. "Have them take out the place through air strike."

"Except those chemical sites were moved constantly," Lucky pointed out. "Even just a few hours later, it might've already been gone."

"*And* this one was in the middle of a residential neighborhood," Crash told them. "Not the most PC site for an air raid." He smiled again. "Jake managed to take out all three targets with no civilian casualties."

"How?" Lucky asked. "Did he find a munitions dump? Get his hands on more C-4?"

"No," Crash said. "He took his time. And he thought it through. And when he was ready, and *only* when he was ready, he placed the explosives he had very strategically. It was risky, but the man's a wizard when it comes to blowing things up. He trusted himself, and he got the job done." He was looking directly at Lucky. "I think we should do the same—trust our team leader to get the job done."

Lucky nodded. "Thank you, Lieutenant."

Message received.

On Tuesday, Zoe was assigned to clean bathrooms. She gave Jake a comically dark look as she headed down the hallway with Edith, a pale ghost of a woman who'd been assigned as her cleaning partner.

Edith looked as if she'd be a breeze to evade. With luck, their pairing would be ongoing.

Of course, it didn't really matter who Zoe was paired with. She would manage to get away from anyone. She was that good.

She was more than good.

She was…

Jake took several steps backward to watch her. Her hips swayed a little as she walked away. Just enough to advertise that the body inside those androgynous jeans was pure female.

They'd taken another late shower last night. Dear, *dear* God. Sex with Zoe was indescribable. It was…

Sex. It was purely physical. Two people having a damn good time with their bodies.

Zoe was so direct, so honest. She didn't play games, didn't try to make him guess what she wanted. She liked having sex the way he did—with her eyes wide open and the lights brightly lit.

He loved watching her eyes as he drove himself into her. He loved the way she seemed to look directly into his soul, the way the connection between them seemed an almost mystical thing. He loved the hunger of her kisses, the sheer intensity of her release. He loved the way she curled against him at night, touching as much of him as possible, as if despite all that they'd done, she still couldn't get enough of him. He loved the way, with just one look and smile this morning, she'd let him know she was anticipating making love to him again tonight.

He loved the way just watching her walk down the hall made him aware of the blood rushing through his veins, aware of his heart's steady rhythm.

Oh, yes, he was feeling very much alive.

Zoe turned to glance back at him, and he didn't look away. He let her know he was watching her. He let her see exactly what he was thinking.

She laughed, and an incredible surge of warmth seemed to detonate within him, radiating out, filling him with happiness.

She waved before she disappeared around the corner, and Jake stood there for several moments longer, struck by the realization that he was going to miss her today. For four days, they'd been together constantly. And as much as the waiting had frustrated him, he'd loved sitting with Zoe and talking for hours and hours and hours.

He'd loved learning about her, loved discovering the intricate ways her mind worked, loved her thoughtfulness and her quick sense of humor.

She'd filled more than the void in his life caused by his lack of a sexual partner. *Far* more.

And that realization shook him.

He'd been so certain of his feelings yesterday, as he'd sat by the waterfall in the early morning light. He'd been convinced that his relationship with Zoe felt so right because it didn't go beyond the physical. And yet his missing her today wasn't just about sex.

And then there was that annoying question he hadn't quite found a way to ask her. "So, babe. When you go undercover, playing husband and wife like this, does, uh, this sort of thing—you know, this intense physical attraction and mind-blowingly great sex—happen all the time?"

He shouldn't care about that, about who she'd been with in the past and why she'd been with them. He shouldn't care about the casualness that she assigned to sexual relationships. Why should he care about anything beyond these immediate moments and the fact that right now she wanted *him?*

He had absolutely no right to be jealous. Jealousy implied love, and…

Falling in love with Zoe Lange would be the mistake of his lifetime. What, did he honestly think she would ever agree to *marry* him? Yeah, right. Oh, she liked him, she desired him, and she probably wouldn't object to getting together and getting it on with him three or four or five times a year, whenever she rolled in to D.C. But marriage? Not a Twinkie's chance in a room full of eight-year-olds.

Get a grip, pal. Jake headed toward Christopher Vincent's office. *You're not looking to marry the woman. It's just the sex messing with your brain.*

Indescribable sex. With a woman whose smile and laughter made him feel truly happy for the first time in years.

Of course he was feeling happy—there was no big mystery to it. Sure, he liked her, sure she was smart and sharp and funny, but the bottom line was that in his mind, Zoe equaled sex. And sex equaled happy. After living like a monk for three very long years, sex definitely equaled very, *very* happy.

All of his warm, fuzzy feelings could be traced to the fact that Jake no longer had to imagine Zoe naked. He could pull her into the shower and see her naked anytime he wanted. See her and touch her and...

And that had nothing, *nothing* to do with love.

Love was what he'd had with Daisy. Slow and easy at times, hot and furious at others, ebbing and flowing like the tides. Love was years of understanding, the ability to communicate volumes with a single look or touch or smile. It was trust, it was faith, it was never to be doubted. It wasn't perfect, but it was the best thing he'd ever had.

There was no way a man could hope to find something so rare twice in one lifetime. And the thought of settling for something that didn't live up to what he'd once had...

No, he didn't love Zoe Lange.

But even if he did, he didn't have to worry. It would never work out.

Zoe would never expect anything long term, Mitch had told him. *Because she leaves, too. And she'll probably leave first.*

And Jake tried to convince himself that that thought made him feel so damned bad only because he would miss the indescribable sex.

"Your position on the high council of the CRO can be secured immediately," Christopher Vincent said, eating a sticky bun as he sat behind his fancy oak desk in his private office, "through your willingness to share your personal wealth."

The room wasn't large. It didn't have one single window. But it did have three doors, all tightly shut, leading off the wall behind Vincent's desk. Jake was willing to bet that behind one of those doors was the CRO surveillance control room—and possibly the missing Triple X.

Jake held out his hands in a shrug. "Chris, you know as well as I do that all my funds are frozen. I've got over four million dollars in liquid assets—that I can't touch."

Christopher stood up and opened the door on the far left. It was only a bathroom. One down, two to go.

He turned on the light and rinsed his hands, raising his voice to be heard over the running water. "Personal wealth isn't limited to finances." He came out, drying his hands on a towel.

"Information," Jake said. "After thirty-five years in the U.S. Navy, I'm in possession of a great deal of information that might be useful to you." He sat forward. "Look, Chris, I've heard people talk about this birthday celebration you're planning. Let me sit in on the meetings, see if there's anything I can contribute—"

"Letting you sit in," Christopher interrupted, "would prove our trust in you. What are you going to give me that proves you're worthy of that trust? Something that proves your acceptance of me as leader of the CRO." He smiled tightly. "Let's be honest, Jake. I know you're a very ambitious man. You wouldn't have gotten where you did in the Navy if you weren't. But if you've got any intentions of coming in here and taking over my show—"

"Whoa," Jake said. "Christopher. You *are* the CRO." He laughed. "Okay, I *am* ambitious, but my goal here is to sit at your right hand at the council table. Be your chief adviser. Your second in command. I'd never try to take you down or undermine your authority in any way." He lied smoothly. "Never."

Chris sat behind his desk. "Then prove it."

"I will," Jake said. "Like I said—through information. I can give you computer passwords. Back door entrances to highly sensitive files. Information on security procedures in government buildings—''

''You have more to give than information,'' Chris said, ''although I'll accept that as a sign of your loyalty—in part.''

Jake shook his head. ''Chris, I came to you empty-handed. As far as wealth goes, I don't have much. Even these clothes I'm wearing are yours and—''

''Zoe.''

Jake sat back in his chair. ''Excuse me?''

''You've got Zoe.'' Christopher smiled. ''I'd say that makes you a very wealthy man.''

Jake laughed, but then stopped when he realized that Christopher wasn't laughing, too. Holy God, the son of a bitch was serious.

Share his personal wealth. Share...*Zoe*. The CRO believed that a wife was a man's possession, but *God*...

''Why don't the two of you join me in my private dining room for dinner tonight?'' Christopher said, standing up. ''Seven o'clock. There's a high council meeting scheduled for noon on Friday, here in my inner chamber.'' He gestured to the door on the far right. ''It would be nice—for all of us—if you could join us.'' He moved to the door that led out of his office, opening it for Jake, dismissing him.

Jake rose to his feet despite the fact that this conversation wasn't over. He had more to say, to protest, to explain, but the phone on Christopher's desk rang. And the guard outside the door gestured for Jake to follow him.

Jake didn't move. ''Look, Chris—''

''I'll see you at dinner tonight.'' Christopher nodded to the guard, who stepped forward and took Jake's arm.

There was nothing he could do short of creating a scene. Christopher's door shut behind him as the guard ushered him into the corridor, closing that door behind him, as well.

And Jake stood in the hallway, certain of what had just been implied and sickened by it.

If Zoe slept with Christopher Vincent, Jake would be in.

If Zoe slept with Chris…

Jake laughed aloud, a sharp burst of disbelieving air, as he headed briskly down the hallway toward his room. No way! He wasn't going to let Zoe anywhere *near* Christopher the scumball Vincent. She was *his,* dammit, and he wasn't about to share.

Except she wasn't really his. Their marriage wasn't really a marriage. It wasn't legal. And even if it were, Zoe wasn't the kind of woman any man could ever completely possess.

He took the stairs down two at a time, moving faster, almost running.

But there was no way he could outrun the truth.

Jake had found a way to get the information they needed. If Zoe slept with Chris, he'd find out on noon, Friday, exactly what the CRO intended to do with the stolen Triple X. And he'd probably even locate the missing canisters.

If Zoe slept with Chris.

He stopped short, gripping the handrail tightly, sitting down right there in the stairwell between the second and third floor, directly in the blind spot between two surveillance cameras.

Oh, God. She would want to do it. Sex just wasn't that big a deal to Zoe. She'd made that more than clear to him many times over. She'd as much as told him she was willing to do anything for this mission. *Anything.*

Except it wasn't knowing that that made his stomach hurt so badly he had to sit down. It was the knowledge that it mattered so much to him. Here he'd been pretending that what he shared with Zoe was only sex.

But it wasn't.

The thought of her with Christopher Vincent—the thought of her with *anyone* else—made him completely crazy. He didn't want to share her, not her body, not her smile, not her laughter, not *any* of her. He wanted her for his own.

Because he was completely in love with her.

God, no, how could he be? He still loved Daisy.

None of this made any sense.

Maybe he just wouldn't tell Zoe. Maybe he wouldn't even give her the option.

Jake pushed himself to his feet.

And maybe the canisters of Triple X would be waiting for him back in their room. Maybe this mission would just take care of itself.

But even if it did, even if Christopher Vincent surrendered the missing nerve gas to them this afternoon, Jake was going to lose because—mission accomplished—Zoe would be off to Saudi Arabia. Or Amsterdam. Or Somalia. Only God would know when she would be back again. Or even *if* she would be back.

The irony was intense. For all those years he'd been a SEAL, *he* had been the one who'd always left.

And Jake had to laugh—it was either that or cry—because only now, by falling in love with Dr. Zoe Lange, did he fully understand just how much Daisy had loved him.

Chapter 16

"I need to see my wife."

Zoe looked up from what seemed like the four hundredth toilet bowl she'd cleaned in the span of three hours.

"I don't care if lunchtime is in thirty minutes." It *was* Jake's voice. "I need her right now. *Zoe!*"

"In here." She pushed herself to her feet as Jake steamrolled over poor pale Edith and came right into the ladies' room.

"Hey." His smile was unnaturally tight and the look in his eyes completely wild. Something was really wrong. "Nice rubber gloves. Yellow looks good on you, babe."

"You all right?" she asked quietly.

He shook his head infinitesimally. No. "Yeah, sure. I'm just breaking you out of here a little early, that's all." He looked behind him. "Do you have a problem with that, Edith?"

Zoe peeled off the gloves and quickly washed up in the sink.

"Well," Edith said. "Technically, we're not—"

"Sorry for any inconvenience," Jake said, grabbing Zoe's hand and pulling her with him into the hallway.

He had her jacket in his other hand and was already wearing his.

Her first thought was that something had gone very wrong and they were evacuating—getting out of there fast. But as Jake punched open the door to the stairwell, he went up instead of down toward the main floor.

Up. Toward the recreation deck.

She had to run to keep up with him, he was moving so fast.

But finally they were there. Jake burst into the open air as if he'd been holding his breath all that time.

She followed. "Jake, what's going—"

He kissed her. He dropped her jacket on the deck, dragged her into his arms and covered her mouth with his in a kiss of pure possession, pure need.

It was electrifying, mesmerizing—his mouth so demanding, his hands slightly rough and very proprietary. The sheer power of his desire sent her instantly aflame.

Was *this* why he'd come searching for her? Because he needed her? Because he finally realized just how very much he needed and—please God—even *loved* her?

He fumbled with the buttons on her shirt, growling in frustration, finally pulling, buttons flying everywhere. The front clasp of her bra gave just as easily, and the shockingly cold morning air hit her naked breasts. But Jake's hands were warm and his mouth was hot as he touched her, kissed her, the rasp of his chin delicious against her skin as he buried his face against her.

"Oh, Zoe," he breathed. "I need—"

He kissed her again, his fingers at the waistband of her jeans, unfastening the button, releasing the zipper.

"Yes," she said. She needed, too.

He stopped kissing her only long enough to shake his jacket off his arms, to throw it onto the deck with hers. Then he pulled her down with him onto the soft cushion

those jackets made. His muscular body was so wonderfully
solid, so deliciously heavy on top of her, cradled between
her legs. She could feel his hardness and she reached for
his belt buckle, wishing the layers of thick denim that kept
him from her would just instantly be gone.

He pulled back onto his knees, easily ridding her of her
jeans as she kicked off her sneakers. He lowered his pants,
covered himself and then, God, he drove himself hard inside of her.

She cried out, she couldn't help it—and he swallowed
her cry of pleasure with the fiercest of kisses as he filled
her again and again with hard, deep, demanding thrusts.

He didn't try to pretend that his need for her didn't completely control him. He didn't hold back, his kisses fever-
ish, his hands and body deliciously possessive.

And Zoe abandoned all pretense, too. She let herself love
him—wildly, furiously, passionately—body, heart and soul.
He was everything she'd ever wanted and everything she
hadn't known it was possible to want. The hero was just a
shadow compared to the humanness, compassion and honest reality of the man.

This incredible man who burned for her with the same
urgent fire that consumed her very soul.

She felt his body tighten and tense, felt him shake, heard
him rasp her name, and the sheer power of his release made
her explode. Pleasure pulsed through her, so intense, so
scorchingly wild. She opened her eyes, and the brilliant
blue of the sky seemed close enough to touch. Her senses
were almost painfully heightened as she smelled the subtle
scent of Jake's cologne and felt the warmth of his breath
against her neck, the slick heat of his body against hers,
the sharply cold air against her legs, the indescribable sensation of him, still hard inside of her as he thrust just one
more time, as the fierce waves of her release finally slowed,
finally subsided.

Zoe closed her eyes, holding tightly to him, afraid that
she might cry from the exquisite wonder of it all. But then

she had to laugh. She would never have believed that she could have had the absolute best sex of her entire life in the so-very-submissive missionary position.

"Jeez," Jake breathed without moving, his mouth against her neck. "What a gentleman. I didn't even wait for you."

"You didn't have to," she told him. "I was right there, with you." Her voice shook. "God, Jake…"

He was still breathing hard as he lifted his head to look at her, acknowledgment in his eyes. What they'd just shared had been as powerful and as intense for him, too.

"When you came looking for me like that, I thought we were in some kind of trouble." She made her voice even lighter. "I had no idea the trouble was physiological."

"Zoe, I…"

She held her breath. This was it. He was going to tell her that he loved her. Please, God, let him love her, too.…

But the expression in his eyes was completely unreadable. His ready smile was nowhere to be found. "I've found out how I can gain access to Vincent's high council."

Not the words she wanted to hear. Still, she managed to hide her disappointment. "But that's *great!*" She searched his eyes. Wasn't it? "How?"

"I need to prove my loyalty to the CRO and to Christopher Vincent," Jake said. "He's got this little share-the-wealth program. I think it's some kind of power trip for him. Whatever his followers have got, he wants a share of. Money. Information." He briefly closed his eyes. "Wives."

Wife sharing. Oh, God.

"Of course the bastard probably wouldn't be as interested in a guy's wife if she didn't happen to look like you, and…" Jake broke off, looking at her more closely, incredulousness in his eyes. "You know about this, don't you?"

She couldn't lie to him. "Chris mentioned something about it to me. I guess he sees himself as the equivalent of some kind of feudal lord and…'' She shook her head. ''I just didn't expect him to approach *you* about it.''

''What, did you expect him to approach *you* about it?'' Jake's eyes were nearly as cold as the freezing air that slapped her skin as he pulled himself away from her. ''And what the hell were you going to do when he did?'' He swore sharply. ''Don't tell me. I don't want to know.''

He had been mostly dressed, and it didn't take him long to pull himself together. Zoe had to search for her underpants, turn her jeans right side out, find her sneakers. Her shirt had no buttons, and the plastic clasp of her bra was broken. She shivered, clutching the front of her shirt together, uncertain what to say, how to explain.

Jake wrapped her jacket around her. ''Dammit, Zoe.'' His voice shook. ''You could've at least let me in on the plan.''

''It wasn't a plan,'' she told him. ''It was…just an option I thought I should keep open. Jake, the man was dogging me for weeks. I thought I could go in there and talk to him. Tell him I was thinking about accepting his offer. I would have told you before I did anything. I thought at least it would be a way into his private office.''

''Well, I've been in his office now,'' Jake said tightly. ''It's small, no windows, one desk, three chairs. Three doors on the wall behind Vincent's desk. The left is the bathroom. The right a room he referred to as his inner chambers. There was no sign of the missing canisters. I'm betting it's in that inner chamber.''

Which he would have access to—provided he share Zoe with the CRO leader.

Zoe's hand shook only slightly as she pushed her hair from her face. ''So what did he say to you about…'' She managed to make her voice sound remarkably calm, but she couldn't say the words aloud.

''It was all implied,'' Jake told her. ''He spoke of sharing my wealth. Mentioned you. Invited us both to his private dining room tonight at nineteen hundred—seven o'clock.''

"Both of us?"

"I asked one of his lieutenants." Jake's voice was raspy. "Apparently the way it's done is, he invites us both, and I send you alone, along with my regrets, pleading I'm feeling slightly under the weather." He laughed, a short bark of disbelief. "Believe it or not, it's considered an honor for Christopher Vincent to mess with your wife." He dropped his head into the palms of his hands. "Crazy-assed, twisted sons of bitches."

Zoe took a deep breath, filled with a sense of dread. "So. Did you tell him yes or did you tell him no? That we'd— *I'd* be there for dinner?"

He looked at her, his eyes nearly as blue as the sky overhead. "We can cancel."

"That's a yes," she said. "You told him *yes.*"

Jake shook his head. "I didn't say yes."

"But you didn't say no."

"I didn't answer him one way or the other."

"Silence generally implies an affirmative," she said tightly.

"Yeah," Jake said, the muscle flexing in the side of his jaw. "I know."

He put his head into his hands, unable to hold her gaze.

Zoe closed her eyes against the rush of tears. Did he actually think… Could he honestly expect… "Are you asking me to have sex with Christopher Vincent?" God, what he must think of her, if he could ask such a thing.

"No." Jake lifted his head. His eyes were rimmed with red, as if he, too, were fighting tears. "I'm not asking you, Zoe. I could never ask that of someone under my command. Except you're not really under my command, are you? And you haven't been completely honest with me about this other *option* you had standing ready. Maybe you've got a better plan in mind to get me into the inner council?"

She shook her head. "I don't," she whispered.

"I'm not going to ask you do this," Jake told her. "But I'm also not going to tell you *not* to do it. I'm giving you the choice." He cleared his throat. "I know this…this sort of thing doesn't particularly bother you, so…" He shrugged as he forced a smile. "It's your choice."

Zoe was dying. She wanted him to tell her not to do it. She wanted him to refuse to let her do it. She wanted him to hold her tightly and tell her that he was never going to let her go, that he honestly didn't believe her capable of such coldhearted self-exploitation.

"Do you…" She had to stop and clear her throat. Amazingly, her voice came out even and clear. "Do you want me to do it?" She had to know.

He looked her squarely in the eye. "This doesn't have anything to do with me."

The last of her hope died, and she turned to look out over the valley. "I see."

She'd done such a good job bluffing. She'd convinced him so completely that she was tough and strong—emotionally made of Teflon. He obviously thought she wouldn't think twice about prostituting herself this way in the name of their mission. He clearly didn't approve, and despite the fact that he'd made incredibly powerful, passionate love to her just moments ago, he didn't think that her buying their way onto the inner council through sex had anything to do with him.

Zoe felt like throwing up. Or bursting into tears.

Instead, she nodded. "What am I supposed to wear?"

Chapter 17

Lucky poured Bobby a cup of coffee and set it down near the video screens in the surveillance trailer.

"Thanks," Bobby said.

"Any change?"

"Zoe got assigned to a two-woman work detail cleaning bathrooms," Bobby stated. "Jake came in a little while ago and pulled her out. They headed toward the roof and have been out of contact for the past hour and a half. I've been cruising around, following Vincent's two top lieutenants—neither one of 'em win any prizes, except maybe Dullest Human Beings on Earth."

Lucky pointed to the screen that showed the CRO mess hall. "Isn't that Jake?"

"Jake." Bobby glanced at him. "Finish reading the book?"

Lucky smiled. "Yeah."

"Like him better now, huh?"

"I'm still working on the like part, considering he's spending all his time kissing my woman."

"You never had a chance with Zoe, and you know it."
Bobby keyed in some numbers, and the screen showed the
camera on the other side of the room, closer to Jake, who
was sitting alone at a table, lunch tray in front of him.
"Yep. It's definitely the admiral."

Lucky leaned closer. "Is it my imagination or… Does
he look okay to you?"

"Looks wound pretty tight. I wonder where Zoe is."
Bobby typed in a steady stream of numbers, and lightning-
quick pictures flashed on the other two screens. "Whoops,
there she was."

"Wait a minute," Lucky said. "You saw her? How
could you see *anything* in that?"

Bobby shrugged, calling back the image he'd spotted.
"I'm pretty good with visuals." On the center screen, Zoe
walked briskly down the hallway, heading toward the room
she shared with Jake. She smiled brightly as someone
passed her.

Bobby hit the commands to show the cameras inside the
room as Zoe went inside.

But no sooner was she inside the door than she leaned
against it, her smile vanishing. It was as if her legs suddenly
failed to support her, because she slid down, back against
the door, so that she was sitting on the floor.

She hugged her legs and bent her head and…

Zoe was crying.

She was shaking, sobbing as if her heart were breaking.

Bobby looked at Lucky and Lucky looked at Bobby.

On the other video screen, Jake toyed unenthusiastically
with his food. He tossed his fork onto the tray and rested
his forehead in the palm of his hand, a picture of total
despair.

But then Jake sat up. And with both hands on the table
in front of him, he made a gesture, a hand signal that the
SEALs used. It was brief but unmistakable.

Get ready.

"Did you see that?" Lucky asked, nearly jumping out of his seat. "Was that what I thought it was?"

"Yes, sir. That was definitely a message for us."

Jake had only made the signal once, but they had it down on tape.

Lucky reached for the phone. "Yeah, Skelly, it's O'Donlon. Is the senior chief there? Bob and I have something we want him and the rest of you guys to see," he said. "Oh, and on your way over? You might want to run."

Zoe pulled her baseball cap down over her eyes as she pushed the cleaning cart into Christopher Vincent's private quarters.

No one had noticed yet that she wasn't a part of the regular cleaning crew. Or if they had, they'd been downtrodden and beaten into submission too often to care.

Melissa, Amy, Ivy, Karen, Beth and Joan. Zoe had had to learn their names from the color of their hair. Their faces were too similar—they looked exhausted and as if they'd lost all hope.

Zoe moved like them, as if she, too, ached both physically and emotionally, as she took the supplies for cleaning the bathroom toward the door to Vincent's private office.

The door was ajar, and she went in without switching on the light.

It was exactly as Jake had described it. Big desk. No windows. Three doors. No sign of the canisters of Trip X anywhere.

The bathroom was on the left. Zoe tried the knob of the far right door as she went past. Locked. So was the center door. The bathroom was half open, and she turned on the light. It was tiny. One toilet and a sink. According to the Frosty Cakes factory layout she'd looked at with Bobby and Wes, there was enough unaccounted-for room in this part of the building for a good-size security headquarters, as well as a conference room-size inner chamber.

She didn't have her lock pick, but she had a paper clip

from Vincent's desk. In the light of the bathroom, she un-
bent the piece of metal and—

The office light went on. "Who are you? What are you
doing in here?"

"Cleaning the bathroom?" Zoe blinked owlishly as she
unobtrusively tried to slip the paper clip into the back
pocket of her jeans. She only got it in halfway before the
long-bearded man got too close.

He was Vincent's second lieutenant. "You're the new
girl. This couldn't possibly be your assignment."

Zoe made her bottom lip start to quiver. "I was told to
clean bathrooms. But I...I got lost, and I didn't know what
to do, so I followed a cleaning crew in here and—"

"Get out." Lieutenant Beard held open the door.
"Now."

Zoe grabbed her cleaning supplies and sprinted for the
door. On her way out, the second lieutenant hit her so hard
on the back of the head that her ears rang and she stumbled
to her knees. It was all she could do to keep herself from
spinning and giving the bastard a roundhouse kick to the
bearded jaw.

But she didn't. She kept her eyes lowered, her head
down. If she was going to make it out of here without
completely blowing her and Jake's cover, she wasn't going
to do it by advertising her black belt in karate.

Beth, the leader of the cleaning team, smacked her, too,
as Zoe pushed herself onto her feet. "What are you, stupid?
You just can't go wherever you want. You were given an
assignment."

Zoe let her eyes fill with tears. It was amazing that she
had any left after the way she'd cried just an hour ago. But
apparently, she still had plenty to spare. All she had to do
was think about Jake, and her tears came in force.

"I'm sorry," she murmured. "I lost Edith, my partner,
and I got scared and I saw you and..."

"Go back to the kitchen," Beth said sharply. "Edith will
probably be waiting for you there."

Zoe stared at her stupidly. This was it? No being dragged in front of Christopher Vincent? No questions about what she'd been doing in his private office?

"Go," Beth said.

Zoe turned and ran.

The computer's alarm sounded, piercingly loud, and Lucky turned to see Harvard leaning over Crash's shoulder, looking at the screen.

"What've we got?" H asked.

"A key word match," Crash told him grimly. "Three words came up. *Zoe. Spy.* And *birthday.*"

Harvard swore.

The computer was programmed to listen to and record every conversation that came in from the heavily wired CRO fort. Harvard had written a program to search for groups of key words that, when used in a single conversation, might signal trouble.

Cowboy joined them. "Play it back," he said.

"We've got video, too," Crash told them as he cued up the digital recording. Lucky rolled his chair closer. "Here we go. Looks like we're in Christopher Vincent's outer office. This can't be good."

A man on the tape spoke. "What's this?" It was Christopher Vincent's now too-familiar voice. On the video screen, the CRO leader straightened and came into camera range. He'd been bending over, picking something off the floor, but now his face was directly in front of the camera. Yeesh.

Lucky had one word for Christopher Vincent. Tweezers. It was his only real hope. Because, damn, that single eyebrow wasn't going to get him a *GQ* cover anytime in the near future.

"I don't know, sir." Another man stepped into the frame. It was Ian Hindcrest, Vincent's second lieutenant—another beauty pageant contestant from hell, what with the six-inch-long ZZ Top beard. He took whatever Vincent had been holding. "It looks like… Yes, it's a paper clip, sir."

"Who's been in here today?" One thing about having a unibrow, when Vincent glowered, he *glowered*.

Hindcrest took a step backward. "You had a series of morning appointments, but the cleaning crew was here after lunch, so I'd guess—"

"The cleaning crew." Vincent's glower became downright scary. "There was a memo on my desk from the crew leader, but she's a moron, I couldn't read her writing. Something about some incident today? Your name was on the page."

"Of course." Hindcrest brightened. "I was intending to type up my report about the event this evening. That rather dim new girl, the blonde, wandered in here by mistake."

"Zoe," Vincent said.

"That's the one."

"Wandered where exactly?"

"I found her in your office." Hindcrest gestured to the door behind him. "Preparing to clean the bathroom."

"In my office." Vincent nodded, his voice getting louder. "And it didn't occur to you that this new girl— who's still only a probationary member of the CRO—might have gone into my *private* office because she's a *spy?*" He was flat-out shouting, and Hindcrest's eyes had glazed over.

"Spy?" the bearded man said weakly.

Wes swore pungently, voicing what they all were thinking. "She's made. She's in trouble now."

"This isn't a paper clip." Vincent snatched the piece of metal from Hindcrest's hand. "It's a makeshift lock pick, dammit! I have no doubt she was trying to break into the inner chamber. Or maybe she'd already been in there, already seen what she needed to see! I knew it. There was something about her."

"The chemical—" Hindcrest cut himself off, aware he'd said too much. He cleared his throat. "The birthday surprise. Is it…?"

"Jackpot," Harvard murmured.

"It's still there," Vincent said, "but we've got to assume she's after it." He swore. "Robinson's probably in on this, too. The son of a bitch!"

"I'll call the guards to bring them in," Hindcrest said.

"We've got to warn them," Bobby rumbled.

"How?" Wes asked. "Send up signal flares?"

"No," Vincent said on the tape. "Not yet. He's got information I need. Let's let them think their cover's intact. In the meantime, let's get my birthday surprise started on its journey. Call Herzog and Jansen. Tell them they're leaving for New York a few days early."

"Yes, sir."

"That's all of the tape," Crash said grimly. "At least it's all that the computer flagged."

Harvard was already on the phone. "We need immediate stepped-up satellite surveillance. We need code-red intercept teams stopping anyone and anything that so much as pokes a nose outside that CRO gate, and we need…" He looked at Lucky and covered the mouthpiece of the telephone. "We need help. Get on the other secured line, Lieutenant. Call in the rest of Alpha Squad. We need 'em here *now*."

Jake couldn't watch as Zoe wove her beautiful golden hair into an intricate, elegant style. But he couldn't not watch, either. A French braid, he remembered it was called. Daisy's hair had been too curly and wild and thick to wear in that particular fashion. So this was a first for him, watching Zoe's long fingers complete the transformation from jeans-clad tomboy to elegant, graceful, coolly formal beauty.

It was another first for him, too.

Jake had never watched Daisy get dressed up to go have sex with another man.

The thought made him sick.

How can you do this? He had to clench his teeth to keep the words from escaping. *Don't go.*

She wore a black skirt that redefined the word *short* and a black tank top that hugged her body and framed the tops of her breasts as if they were some kind of work of art. Her long, shapely legs were clad in the sheerest of stockings, her black heels at least three inches high.

She leaned closer to the mirror to apply a final touch of lipstick and then stepped back to survey herself as she closed her makeup bag with a snap.

She met his gaze only briefly in the glass.

"Well," she said.

Jake couldn't speak.

"I guess it's time," she said.

He found his voice, but he had to clear his throat about four times before his words could be understood. "It's still a little early."

Don't go.

"I can't walk very fast in these shoes."

"Ah."

She turned to face him, squaring her shoulders and lifting her chin slightly. She finally met his eyes, but she somehow kept her *own* gaze cool, distant. "So. I guess I'm out of here."

Don't go.

He couldn't believe she was actually going to do this.

"I guess I'll see you later," she said, heading for the door.

Don't go.

She reached for the doorknob, opened the door. And she closed it behind her, leaving without even looking back.

Chapter 18

Zoe had to stop and sit down, drop her head between her legs to keep herself from fainting.

God, she was going to throw up.

Jake hadn't stopped her.

He'd just watched her get ready, watched her walk away.

This didn't have anything to do with him. He'd told her that himself.

She couldn't keep her breathing steady, couldn't stop herself from being buffeted by the raggedness of each breath she took in and out, couldn't stop her hands from shaking and her stomach from churning.

Ask not what your country can do for you. Ask what you can do for your country. Whoever would've guessed it could be *this?*

When Jake stood by the mirror, he could still smell Zoe's perfume. It was a subtle fragrance, mysterious and light. He'd watched her put it on—just two short spritzes into the air that she'd then walked through.

She usually didn't wear any scent at all, but she'd worn this on their wedding day. Their *mock* wedding day.

He closed his eyes against the memory of Zoe standing in her trailer, bags already packed, chin held high as she'd prepared to confront him, tough and strong and ready to do whatever she had to do to get inside the CRO gates.

Whatever she had to.

She'd looked at him that same way tonight. Right before she'd walked out the door.

She was cool, she was calm, she was completely in control. She was prepared to do whatever needed to be done, regardless of the sacrifice to herself. She was strong enough and tough enough.

But Jake wasn't, dammit. He *wasn't* strong enough. And even though love didn't seem to be part of Zoe's working vocabulary, the fact remained that he loved her.

Whether he liked it or not, whether he wanted to or not, he *loved* her.

And despite telling her otherwise, despite her matter-of-fact indifference to this entire situation, he was *not* going to allow her to do this.

He was the team leader, dammit. He had every right to tell her what she could and could not do.

And she *could not* do this.

Jake burst out of the door and headed down the hallway at a dead run.

Please, God, let him catch her....

Zoe stood up.

Holy Mike, she hated wearing heels. Sure, she'd taught herself to in them—for those times when she had to. But despite the hours of practice, she never quite felt as confident when she was wearing heels as when she had on her sneakers.

She smoothed her skirt and took a deep breath. She'd made up her mind and she knew beyond the shadow of a doubt exactly what it was she had to do.

Resolutely, she started walking carefully on those high heels, her heart firmly in her throat.

This wasn't going to be easy.

As a matter of fact, it was, quite possibly, going to be the hardest thing she'd ever done in her entire life.

Dick Edgers stopped him in the stairwell.

"Hey, Jake! I understand you're joining us in the inner council Friday. Congrats."

"Sorry, Dick, no time to talk." But when Jake moved right, to go around the man, Dick moved to his left, blocking him. And when Jake moved left, Dick moved right.

"Whoops," Dick said, laughing. "Sorry!" Jake all but lifted him up and moved him out of his way.

Jake cursed the delay, cursed the fact that he'd waited so long to go after Zoe, cursed the entire situation, cursed himself for letting the charade go this far.

And when he was done cursing, he started to pray. Please, God, let him catch her. Please, God...

He took the stairs three at a time and hit the door onto the floor that led to Vincent's quarters at a full run.

And nearly knocked Zoe onto her rear end.

He caught them both, holding her tightly, relief flooding through him. He hadn't been too late. Thank God. Thank *God*.

"What are you doing here?" she asked as he pulled back to look at her.

"You're going the wrong way," he said. Vincent's quarters were to the right, all the way down at the end of the hall, but she'd been heading toward the stairwell.

He realized that her eyes were filled with tears and she was shaking. Still, she lifted her chin as she met his gaze. "I'm drawing the line," she told him.

He realized instantly what she meant. He'd told her once before that he didn't trust her to draw a line marking what was and was not comfortable for her on this mission.

But she was telling him, right now, that she was not going to go through with this farce. *She* was telling *him*.

He kissed her—hard—right there in the hallway. He didn't care who could see them, he simply didn't give a damn anymore. She kissed him just as fiercely, clinging to him as if she were never going to let him go. But a kiss wasn't enough. He had far too much to say.

Jake pulled her with him into the stairwell and down the stairs. There was a men's room on the next floor.

She could move pretty fast in those heels when she wanted to, and he led her down the other hallway. Still holding her hand, he pushed open the men's room door, pulled her inside and locked the door behind them.

Releasing her hand, he turned the water on in all three sinks. As the roar from the faucets filled the room, he knew they could be seen but not heard. Zoe knew it, too.

She stood hugging herself as if she were cold.

"You were coming after me," she said.

"I was," he admitted. "I couldn't let you do this. It was crazy of me even to pretend that something this insane would be all right, because it's *not*." He swore. "I was ready to order you to back down, to forbid you from going further. And if that didn't work, hell, I was ready to get on my knees and beg you if I had to."

She was in his arms then, holding him as if he were her salvation. And she was crying. Brave, strong, tough Zoe had dissolved into tears.

"I didn't want to do it," she told him. "I wanted you to tell me not to. I kept hoping you'd stop me, but you just seemed to think it was something I'd do, something you expected of me. And when you said it had nothing to do with you…"

Her face crumpled, and she clung to him.

"I'm sorry," he murmured. "Jeez, Zo, I'm so sorry."

"I wasn't completely honest with you, Jake." She drew in a deep breath as she pulled back to look into his eyes, wiping her face with her hands. "I wanted to impress you, make you think I was like, I don't know, James Bond or something.''

He had to laugh at that.

''And you *believed* me, even when I tried to tell you it wasn't true. And then it got even worse because I...'' She lifted her chin a little higher. ''I fell in love with you.''

Jake stopped laughing.

''That's what I was coming back to tell you.'' Fresh tears brimmed in her eyes. ''I've never used sex to get information or...or anything. Not ever. I've never slept with anyone I didn't love at least a little, only with you I...I don't know what happened. I thought it would be safe to fall a little bit in love with you because I know you can't love me, but somehow a little bit became a little bit more and then more and... And it's good, it's a *good* thing because I didn't think I'd ever feel this way about anyone, but now I know, and it's wonderful and...and tragic, too, because now I also know what you lost when Daisy died, and I'm so, *so* sorry.'' Her tears again escaped.

Jake held her tightly, bemused, amazed, a lump in his throat. Zoe was crying for *him*. Her tears now were for his loss. She was, without a doubt, one of the most remarkable human beings he'd ever met.

''I know you still love her,'' she said softly, her face wet against his neck. ''I'm not asking you to stop loving her. And I know I can't replace her. But maybe, if you don't mind, we can keep seeing each other for...I don't know, a while, after this mission is over?''

Jake tried to clear the lump from his throat, but it wouldn't budge. ''A while,'' he repeated. ''About how long is a while?''

He could feel her breath warm against his throat. He could sense her weighing her responses, wondering the best way to answer his question.

''Honestly,'' he told her. ''Tell me honestly, babe. How long—honestly—would you want that while to last?''

''I guess,'' she said carefully, ''I was hoping for anything between, say, thirty years and forever. Leaning heavily toward forever.''

Forever. Jake closed his eyes as he held her even closer. ''Oh, Zoe, your forever's a whole lot longer than mine. My life's half over—yours is just starting and, jeez, I'm—''

She covered his mouth with her hand. ''It's okay,'' she said. ''You asked me to be honest, so I was. I know you're not ready for anything like this. And I know now's not the best time for another installment of the you're too old for me debate. Right now we've got a different problem to deal with.''

''Vincent's expecting you in his dining room,'' Jake agreed. ''You're already five minutes late.''

''What are we going to do?''

''I signaled the team this afternoon,'' Jake told her. ''They're on standby, waiting for my next command.''

''I keep coming back to our theory that Vincent doesn't truly know what he's got—that he doesn't know what the Trip X is capable of,'' Zoe said. She wiped the last of her tears from her face. ''We haven't found any kind of delivery method, no missiles lying around. No bombs—unless they're already locked up tight with the Triple X and—''

''I'm ready to gamble,'' Jake said. Hell, Zoe loved him. He was feeling pretty damn lucky tonight. ''Are you?''

She could read his mind. ''Gamble that the Trip X is somewhere in Vincent's private office behind one of those two locked doors?''

''It's either there or it's somewhere outside this facility,'' Jake said. ''I'm convinced of that.''

She nodded. ''I am, too.''

''Okay,'' Jake said, thinking fast. ''Here's our plan. We take control of Christopher's private quarters. You and me. Between the two of us, we can hold off the entire CRO until the SEALs arrive.''

Zoe looked skeptical. ''Without a weapon?''

''I'm sure Christopher has something in there we can liberate. And have you seen the door to his office? You would need a serious explosive to get that open after it's been locked. The trick is in getting it locked *behind* us instead of in front of us.'' He started to pace. "Look, here's what we do. You go to Christopher's dining room. Make a big deal over the fact that you've heard his chef is a four-star gourmet, that you've been really looking forward to this meal. Don't let him skip right to the dessert—which I've got to assume is you.''

"I won't.''

He stopped pacing to look searchingly into her eyes. "Are you really okay with this, because if not—''

"I'm okay with this.'' Zoe's smile was tremulous. "I'm *really* okay that you trust me to be able to handle Vincent.''

"While you're doing that,'' Jake told her, "I'm going to rig the main power supply and the backup generator to blow. I'll try to take out the main computer while I'm at it.''

"Are you telling me you can make a bomb from cleaning supplies—things that are just lying around—that will do *that* much damage?'' she asked.

"Well, I probably could, but I don't have to.'' Jake smiled. "I brought two bricks of C-4 plastique into the fort, inside your duffel bag.''

She stared at him. "Holy Mike! What if my bag had been searched?''

"It was,'' he said. "I hid the C-4 in with a couple slabs of modeling clay and some other art supplies. No one knew.''

"Including *me*.''

"I thought it would be better if you didn't know.''

"That's what *I* thought about Vincent's proposition.''

"No more secrets,'' Jake said. "Okay?''

Zoe smiled weakly. "Then I guess I better tell you that this afternoon I snuck into Vincent's quarters with a cleaning team.''

Jake closed his eyes. "Zoe. God.''

"It was all right. Ian Hindcrest found me in there, but I

played dumb, and all he did was send me back to the kitchen.''

''Why would you risk everything to—''

''Because I thought if I found the Trip X I wouldn't have to have sex with Christopher Vincent!''

There was absolutely nothing Jake could say in response to that. Nothing but, ''I'm sorry.''

''It was okay, Jake. I got shoved around a little, but Hindcrest bought my story.''

Shoved around a little. Coming from the queen of the understatement, that could mean anything. It helped a lot that she was standing in front of him, looking to be in one piece.

''What are the odds he didn't tell Vincent about the incident?'' he asked.

''I'll take care of that,'' Zoe promised. ''When I go in there, I'll confess to Chris I was so eager to have dinner with him, I snuck into his office this afternoon, hoping to get a chance to talk to him.'' She turned his wrist, looked at his watch. ''Meanwhile, I'm now *ten* minutes late.''

''I'm not sure I want you to go at all now.''

''Just tell me your plan,'' Zoe said. ''*Please*. You just rigged the power and computers with a bomb. Then what?''

''I'll set a delayed fuse and go up to Christopher's quarters. I'll make a stink, play the part of the jealous husband, make like I've reconsidered this whole sordid deal, push my way into the room. Once I'm there, the bomb will go off, power will go down and in the confusion, we'll overpower Vincent—''

''With what? The salad fork?''

''That could get messy. I was intending to just use my hands. Get a grip on him, threaten to snap his neck. Hopefully there'll be a guard or two in the room. Once they drop their guns, we'll be armed.''

Zoe nodded. She didn't say a word about the fact that Christopher Vincent had at least fifty pounds and several inches on Jake. She didn't doubt his ability to do precisely what he'd said. She didn't make a single comment about his age, about the fact that it had probably been years since he'd threatened to snap another man's neck. She had complete and total faith in him. He couldn't keep himself from kissing her.

"We'll lock ourselves into Vincent's private office," he continued, "and we'll sit tight until the rest of the team arrives. Your job is to not let the scum bag touch you and to be ready for me, you got it?"

"I do."

"Good," Jake said. "Now go. And make it look as if you're going even though I don't want you to. Let's get that jealous-husband thing happening starting now."

She pulled away from him, twisting free from his arms, her words contradicting her body language. "Be safe, Jake."

It wasn't hard for him to look as if he didn't want her to leave. "You, too, babe."

Zoe hesitated at the door, looking at him. "I love you."

How could three little words make him feel both so damn good *and* so damn bad? "Zoe—"

She was gone.

Lucky had been left behind to man communications.

He wasn't completely certain how it had happened. One minute he'd been ready to move out with the rest of the team and the next he was waving goodbye from the window of the trailer.

Somebody had to stay behind. Somebody had to watch those video screens, hoping for another communication from Admiral Jake Robinson. Somebody had to be ready to relay that information to the team.

Lucky had hoped that that somebody was going to be Bobby or Wes. Or Cowboy.

He had his headset and lip mike on, connecting himself to the rest of the team, now split into two groups, one led by Cowboy, the other led by Crash and Harvard. He could hear the second group's chatter over his phones as they circled the sky in a plane above the Frosty Cakes factory.

Jake and Zoe had split up, and Lucky was following them both, keeping them both on screen—no easy task for anyone besides Bobby.

Zoe was in the stairwell, looking as if she'd stepped out of his own personal sexual fantasy. He liked women dressed in what he thought of as contradictions. And Zoe's breathtakingly short skirt and low-cut top combined with the rather formal, opera-bound debutant-style of her hair really worked for him.

He forced his attention away from Zoe and onto Jake. The admiral left the men's room on the fourth floor and went into the same stairwell, heading down, though. But then he stopped, looking up, and Lucky realized Zoe had run into trouble.

She'd left the stairwell. He could hear raised voices from the other side of the door on the stairwell camera, and he quickly adjusted, keying in the numbers to pull in the picture from the security cam in the hallway.

It jumped onto the video screen. Ian Hindcrest and a half a dozen armed guards had surrounded Zoe.

Lucky swore, and over his headset, Harvard's voice responded. "What's happening, O'Donlon?"

"We've got six zealots with Uzis, aiming them at Zoe."

"I don't know what you're talking about." Zoe didn't look frightened, only amused.

Jake had moved silently up the stairs, and he stood, right outside the door, listening and looking out, the door open infinitesimally.

"So you deny you were in the leader's office today as a spy."

Zoe laughed. "Spy? Me? Do I look like a spy?"

"She's definitely made," Lucky reported. "We've got some serious trouble here, Senior Chief."

He knew exactly what Jake had to be thinking. Every

instinct the man had was screaming for him to go out there and start kicking butt, to rescue Zoe.

Except one unarmed man against six men with automatic weapons… There was no way in hell he could possibly succeed. Three seconds after he leaped out from behind the door, Zoe would still be in trouble, but he'd be too dead to help her. One of those grim-faced cleaning crews would be mopping what was left of him off the floor.

No, it was definitely neither the time nor place to attack.

"Take her to General Vincent's office," Hindcrest ordered the guards.

General. Talk about a sudden promotion. Of course, when you run your own little fantasy world behind a high electric fence and walk around with security guards with Uzis, you can call yourself Lord God Almighty if you want.

"Does Jake know about Zoe?" Harvard asked over his headphones.

"Yeah. He's on it, Senior. But there's only one of him and he's not armed."

As Zoe was led away, Jake turned and went down the stairs, moving fast.

Lucky followed him via camera down the stairwell, down the hall to his room. The admiral grabbed what looked to be—hot damn!—two solid bricks of C-4 explosive and a bunch of fuses and was back out in the hall, moving fast.

It wasn't until then, until Jake hit the stairwell going down again, that Lucky realized the man was sending him a steady stream of hand signals.

Now, Jake was signaling. *Now. Over and out.*

God, Lucky had missed it all. Do *what* now?

He quickly rewound the tape. "Got a message incoming from the admiral," he announced as he watched it. "He says he's taking out security, power and computers, *and* he'll blow a hole in the electric fence, as well." He snorted. "Well, sure, why not? One guy doing the job of ten men. Who does he think he is, one of the X-Men?"

"No, just Jake Robinson," Harvard responded.

"He says five minutes—oh, is that all? Or maybe even less till it blows. He says he needs support. He says come in as covertly as you can, as quickly as you can. He says he's ready to guess where the package—meaning the Trip X—is, but it's just a guess. Wear gas masks, be ready for anything, don't forget there are women and children here. He says come now. *Now.*"

On the other video screen, Zoe had arrived in Christopher Vincent's outer office.

She looked so small, so fragile compared to the CRO leader's bulk. She was looking at something Vincent held in his hand.

"That's a paper clip," she said. "You're all worked up over a *paper* clip?" She laughed. "Chris, I'm a *waitress*. I'm not a *spy*. That's crazy!"

Christopher hit her with his fist, like a club against the side of her head, and as Lucky watched, Zoe went down, hard.

"Move fast, team," he said, his heart in his throat. "Zoe's in serious trouble."

The room spun, and Zoe clung to the floor, trying desperately to regain her senses, fighting the waves of nausea and dizziness that made her want to retch.

That was her fault. Her fault. Crazy. She should have remembered that Crazy Christopher went ballistic when he was called crazy.

Her head pounded and her vision blurred as two of the guards dragged her to her feet. She fought to focus her eyes. Christopher stood in front of the open door to his private office. That door was heavy duty, as Jake had pointed out, with dead bolts that would withstand anything short of explosives. If she could get in there and lock that door behind her...

"Here in the CRO fort, like most countries, treason is a capital offense." Vincent was holding a gun on her.

Zoe blinked, but the gun was real, not a result of the problems she was having with her eyes.

It was a German-made Walther PPK twenty-two caliber. The kind of gun any inbred militia leader with Hitler aspirations would take pride in owning. "Is Jake Robinson also here to spy on us?" he asked her.

Zoe let herself start to cry. "Chris, I don't know *what* you're talking about—"

"Yes," he said. "He is, isn't he? He's here because of the anthrax."

Every now and then, there came a mission in which it was necessary to accept that her cover had been blown. And if Christopher Vincent thought that the poison he'd appropriated from the Arches test lab was merely anthrax...

It was definitely time to lay all of her truth cards out on the table.

Zoe stopped crying, stopped pretending. "Chris, you don't have anthrax. What you have is called Triple X. It's a nerve agent. A chemical weapon that's deadlier than even *you* can imagine."

"So you *are* a spy."

"I'm here to try to help you," Zoe told him. "If you give me the missing canisters of Triple X now, I'll make sure it's known that you cooperated fully—"

"Guilty," Christopher said. "I find Jake and Zoe Robinson guilty as charged. Their sentence is death, to be carried out immediately." He looked at his guards. "Find Robinson. *Now.*"

Zoe kept talking. "Chris, this is the dead last thing you want to do. If you kill me, if you harm *anyone,* if you even attempt to use the Triple X, the CRO will be crushed."

Christopher Vincent lifted his gun, and as Zoe stared into the deadly blackness of its barrel, she prayed. God, please don't let Jake come bursting in the door right now. Please, God, keep him far, *far* away from here.

"Oh, God," Lucky said. "Oh, God, he's going to kill her!"

There was nothing he could do. He could only watch on the video monitors, completely unable to stop the murder that was about to happen miles away in the CRO compound. It was the most awful, completely impotent moment of his entire life.

He was going to watch this woman he admired so much, his *friend,* die while he sat here, unable to lift a finger to save her.

Zoe could barely stand after that blow Vincent had given her to her head, but the guards moved back from her, out of their leader's range.

Zoe was still talking, telling Vincent about the Triple X, trying to make him understand that the United States Government would not rest until they recovered it.

Vincent smiled, and…

"No!" Lucky shouted. *"No!"*

The bastard fired the gun, the roar deafening over his headphones.

And the screens all went black.

"Sit-rep, O'Donlon." Harvard's voice came in. "What are you shouting about?"

Lucky worked frantically to get some sort of signal. But there was nothing. There was no signal to receive.

Jake, true to his word, had taken out the security system.

"Security's down," Lucky rasped. "But, God, H! Vincent shot Zoe. Point-blank. The bastard executed her." His voice shook, and he couldn't stop the tears that came to his eyes. "I've got it all on tape."

"Oh, God."

"Cowboy's team intercepted all six canisters of the Triple X about ten minutes ago." Zoe would've been so glad to hear that. Lucky pushed his lip mike away from his mouth so the senior chief wouldn't know he was sitting here crying like a baby. But, dammit, this operation wasn't over yet. He didn't have time to lose it this way. He took a deep breath and repositioned his mike. "As far as I know, Jake's still alive. But they're looking for him, Senior. Let's make sure we find him first."

"We will. But we're still about two minutes from contact." Harvard's voice was grim, cold.

"If you come face to face with Christopher Vincent," Lucky said, doing what he knew Harvard was doing—turning his grief into frozen hard anger "—hurt him bad for me."

Jake covered his head as his fourth and final bomb took out a big piece of the fence surrounding the CRO fort. It was hard to blow a fence like that, and he'd used a little too much of the C-4. Bits and pieces of what once had been trees and underbrush rained down on him.

He shouldered the Uzi he'd appropriated from a careless guard. A guard who'd have one hell of a headache when he finally woke up.

Jake moved silently through the darkness toward the factory—toward Zoe.

She was still in there. He prayed she was able to take advantage of the sudden explosions, of the power going out. But even if she wasn't, it didn't matter. Because he was going in after her.

Smoke alarms were wailing, and he could hear shouting, sounds of confusion from inside.

He hadn't used enough of the explosive to start a real fire, but the smoke and dust were thick. And the complete darkness had to be daunting to a group of people used to living under the constant scrutiny of bright spotlights.

Jake was nearly to the door of the building when he looked at the velvety blackness of the night sky.

It wasn't so much that he'd heard them or seen them. It was more that he'd sensed them.

And sure enough, it was his SEAL team, parachuting in, dropping out of the sky.

So much for blowing the hole in the fence to let them in.

The SEALs gathered their chutes as they landed, unhooking themselves, instantly armed, weapons locked and loaded.

Senior Chief Harvard Becker recognized Jake almost as quickly as Jake recognized Harvard.

"Sir. Are you all right?"

"I'm fine." Jake had smeared himself with dirt in an attempt to cover the reflective paleness of his face as he'd crossed to the fence in the brightly lit yard. "But Zoe's still in there. I could use some help getting her out—and finding that damned Trip X, as well."

"Sir, the Trip X was intercepted by Lieutenant Jones and his men. Christopher Vincent tried to send it to New York tonight." The door to the building opened with a crash, and they all stepped further into the shadows. Bobby and Wes had joined them, as well as Billy, and two other men Jake recognized but didn't know—Joe Catalanotto and Blue McCoy, the Captain and XO of SEAL Team Ten's Alpha Squad. Harvard apparently didn't call just anyone for backup. And despite their higher rank, they were standing back and letting Billy and Harvard run this show.

"Jake, I think it would be really smart if we got you out of here right now," Billy said.

"You better think again, kid, because I'm not leaving without Zoe."

Billy looked at Harvard, who shook his head very slightly. Bobby looked at his feet.

"You guys gonna help me help Zoe, or what?" Jake asked.

Silence. Complete, total silence.

Then Harvard put his hand on Jake's shoulder. And Jake realized Bobby Taylor was crying.

"Jake," Harvard said, his voice thick with emotion. "Zoe doesn't need our help anymore."

No. Jake knew what they were telling him, but he couldn't believe it. He looked at Billy and saw the awful truth echoed in the kid's eyes.

"She's dead," Billy said. "I'm sorry, Jake."

Chapter Nineteen

Zoe was dead.

Jake stood there. Somehow he managed to stand there, to keep his knees from crumbling, to keep himself from folding into a ball of pain and anguish. "No," he said.

"Lucky saw that prick Vincent kill her. He shot her right before the power went down." Wes sounded strangled.

Zoe was dead.

Pain screamed through Jake, growing louder, stronger with every beat of his heart, with every ragged breath that he took. And as it grew, it changed. It boiled and churned and hardened and blackened, and it numbed him. It deadened him, and all the joy and the life that Zoe had breathed back into him with her laughter and brightness over the past few weeks dried up and skittered away like leaves in the cold winter wind.

Zoe was dead.

"Please, Jake," Harvard said again. "We've got what we came for. The Triple X has been recovered. It's time to move you to safety, sir."

* * *

Zoe's arm was on fire.

She sat on the floor of Christopher Vincent's inner office in the dim emergency light, bleeding onto the carpet, listening to the sound of the CRO guards pounding on the steel-reinforced door.

She'd surprised Vincent by rushing toward him rather than away right before he'd discharged his weapon. She'd dived for his feet, and he'd tried to compensate, but his bullet had only skimmed her.

It was just enough to make her bleed like crazy and hurt like hell.

But at least she wasn't dead.

And the pain was a good thing. She could use it to keep her focus—to keep herself from blacking out from that blow to the head he'd given her.

She crawled toward Christopher's desk on her hands and knees, afraid if she stood up, she'd fall over.

She searched the desks, hoping for some kind of weapon—a handgun, a switchblade, anything.

She found a book of matches and… She had no pockets. Damn, not wearing her jeans was so inconvenient. She tucked it into her bra, hoping she wouldn't inadvertently light herself on fire.

The door to the fabled inner chamber was still tightly locked, and she searched for a paper clip. She unfolded it and set to work on the lock.

Jake looked at the Uzi in his hands. "Does somebody have an M16 for me, or am I going to have to use this piece of crap?"

The captain finally cleared his throat and spoke. "Begging your pardon, Admiral—"

He looked into the man's compassionate brown eyes. "No," he said. "No, Captain, I'm not ready to be taken to safety. I suggest if you have further support available, you talk to them via radio and tell them about the hole I just blew in the fence. Remind them that there are women and children here. I need eyes open and brains working. No autopilot. The same goes for the rest of you. Because we're going in there. Our goals are twofold, gentlemen. We're going to apprehend Christopher Vincent. And we're going to recover Zoe's body. She was a member of this team, and SEALs don't leave teammates behind. Even when they're KIA.''

Killed in action. Jake's voice shook. Even the numbness spreading through him couldn't keep him from hurting as he spoke the acronym he'd hated so passionately for so many years.

Zoe had loved him. A miracle had happened, and he'd been given a second chance to find happiness. She hadn't been Daisy, but no one was. No one could have replaced all that he'd had with Daisy. But in the exact same way, Daisy hadn't been Zoe. Zoe had touched parts of Jake's soul that Daisy would never have been able to reach even if their life together had lasted another thirty years.

There was no way really to compare, no contest as to which woman he had loved most, because although he had loved them both, he'd loved them differently.

And yet, when Zoe had offered him forever, he'd been too obsessed with doing the math. He was too old for her. When she turned fifty, he'd be seventy-four—if he even lived that long. It had seemed so absurd, and he couldn't understand why she would want that, why she would want him.

But he understood now. Because love didn't always make mathematical sense. And forever was completely relative. Zoe wasn't ever going to turn fifty now. Not ever. Her forever had been obscenely short.

And Jake had forsaken every opportunity in the far-too-briefness of their time together and hadn't even told her that he loved her.

He felt ancient as he looked into the still-young faces of

his SEAL team. "I loved her," he said, his words far too little, far too late. "Who's going to help me bring her out?"

Bobby stepped forward, pulling a twelve-gauge shotgun from a holster he wore on his back. "Since you're taking the point, Admiral, you might want to carry this."

Admiral. When Bobby said it like that, it wasn't a title, it wasn't a rank. It was his old nickname from Nam.

Harvard nodded, his dark brown eyes deadly. "We're right behind you, Admiral. Lead the way."

Zoe found it.

The Triple X.

Behind the locked door to Vincent's inner chamber, inside a cheaply made safe.

It was no longer stored in the testing lab's metal canisters. Instead, someone had put the powder in old coffee cans. Here at the CRO compound, they'd replaced the Folgers crystals with the dried ingredients of a deadly nerve gas.

In the office, the door strained against the battering it was receiving from Vincent and his guards.

Zoe closed and locked the door to the inner chamber, and using all her Girl Scout training, she set about building a campfire in a small metal trash can right on top of Christopher Vincent's conference table.

She could only destroy half of the chemicals. There was no sprinkler system in this part of the factory, but the possibility of someone bursting in and spraying the fire with water and creating a massive amount of potent Trip X was not worth the risk.

She used single sheets of paper as kindling and twisted chunks of computer reports in place of wood.

She took the matchbook from her bra and lit the fire, waiting for it to really start burning before she added the A component of the Triple X.

She knew that the chemical would burn clean. The

smoke would be nontoxic. But smoke didn't have to be toxic to kill.

This room had no windows and only the one door.

Already the smoke was chokingly thick.

She added the first coffee can of chemicals to the fire, then stayed low to the floor. She stayed as far away as she could from the flames, praying she'd have time to destroy all the chemicals before the smoke overcame her.

The fire alarm went off.

Jake and his team had just moved out of the stairwell and onto the fifth floor.

The noise was deafening—it came from one of those old-fashioned bells attached to the concrete block wall. It was good. It would mask their approach. No one would hear them coming.

There was one emergency light at the end of the hallway. It was old, with a bulb that sputtered and flickered, giving the impression that they were lit by leaping flames.

Welcome to hell.

Jake slowed as they moved closer to the door that led to Christopher Vincent's private suite of rooms. And when the door opened, he moved against the wall into the shadows. He didn't need to look behind him to know that Harvard and the rest of the team had disappeared, as well.

Christopher came striding out.

He was followed by his entourage of guards and lieutenants.

"Get the car, Reilly," he ordered. "Bring it to the front and—"

Jake stepped into the light, shotgun held high, finger heavy on the trigger. "I think you can probably leave the car in the garage for now, Reilly," he said, shouting over the noise of the alarm.

Christopher Vincent froze, but behind him, a half a dozen guards shouldered their weapons.

Jake didn't have to turn around to know that his SEALs

were standing behind him, their weapons already locked and loaded. He could see them in the eyes of Vincent and his men.

"What do you think, Chris?" Jake shouted over the alarm. "My guess is we could have it out right here. Maybe some of your guys will get away, but *you* sure as hell won't. Do you know what a twelve-gauge can do to a man at ten feet?" Jake turned his head slightly without ever letting his eyes leave Vincent. "Hey, Bob, what you got in here? Double ought buckshot?"

"Five rounds of it." Bobby's deep bass voice had no problem cutting through the racket.

"One round'll do," Jake told the CRO leader. "Think of it as the equivalent of me firing, oh, about six or seven regular bullets all at the same place at the same time. It'll put a big hole in you, Chris. And while I'm looking forward to doing that, you may not be, in which case it would be really smart of you to tell your men to drop their weapons. *Now.*"

Jake had played mind-game poker plenty in his career, but this was no bluff. He suspected Chris recognized the edge of insanity he saw in Jake's eyes.

"Do as they say," Christopher ordered his men.

Harvard took over, collecting their weapons, pushing the men onto the ground and searching them none too gently for anything they might be carrying concealed.

"Can someone shut that damn thing off?" Jake asked. His head was aching and his stomach hurt. Part of him wished Christopher Vincent hadn't given in. It didn't seem fair that he was still alive while Zoe…

He was going to have to go in there, into Vincent's quarters, and carry Zoe's lifeless body out of here.

Bobby raised his MP-4, and, firing a single burst, shot the alarm bell right off the wall. The silence seemed only to emphasize Zoe's absence.

"McCoy and I'll hold Bozo and his clowns here," Captain Joe Catalanotto of Alpha Squad volunteered. "We've got another team already inside the gate coming up to meet us, but it might be a good idea to use Vincent as a hostage, guaranteeing our safety out of here.''

"I've got a sit-rep if you want one, Admiral," Harvard said.

Jake didn't have a headset, but the other men did. "Any casualties?"

"None so far." Harvard corrected himself. "Besides Zoe." He cleared his throat. "The other teams have run into some opposition, but not a lot. A couple of men have locked themselves in one of the storage sheds. And we had a sniper on the roof with the lousiest aim in the Western Hemisphere. He's been taken care of.''

Jake looked at the captain. "These dirtwads are going to be charged with treason, conspiracy and murder. If they so much as look at you funny," he ordered, "shoot them."

"With pleasure."

Wes stepped forward. "Admiral, I want to bring to your attention the fact that there's a raftload of smoke coming from Vincent's quarters.''

Smoke.

It was rolling out the door, already thick against the high ceiling of the hallway.

Holding his shotgun at the ready, Jake pushed through the door into Christopher's outer office. The smoke was even thicker in there.

He braced himself as he made a quick visual sweep of the room, but there was no sign of Zoe, no broken body bleeding on the floor.

The door to Christopher's private office was hanging on its hinges. The smoke seemed to be coming from there. Covering his face with one arm, Jake again took the point.

Zoe wasn't in Christopher's private office, either.

The smoke was coming from behind the door to Christopher's inner chamber.

Hope hit Jake hard in the chest, taking his breath away.

Somehow Zoe had survived. Somehow she'd gotten in here, found the Triple X and was now…burning it?

But Harvard had told him they'd recovered the missing canisters, and Lucky had seen Zoe….

Die? Or fall? And what exactly had been inside those canisters Lieutenant Jones had recovered? No one besides Zoe would be able to identify whether or not it actually was the Trip X.

The door to the inner chamber was locked, and Jake pounded on it. "Zoe! It's me! It's Jake—open up!"

Harvard was beside him, compassion in his eyes. "Sir, I don't—"

"She's in there!" Jake was sure of it. But the smoke was in there, as well. And just standing out *here* was making him choke and cough.

This door was as heavily reinforced as the other. The lock was a piece of junk, but it would take too many precious minutes to pick it. If Zoe *was* in there, she'd been breathing in the smoke for quite some time. If she *was* in there, she was dying.

Jake hadn't been able to do a damn thing when Daisy had died. He hadn't been able to fight her cancer, to wrestle it to the ground and even *try* to save her life.

But he sure as hell could try to save Zoe.

"Stand back," Jake ordered, tossing the shotgun to Bob and taking the last of his C-4 from his pocket. It wouldn't take much, just a little around the lock. He lit the fuse, moved behind Vincent's desk and…

Boom.

The door swung open, and smoke billowed out, chokingly thick, coming from a garbage can that flamed atop a huge conference table.

Jake was the only man without a gas mask but the first one inside. He couldn't see a damned thing, but if Zoe *were* in here, she'd be on the ground.

He found her in the corner. She'd torn nearly half the

carpeting off the floor, yanking and pulling it on top of her to create a small pocket of air for herself.

She was unconscious and streaked with blood from a bullet wound on her arm and soot from the fire. But she was still breathing.

She was still alive.

Jake didn't pretend that he wasn't crying as he carried her out of there.

"She's alive!" Wes was practically running in circles around him.

Harvard followed him, too, taking off his gas mask as they hit the fresher air in the hallway. "Sir, we intercepted six canisters of what we thought was the Triple X outside the gates. But it sure looks as if Zoe thinks she's found the chemicals right here. There are six coffee cans in there, three empty. I think that's what she was burning."

"Stay with the rest of it, Senior," Jake ordered him. "Don't let it out of your sight." He raised his voice. "I need to get Zoe down to the medics *now*. Let's get this sideshow moving!"

With Vincent and his men in handcuffs, Bobby's shotgun aimed at the CRO leader's head, and with the rest of the SEALs surrounding Jake and Zoe, they went down the stairs and into the yard without mishap.

FInCOM had arrived, and as the dark-suited agents read Christopher Vincent his rights, Jake carried Zoe through the hole he'd blown in the fence to a waiting ambulance.

The medic gestured to a cot inside the vehicle. "You can put her there, sir."

"No," Jake said.

The medic looked at him in surprise.

Jake smiled to soften his words. "No, you see, I'm…I'm not going to let her go."

"Ever?"

He looked down to see Zoe's eyes had opened. Her voice was whispery from a throat that must've been raw from all the smoke she'd inhaled. Her hair hung in strings from her

French braid, and her face was streaked with soot and blood. He was certain he'd never seen her look more beautiful.

"No," he told her. "Not ever."

The medic was about twenty years old and trying as hard as he could not to listen as he gently slipped several thin tubes from an oxygen tank into Zoe's nose.

"Give us a minute," Jake said to him. "Will you, pal?"

The medic faded back. Or maybe he didn't. Maybe Jake just stopped seeing him as he lost himself in the depths of Zoe's eyes.

He touched her then, her face, her hair, her throat, unable to keep his eyes from filling again with tears. "I thought you died," he told her quietly. "Lieutenant O'Donlon saw Vincent shoot you, and…we all thought he'd killed you, Zo."

"Oh, Jake," she whispered.

"But then you really could've died," he said. "What the hell were you doing, starting a fire in a room without ventilation?"

"I was doing my job," she said quietly. "And I trusted that you'd do yours and come get me out of there. I took a gamble that this teamwork thing would pay off." She smiled. "I won."

"Yeah," Jake said. "I did, too."

"I think this would be a really great time for you to kiss me," she said.

Jake laughed and kissed her. "I love you, Zoe."

She shook her head. "Oh, Jake, I don't need you to say that."

"Yeah, but I need to say it," he said. "I thought I would never get a chance to. I thought…" He had to clear his throat before he could go on. "Zoe, I would be honored if you would agree to make this craziness legal and stay Zoe Robinson. You see, I'm too old to—"

"Jake, how can you ask me to marry you—in a completely half-assed way, might I add—and then in the same breath claim to be too old—''

''You want to let me finish? I *am* too old. I'm too old not to learn from the past. I didn't expect to outlive Daisy,'' Jake told her. ''And let's face it, babe, your job being what it is, it's entirely possible that I could outlive you, too. I had a taste of that today, and it was pretty damn sobering. The truth is, neither of us can possibly know how much time we'll have together. And we're both of us too old to waste another precious second of it.''

Tears were leaving clean tracks in the soot on her face. For a tough operator, Zoe cried more than just about anyone he'd ever met. He kissed her. ''Marry me.'' He kissed her again, longer this time. ''I want you to be my friend and my lover and my wife for however long forever lasts.'' He smiled at her. ''How was that? Not quite so half-assed that time?''

She was smiling through her tears. ''That was…inspirational. And very persuasive.'' She laughed. ''Not that I particularly needed persuading.''

''If that's a yes,'' Jake said, ''it's very half-assed.''

Zoe laughed. ''Yes,'' she said. ''It's a yes.''

Jake lost himself in the sweetness of her lips. He'd thought she'd been taken from him. He'd lived an entire wretched lifetime in that endless fifteen minutes in which he'd believed she was dead. He loved this woman completely. But there would be people who looked at them and wondered, people who wouldn't understand.

''I have to be really honest with you,'' he said, looking into her dark brown eyes. ''There's a big difference in our ages, and nothing we do or say is going to change that. I know you don't care, and I don't care anymore, either. But people—my colleagues—are going to look at me and look at you and think I'm getting away with something here.''

Zoe reached up and touched his face. ''Your colleagues and friends are going to look at me and think I'm a poor substitute for Daisy.''

"You are," Jake told her. "But then again, Daisy would be a tremendously poor substitute for you." He kissed her hand. "I'm not looking for a replacement for Daisy. There's no such thing. I'll always love her—it's important you know that because she's part of my past. But there's room in my heart for both the past and the future. And babe, you're my future."

There was so much love in her eyes as she looked at him he nearly started crying again.

"I love you," she said.

Jake smiled. "I know."

Epilogue

"You all right?" Billy Hawken asked.

"Yeah," Jake said as the limousine pulled up to the church.

He looked at the kid. *Kid.* Jeez. The kid was a Navy SEAL with the somewhat dangerous-sounding nickname of Crash. The kid was also older than Zoe. The kid hadn't been a kid in fifteen years. Heck, even back when Billy was ten, he hadn't really been a kid. He was still far too serious, far too intense—except when he was with Nell, his wife.

Jake had heard the two of them giggling together until nearly two last night, up in the guest bedroom. Crash Hawken—giggling. Whoever would've thought it possible?

"Are *you* okay with this, kid?" he asked as they got out of the car. *Kid.* Jeez. Old habits died hard.

Billy didn't hesitate. "I am. Completely," he said. He smiled. "Zoe looks at you the way Nell looks at me. I'm happy for you, Jake."

"I love her," Jake told the young man who was the

closest thing to a son he'd ever had, the young man to whom Daisy was the closest thing to a mother *he'd* ever had.

"I know," Billy said. "I've seen the way you look at her, too."

"This isn't just a…a second-best kind of thing." Jake felt the need to explain. "Zoe and me, I mean. But that doesn't mean that Daisy wasn't—and isn't—first, too. God, does that make any sense at all?"

Billy hugged him. "Yeah, Jake," he said. "You know, I had a dream about Daisy last night. She was having lunch with William Shakespeare. It was weird, but nice. One of those dreams where you wake up and feel really good."

"Shakespeare, huh?" Jake laughed. "Cool."

"Yeah." Billy motioned toward the church. "You want to go in?"

"Yeah," Jake said. "Come on, kid. Let's go get me married." He put his arm around Billy's shoulders, and together they walked up the stairs.

Zoe was a vision.

Walking toward him, down the aisle of the church, on her father's arm.

Sergeant Matthew Lange, USMC, Retired.

Matt seemed like a really nice guy, a straightforward, honest guy. He seemed genuinely pleased that Zoe was marrying Jake. Lisa Lange, Zoe's mother, was also honestly happy for her daughter. They were good people, solid people.

It was kind of cool, actually. He'd never had in-laws before.

His children had a chance of knowing at least one set of their grandparents.

His children.

Zoe smiled into his eyes as she took her place beside him, and he couldn't help but think about last night. While

Billy and Nell had been giggling in the guest bedroom, Jake and Zoe had been sharing their own secrets.

Such as the fact that Zoe wanted his baby. Enough to retire from her job as a field agent—at least temporarily.

It hadn't been an easy decision to make. She was good at what she did. And the Agency would miss her, badly.

Jake suspected her decision was at least partly based on the fact that she knew how badly *he* wanted children. Daisy had been unable, and found the adoption process too painful, and…

He'd tried to convince Zoe that he would be okay with whatever decision she came to, but the truth was, *his* biological clock was ticking. Sure, he could father a baby when he was sixty-five, but how long would he be around to take care of that child?

Last night, she'd come to him with the ultimate wedding gift. And last night, they just may have created a small miracle.

Jake took her hand.

And as he promised Zoe all that he could promise her, he smiled.

"I love you," he whispered as he bent to kiss his bride.

Zoe smiled, too. She knew.

*   *   *   *   *

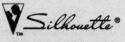

If you enjoyed what you just read,
then we've got an offer you can't resist!

Take 2 bestselling
love stories FREE!
Plus get a FREE surprise gift!

Clip this page and mail it to Silhouette Reader Service™

IN U.S.A.	IN CANADA
3010 Walden Ave.	P.O. Box 609
P.O. Box 1867	Fort Erie, Ontario
Buffalo, N.Y. 14240-1867	L2A 5X3

YES! Please send me 2 free Silhouette Intimate Moments® novels and my free surprise gift. Then send me 6 brand-new novels every month, which I will receive months before they're available in stores. In the U.S.A., bill me at the bargain price of $3.57 plus 25¢ delivery per book and applicable sales tax, if any*. In Canada, bill me at the bargain price of $3.96 plus 25¢ delivery per book and applicable taxes**. That's the complete price and a savings of over 10% off the cover prices—what a great deal! I understand that accepting the 2 free books and gift places me under no obligation ever to buy any books. I can always return a shipment and cancel at any time. Even if I never buy another book from Silhouette, the 2 free books and gift are mine to keep forever. So why not take us up on our invitation. You'll be glad you did!

245 SEN CNFF
345 SEN CNFG

Name	(PLEASE PRINT)	
Address	Apt.#	
City	State/Prov.	Zip/Postal Code

* Terms and prices subject to change without notice. Sales tax applicable in N.Y.
** Canadian residents will be charged applicable provincial taxes and GST.
    All orders subject to approval. Offer limited to one per household.
    ® are registered trademarks of Harlequin Enterprises Limited.

INMOM99   ©1998 Harlequin Enterprises Limited

**Start celebrating Silhouette's 20th anniversary
with these 4 special titles by
New York Times bestselling authors**

Fire and Rain
by Elizabeth Lowell

King of the Castle
by Heather Graham Pozzessere

State Secrets
by Linda Lael Miller

Paint Me Rainbows
by Fern Michaels

On sale in December 1999

Available at your favorite retail outlet

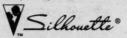

Visit us at www.romance.net

PSNYT

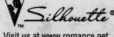

In December 1999
three spectacular authors invite you to share the
romance of the season as three special gifts are

Delivered by Christmas

A heartwarming holiday anthology featuring

BLUEBIRD WINTER
by *New York Times* bestselling author

Linda Howard

A baby is about to be born on the side of the road. The single
mother's only hope rests in the strong arms of a dashing doctor....

And two brand-new stories:

THE GIFT OF JOY
by national bestselling author **Joan Hohl**

A bride was not what a Texas-Ranger-turned-rancher was
expecting for the holidays. Will his quest for a home lead to love?

A CHRISTMAS TO TREASURE
by award-winning author **Sandra Steffen**

A daddy is all two children want for Christmas. And the
handsome man upstairs may be just the hero their mommy needs!

*Give yourself the gift of romance in
this special holiday collection!*

Available at your favorite retail outlet.

Silhouette®

Visit us at www.romance.net   PSDBC